AZAZEL
ALIEN LEGACY BROTHERHOOD BOOK FOUR
FOUR
KERI KRUSPE

STARCHANCE PRODUCTIONS

CONTENTS

AZAZEL

He was sent to rescue her, but she may be the only one who can save him from himself.

Azazel is a psychic warrior, one of five brothers engineered for a battle that was lost millennia ago. Now, he has a new mission: infiltrate a soul-crushing alien mothership and rescue a captured human female. But the oppressive psychic energy of the Krystalii invaders awakens the one thing he fears most—the savage, uncontrollable beast chained within his soul. To succeed, he must maintain absolute control. But one look at the woman he's meant to save, and the beast roars in recognition—*Mate*.

Toni Choi traded her soul-sucking Hollywood job for a once-in-a-lifetime adventure, only to be abducted and imprisoned by a galactic tyrant. Now, she's a pawn in a terrifying genetic experiment. When a dark, powerful warrior with haunted eyes appears in her cell, she doesn't know if he's a savior or a more dangerous kind of trap. But as they're thrown together in a desperate escape, Toni discovers a shocking secret: she has an uncanny connection to the enemy's technology, a gift that could turn the tide of a galactic war.

Trapped in the heart of enemy territory, their only hope is the undeniable, searing bond that ignites between them. But to protect her, Azazel may have to unleash the very monster he's sworn to contain.

AZAZEL

And to survive, Toni must place her trust in a man whose inner demon could be their salvation... or their ultimate undoing.

"Azazel" is a gripping tale of action, adventure, and romance, exploring themes of destiny, redemption, and the enduring power of love in the face of intergalactic turmoil. Fans of science fiction romance will be captivated by this epic conclusion to the Alien Legacy Brotherhood series.

CHAPTER ONE

I *diot.*

Azazel grimaced, rubbing the side of his head with his eyes closed. The dull pain of a relentless headache made him moan.

You should know better than to teleport to somewhere you've never been before. Especially to an alien spaceship traveling at light speed to goddess-knows-where.

Wouldn't his tease-loving brother, Arakiba, love to see him now? Frozen in agony, unable to protect himself if anything threatened him. He could just imagine the endless harassment he'd have to endure... from all four of his siblings.

Sucking in a fortifying breath, he forced his eyes to flutter open. The blur of unconsciousness lifted just enough to let the world above him seep in. His fuzzy gaze drifted to the cracked ceiling.

Grime clung to it in thick smears. Dark stains etched across the surface like scars that time and neglect brought. Even a slow drip from one of the cracks above him hesitated, as if waiting to fall.

Forcing his sluggish mind to function, he frowned. Maybe once his mind cleared, he'd figure out if he was on the ship he'd aimed for. The uncontrollable twitch of his fingers against the hard, icy surface beneath him made him grimace. Turning his head slowly, he groaned as his muscles resisted with a dull ache at each movement. With a grunt, he wiped the unexpected sweat from his brow. Blinking against the gloom, he scanned his surrounding for anything familiar. But the only thing clear was he'd landed in some kind of dingy corridor.

Well, hopefully he'd made it where he meant to go. Before he teleported, he envisioned an unused place to land on the ship that held the essence of the human woman he'd latched on to. Not that he imagined it'd be in some hallway. His gaze returned to the drip waiting to fall above him. The rough, cracked, and battered surface around it testified to its neglect. Taking a deep breath, he let a moment of serenity in to calm his mind before panic snuck in.

Focusing, he concentrated on controlling his breath. After a few moments, he rubbed his eyes with the heels of his palms, then let his arms flop beside him. Damn his head for the continued pounding. Guess he was lucky a headache was the only thing he suffered from. Teleporting straight from the gangster planet FiPan to a spaceship traveling through deep space could've ended up worse. Even with the ship at a minimum light-speed setting, he and his spider-bot AI companion, JR14, were lucky to survive in one piece. He grunted. Why he thought it'd be effortless was beyond him. That's what he got when he let his pride take over—showing off in front of his brothers. No matter how much introspection he practiced, once in a while he couldn't help himself when he gave into the petty temptation of grandstanding.

Something to consider later. Much later.

For now, he'd better make sure his android partner survived the experience. There, in the middle of his closed palm, lay JR14. Azazel widened his fingers. The bot was curled in the center with his spindly legs tucked under his bulbous body.

The bot opened his two primary rounded optical sensors on the front of his head and looked back at him. His eyes held a serene sky blue. His spider frame of gold and red gleamed in the low light, a testament to his advanced design.

JR14 stood on his sleek, eight, spider-like legs that tapered with mechanical precision. The bot turned his rotund head around as if to analyze where he was. Besides his arachnid-like legs, he had shorter front limbs that ended with metallic claws, which now clicked. A sure sign he was analyzing the situation.

"Are you well, JR14?" Azazel asked.

"Confirmed. My systems are functioning at optimal capacity." The droid responded as his iridescent wings slid out of the concealing panels on his back. The bot fluttered off his palm and landed on Azazel's chest. His wings once again folded out of sight under his red exoskeleton. "Teleportation was successful. However, your vital signs indicate post-transit disorientation. Recommendation: stabilizing self promptly. Sentient organics are notoriously inefficient under duress. This could place us in unnecessary danger from the hostiles of this ship."

Azazel did his best to focus on the small android now poised on his chest. Close enough he might go cross-eyed.

"I'll be alright, JR14." He reassured his companion. "Just give me a moment to clear my head." Sighing, he closed his eyes once again and concentrated on stabilizing the spinning wheel in his head that made him dizzy and nauseous. After a few precious moments, he took a chance and opened his eyes again. He breathed a sigh of relief. The mind-fog had faded somewhat. His sentient AI companion hadn't moved, those two main ocular orbs still trained on him, their glow now a soft red. The bot's eight pointy legs dug lightly into the shirt of his tunic.

"Query: Azazel, is your physical equilibrium restored?" JR14's monotone voice had a low pitch. "As previously stated, suboptimal performance compromises mission efficiency."

"You are so right, *kalu*." Azazel swallowed with a dry throat.

Without a word, JR14's wings slid from beneath his outer exoskeleton on his back, and he whirled to lift himself off Azazel's chest and buzzed in front of his face. "*Kalu*, an ancient word, means a close, loyal companion or friend." After that statement, the bot zoomed to settle on Azazel's stomach. "While my designation of JR14 remains more efficient for identification," JR14 continued. "I accept the notation for future usage."

At least the droid was in a better position for Azazel, so going cross-eyed wasn't going to happen. He grunted in acknowledgment. But, pleasantries aside, it was time to gather information instead of lying here doing nothing.

"JR14, can you interface with the computers on this vessel and determine our location?" He glanced up at the depressing ceiling. "And any other pertinent information you deem necessary?"

"Affirmative," JR14 stated as a soft, pulsating effect shone in his two primary lenses, now emitting faint flickers of glowing amber.

While the bot did as he asked, Azazel opened his senses to determine what he could. He had to be on a small ship that housed... one other person? Being? A wave of harsh malevolence hit him. It was cold, hard, and had a strong sense of psionic abilities.

Azazel shut down his psychic senses before the entity connected with him. His heart raced. He hadn't felt anything that powerful since he was a child when he accidentally touched his mind with one of the previous slaves the Akurn scientists created and tried to destroy. The being, known as a Titan, almost gained control over his mind to force Azazel to free him. The only thing that saved him was mentally calling his brothers to come and help him. Joining their minds together allowed him to snap away from the creature's clutches. He'd vowed to never let something like that happen ever again.

The sinking fear from the memory nudged his inner beast awake. Azazel sucked in a breath at the new threat. With his fingers clenched, he tightened his hold on that hidden part of himself he kept locked down deep inside, where it belonged. Long ago, he vowed to never, ever let the thing loose. With a final harsh shove, he pushed that unpredictable part of himself back into the dark pit he'd created for it when he was young.

"JR14," he croaked. Clearing his throat, he tried again. "JR14, are there any Krystalii on this ship?" That would explain the powerful wave of intense psychic energy he'd touched.

The Krystalii were the reason he was here in the first place. The crystalline alien race was from another dimension vastly different from the one he lived in. The sentient beings were composed of various mineral and crystalline structures and were ruled by a brutal dictator with the name Lord Baelon, of all things. Baelon, a being made of rough blue Apatite was an extremely powerful psychic as well as a ruthless despot who ruled his people through fear and intimidation.

For reasons no one understood, Baelon had targeted this dimension. And not to just strip it of its natural resources. He'd also grown obsessed with capturing human women for his twisted experiments.

Azazel's brother, Abalim, stated Baelon believed human DNA could merge with Krystalii genetics to shorten their incubation period and boost reproduction. Apparently, their scientific capabilities would somehow make that possible. Or he was dangerously delusional. Crazy as an Akurn scientist. Those aliens who created him and his brothers suffered from the delusion they had control over them. Especially when the fools drank too much *kakkaru* wine.

Either scenario wasn't good for anyone. This was especially true for the human women he and his three brothers were sent to rescue from the Krystalii's brutal intent.

"Analysis complete." JR14 announced.

When the droid remained silent, Azazel prompted him.

"Please share." He sat up and leaned against the metallic wall, ignoring the crusty surface coated with a hard, slimy substance he didn't dare examine.

JR14 hovered before resting on Azazel's thigh. "Designation: We are on a ship owned by an alien race called the Ozevroc, who are galactic criminals wanted in the civilized galaxy." The bot plopped onto his belly with his legs folded underneath him as he continued his narrative. "I have compared their readings with the ones on FiPan and determined they are a match. Further analysis has determined these are the beings that absconded with the human women from that planet."

Azazel raised his eyebrows.

"I didn't sense a being like that on this ship. The one I sensed has the same outliers that my brother, Abalim, brought back to share with us concerning the Krystalii."

"Affirmative." JR14 nodded. The steady, pale-blue light in his eyes dimmed. "I have determined that a Krystalii has commandeered this ship that formerly belonged to an Ozevroc. We are now proceeding to the Krystalii mothership called the *Nyrlith,* which, in the Krystalii language, means soul-prison."

That, as his brother Arakiba would say, didn't inspire any warm fuzzies.

Sucking in a sharp breath, Azazel said, "Then I'd best not use my psychic abilities to read the Krystalii here. So, I have two questions." Azazel rubbed his chin. "First, is the Krystalii aware we are here? And second, is the human woman on this ship? If so, where?" If he got to her before they docked with the Krystalii mothership, he'd be able to teleport the three of them from this ship back to FiPan. From there, he'd figure out a way to get back to Earth.

"Inconsistent." JR14's back wings came out and flicked before being covered again. "Instead of two questions, that was three. You must refrain from misrepresenting the number of your queries."

Azazel pressed his lips together to keep from grinning. *Darn bot was so literal.*

"My apologies." He put a hand over his heart. "But I tend to ask questions as thoughts occur to me. Please overlook that propensity and answer my questions to the best of your abilities."

JR14's front claws clicked.

Azazel understood the sound as a sign the bot was either irritated or considering the request.

"I understand your limitations."

At least the bot's tone wasn't condescending.

"I agree to respond to your illogical way of conversing." JR14's front claws were silent. "Firstly, the Krystalii is unaware we are on board this ship. He is focused on approaching the *Nyrlith* to land this vessel. Secondly, the human woman is here and is unconscious in a stasis pod. Thirdly, her stasis pod is just through that doorway." JR14's front claw pointed to an obvious open doorway Azazel hadn't noticed.

He swallowed a sigh. *It wouldn't do any good to chastise the bot for not telling him that in the first place. After all, the little droid had only been online for less than a month.* "All right, let's get out of this corridor and go get her."

"Affirmative. Optimal decision to recover the human woman first minimizes detection from the Krystalii by 42%. Let us proceed."

Toni led a glamorous and fulfilling life.

Ask anyone.

Those looking at her life from the outside would tell you she led one of the most fascinating, exciting lifestyles imaginable. Professionally, she was a woman in great demand as an assistant film producer, who lived in one of the most exciting cities on the planet. She surrounded herself with dozens of friends and thrived in a tight-knit, like-minded community nestled in the heart of Koreatown, Los Angeles.

She'd bought a small condo on her own (at the express disapproval from her *eomeoni*—mother), and she dated occasionally with intelligent, handsome men who respected and admired her.

Yep, she should be happier than a teenager discovering Wi-Fi in a blackout.

But... she wasn't.

Instead, she hid from everyone how lonely and bored she was. Most days were filled with mindless tasks and useless things those above her pay grade demanded she do. Day in and day out. And, in those rare flashes of honesty, especially in the middle of the chaos, she admitted her life sucked and she'd better change it before it was too late.

To add to that pile of self-loathing, from an early age, she wrestled with the gnawing sense that something essential was missing from her life. And nothing she did came close to filling that void. Searching for meaning in a life partner was spotty at best. It didn't take her long to relegate most of the men she dated to the "friend zone"—that is, if she let any of those men stay in her life at all. Most of them only got close because they thought she held sway in the film industry. Good thing it didn't take long to see through those charmers. Damn asses were so predictable. And the ones who ended up in that friend zone? If she was honest, she couldn't care less if she ever saw them again. None of them lit that spark of passion she'd read or made movies about.

As for her personal life—raised as an only child, she didn't have any siblings to bond with. And, since her parents migrated alone to the United States in the early 1970s, she didn't have other family to connect with. Any aunts, uncles, cousins or grandparents she had were all in Korea, a place Toni never had the chance to visit.

But one unexpected night, that all changed. She was given a chance to do something so crazy, so outlandish, so irresistible, she couldn't bear to turn it down. When an alien race called Zerin contacted... er, abducted her, they presented her with a once-in-a-lifetime opportunity to leave Earth and find a meaningful relationship with an alien who would love and adore her for the rest of her life.

Unlike most of the science-fiction romances she'd read, these aliens gave her a choice—join their exchange, or they'd return her home none the wiser, with the reassurance they'd erase her memories of the encounter with no harm done to her. After she heard their tempting offer, she felt an underlying sense of fate aligned within her for the first time. This... this was what she'd been waiting for. She'd always adored anything with a sci-fi twist combined with a hint of romance. How could she resist?

Toni, by nature, wasn't impulsive. She took her time and contemplated their offer, especially since she couldn't return to Earth if she went with them. Before she gave them an answer, she relived her life, piece by piece. Her job, which she adored at first, had been exciting; she was part of producing movies and TV shows that she'd felt were worthwhile.

But as time went by, the fierce competition turned into something she loathed, forcing her to choose between backstabbing a good friend to get the job done or losing any credibility she had in the industry. And lately, the projects she'd worked on weren't worth the effort. They were flat and uninspiring. It was the same old grind. Like a bad rerun.

Disgust couldn't describe how mind-numbing and soul-sucking the entire industry had turned out for her.

The only regret she had was leaving her *eomeoni* behind. Although not estranged, Toni's refusal to live as her mother decreed forced her to move out and reject her mother's traditional lifestyle. Lately, whenever they got together, her mother became increasingly demanding.

"Toni-ah, look at you! You're not young anymore. When I was your age, I already had you. Do you want to be alone forever? No husband, no children! How can you live like this?"

As if Toni being in her early thirties counted as old age. Then her mother would spout this gem:

"How will I get to hold grandchildren at my advanced age?"

Toni was smart enough not to point out her mother was barely in her sixties. Then her favorite would follow:

"You don't think about me at all! Do you want me to grow old and feeble with no one to call me *halmoni*? You don't want to have *han* in my heart, do you?"

Her mother had the emotional blackmail trope down to a science. As if Toni was responsible for all her mother's unresolved sorrow, resentment, and longing for how her life turned out. While she loved her *eomeoni* with all her heart, her mother had developed her own interests after Toni's father died several years ago. She'd joined a group of widows from their community and traveled all over the world. If Toni saw her mom twice a year, that was considered a lot.

She shuddered. The only question was, how to tell her mother she was going away for a long time without starting in a guilt-ridden argument? Which turned out to be a no-brainer. Her only choice was to leave a note explaining she'd be unavailable for a year because of a remote job. After all, it was normal for either of them to be out of touch for long periods before. Besides, if she found a mate on an advanced world that had space travel, who's to say he wouldn't bring her back for a visit occasionally?

The final decision came down to this. Was she willing to take a risk of going to the ends of the galaxy for something as bold as a fulfilling life filled with love? Could there be anything nobler? Here was an opportunity to uncover parts of herself she never dared to understand—one with no outside influences. A chance to reclaim her identity away from the roles and expectations placed on her.

And wasn't that what being alive was all about?

Of course, fate loves nothing more than to slap you upside the head with your own stupidity the second you dare to chase something better. Just a little reminder to let you know what a complete idiot you were for even thinking you had the right to change your life.

Or that you even had a chance.

Instead of finding love with a hunky alien and living a life of love and adventure on an exotic planet, Toni's butt was stuck in a holding cell with four other women on a gangster planet called FiPan. To make matters worse, their android jailers—called, of all things, *sexbots*—stopped working some time ago, leaving her and her friends to die either of starvation or thirst.

Or monotonous boredom.

Just when Toni feared all hope was lost, a clatter of alien footsteps echoed down the abandoned corridor. She blinked against the light that clicked on in the hallway, spilling its dull glow into the dreary cell. What came toward them made her eyes widen. They were strange-looking creatures she could only describe as a nightmarish mix of dingoes and beavers on two feet. That is, if a dog walked on its hind legs. They scrambled to a stop at the entrance of the cell. They were short suckers, only around four feet tall. All of them had six arms—three on each side of their furry, matted torsos. In the middle of their foreheads, above their snouts, were four black-beady eyes that gleamed with identical malevolence.

Each one fixated on her and her captive friends.

Her stomach tightened as one of them ran a scan around the cell with some kind of device it held in its clawed middle paw while others focused on the frozen red sexbot poised at the entrance to their cell.

Together, they dragged the android away while uttering growls and hisses.

Toni's faint hope of freedom evaporated once the force field covering the entry dissipated when the sexbot was gone. She gritted her teeth in a vain attempt to steady her breathing. These creatures weren't rescuers. They had to be something far more dangerous.

Sudden pain from the thick slave collar around her neck shocked Toni. She dropped to the floor like a stone, every nerve in her body blazing with agony. With everything she had, she did her best to cry out, but before any sound escaped, one of the creatures slammed a putty-like gag ball over her mouth. It expanded and covered her frozen lips.

Cold metal bands snapped onto her wrists with mechanical precision over her wrists, binding her hands in front of her. The icy metal bit into her skin, making her fingers numb.

The pain bled away, giving her a chance to breathe through her nose. Her captor yanked her upright, and the sudden movement left her dizzy. She stumbled forward, dragged along by the six-armed alien who gripped her with unnerving ease with his middle paw-hand. The other women in the cell with her were similarly held captive.

Their expressions over their gags were a mixture of fear and defiance. Toni's heart wrenched when she caught sight of Morgan's narrow-eyed determined stare at the alien manhandling her. Izzy—gentle Izzy—whose brown eyes were now wide with tears. She couldn't see Althea or Lisa, who sounded like they were behind her.

The elevator ride from the cell block was suffocating, both from the stench of their captors and the oppressive silence they forced on them. Toni's fingers flexed against the restraints as her mind raced for an escape plan. But nothing jumped out how to get free. The only thing she could do was glare at the short alien holding her. Not helpful, but it made her feel better.

When the doors of the elevator slid open, chaos greeted them. The once-pristine facility was in shambles, its halls reduced to a battlefield of destruction. Aliens of all shapes and sizes looted, fought, or reveled in chaos. Toni's captor pushed her onward, ignoring the scene as though he couldn't care less about the twisted spectacle going on around them.

Her breath hitched when they emerged outside. The outside world was a blur of dull sunlight and rancid air, but it was the looming metallic structure ahead that scared the crap out of her. The octagonal vessel radiated menace, its surface marred by years of wear and stained with substances she didn't care to think about.

Toni stumbled, and her knees pounded onto the crumbling asphalt. The rough ground scraped holes in her pants and scratched deep gouges in her skin. Her muscles screamed in protest as the collar around her neck tightened and hoisted her off the ground like she was a puppet on invisible strings. She thrashed, desperate for air. But her struggles only made the pressure worse. Her captor's grip didn't falter as he propelled her toward the ship.

Once they reached the side of the battered vessel, a metallic slab slid out. The collar around her neck tightened, making it hard to breathe. Its hold lifted her into the air, and she hovered for a moment before it settled her onto the slab. She shivered. The icy surface seeped through her clothes, a frigidity that burned the skin on her back. Straps emerged automatically, binding her with ruthless efficiency. Toni's mind screamed in defiance, as if her mental struggles made a difference. This couldn't be the end! Not here, not like this.

Her only answer was the hiss of something piercing her neck. Her gasp of welcome air was the only good thing before darkness claimed her and put her out of her misery.

Azazel slid up the wall he'd leaned against, straining to stand as his thigh muscles screamed in protest with every movement. It took a while, but once the spinning in his head slowed to a dull ache, he rested his hands on his thighs and raised his head to look around. He couldn't believe how weak he still was. JR14 flittered in front of him like a ladybug in flight, his wings beating faster than the eye could follow. The droid turned down the corridor toward the open doorway next to them. With slow, sure steps, Azazel trailed him, watching the bot's eight golden legs with their red trimmings dangle.

The room they entered was barely big enough to hold the coffin-like stasis pod. Its clear casing was as grimy and crusty as the rest of the ship he'd seen so far. A rancid smell hit him, making his eyes water. The closest Azazel could describe the stench was a mix of something rotting and sharp, like sour meat soaked in cleaning chemicals. It also carried an underlying bouquet of feces, vomit, and urine, all marinating in a vat of ammonia.

"Son of a lilit!" Azazel wiped the tears from his streaming eyes. "What is creating that odor?"

JR14 buzzed beside him, his small metallic head tilted. "Hold for determination." The bot flew to the other side of the pod, then hovered. "Analysis complete. Organic classification: Ozevroc male, deceased. Cause of death: undetermined."

Azazel strode in the direction where JR14 pointed one of his front claws.

"Olfactory analysis indicates advanced decomposition." JR14 continued, his front claws clicking as he processed. "The odor is consistent with sulfuric compounds and putrefying proteins. Summary: the specimen is dead, thus creating what you organics would specify as a very smelly experience."

Azazel's mouth twitched into a small grin when the droid said "smelly". Glancing at the dead Ozevroc, he frowned. Even though he was unfamiliar with this type of creature, it was clear it had died a painful death. The Ozevroc's six arms twisted at awkward angles, and its long, clawed fingers curled inward, as if clutching something unseen in its last moments. The alien's snout gaped open, exposing sharp yellowed teeth now bared in a silent scream of agony. The creature's matted, dull, navy-blue fur clung to its emaciated frame. Two sets of glossy black eyes stared at the ceiling.

Azazel crouched closer. No obvious wounds marred the Ozevroc's body. No gashes or punctures to suggest how it had died. And yet, every detail of the scene—the tension in its limbs, the unnatural arch of its back—spoke of unbearable suffering. It was as if an invisible force had crushed the creature from the inside out. Sheer, unrelenting pain had snuffed out its life.

"JR14," Azazel said, his voice tight, "please analyze the cause of death."

The tiny spider-like AI perched on his shoulder and his front claws clicked softly in response. "Analyzation in progress: death likely caused by severe internal trauma or system failure. No external injuries detected. Pain levels during expiration—estimated as extreme. Final determination: This organic suffered before dying."

Azazel's jaw tightened, his hands balling into fists. Whoever caused this Ozevroc's death wasn't looking to just eliminate a foe, they reveled in causing extreme pain and suffering. He looked up at the stasis pod holding the woman.

"JR14, please examine the woman in the pod to ensure her health."

"Affirmative." JR14 buzzed away.

Azazel turned his attention back to the dead alien. He couldn't let someone who suffered like this to be ignored in its final moments.

"May the universe cradle you once more in her tender embrace, my friend, and renew your spirit in the boundless warmth of her eternal grace." He closed his eyes and ran an open palm over the torso of the Ozevroc. With his psychic ability, he scrambled the creature's molecules into the finest stardust, then waved them free to be absorbed into the cosmos. When he opened his eyes, the alien's body was gone, as if it had never been there.

"Spatial analysis of the unconscious human female is concluded." The bot returned. "I confirm this is the human female known as Antonia Soo-min Choi, who prefers to be called Toni. The female suffers from dehydration and malnourishment but is otherwise in optimum health."

Azazel went to the pod and peered in. He'd only gotten a brief glimpse of her when JR14 zipped in front of his face. He jerked back. "Why did you do that?"

JR14's front claws became silent. "Recommendation: hide. This ship has docked within the Krystalii mothership. Conclusion: Krystalii forces will be upon us momentarily. Thus, we will not have ample opportunity to discover how to release the female from her containment device."

"Ezeru!" Azazel cursed in his ancient tongue. "Quick, take your place on my shoulder and do not speak."

His sense of urgency must have penetrated the android's unemotional makeup. JR14 zipped and landed on Azazel's shoulder.

Satisfied the bot was secure, Azazel closed his eyes and visualized himself and the droid becoming invisible to the naked eye. He opened them when a mammoth creature made of clear crystals strode into the room. His form was like a humanoid male made of translucent, shard-like material that reflected the dim light into sharp, prismatic bursts. The Krystalii's movements were eerily smooth and deliberate, more like a being of fluid than one of solid crystal.

Azazel doubled his efforts to keep his mind blocked and his breathing and heartbeat remained shallow and slow.

The crystal man paused in front of the stasis pod containing Toni.

Azazel's fists clenched as the creature's jagged fingers curled around the pod's reinforced frame. Without so much as a grunt, he lifted the pod from its pedestal, one-handed, as though it weighed no more than a fluffy pillow.

Azazel's jaw tightened. An apparatus like that had to be made of dense alloys designed to contain volatile energy—materials that would crush even a trained warrior under their weight.

The Krystalii hoisted the pod onto his angular shoulder, his spiked frame absorbing the load without strain.

Azazel glimpsed Toni inside, suspended in the pale light, her features serene but vulnerable. His pulse quickened, and JR14's metallic legs clicked against his collar as the AI shifted.

The creature turned toward the exit with the same unhurried precision, the stasis pod balanced like a trophy.

Azazel's mind raced, calculating the sheer power required for such an effortless display. His psychic senses caught faint ripples of energy radiating from the being—controlled, focused, unrelenting.

His eyes narrowed as the being disappeared into the corridor, the faint chime of his movements fading.

For a moment, the room was still, save for the soft hum of the machinery.

Exhaling, he let go of his invisibility and hung his head to catch his breath and regain his strength.

JR14 whispered in his ear, his tone sharp and analytical. "Opinion: current intervention is not advisable."

Azazel nodded and straightened. "Agreed," he murmured. His gaze lingered where the pod used to be, a flicker of awe at the Krystalii's strength warred with his hardening resolve. "Inform your father, JR10, that the Krystalii are already here in our dimension." He didn't dare communicate with his older brother, Adapa, telepathically on the chance the Krystalii would pick it up. "And that we are going to infiltrate their mothership. Send whatever schematics you can to aid them."

"Affirmative," confirmed JR14. "I will apprise you upon completion of my communication."

In the meantime, Azazel closed his eyes and concentrated on formulating a viable plan to not only rescue Toni but get them out of the forbidding psychic mothership.

Azazel managed to teleport inside the docking bay on the Krystalii mothership while keeping himself invisible. Glancing around to make sure no one saw him, he scurried through a closing doorway. Because the walls were composed of clear crystals, glass, and mirrors, he watched the Ozevroc ship float back into space, empty and free. His heart thundered at the narrow escape. If he hadn't left when he did, he'd be stuck on that floating ship, far from where he needed to be.

Taking a deep, fortifying breath, he paused and took in his surroundings. The purity of the oxygen was a pleasant surprise, even with its strange, subtle scent. It reminded him of damp stones after a rainstorm with a faint mineral-like undertone. Not seeing or sensing anyone around, he released the tension between his shoulders, satisfied he was as safe as possible. At least for now.

The corridor stretched out, the crystal walls a mesmerizing blend of cool blues, deep purples, and ghostly whites with vein-like streaks of colored glass under dim, pulsing lights. Since he was at a dead end, he turned around and moved the other way. As his feet touched the ground, the colors on the floor shifted and shimmered, creating a kaleidoscope of corresponding hues where his feet touched. The surrounding silence was dense, like a weight pressing against his senses. The only sound was a faint hum of energy that radiated through the crystalline walls. The shifting shadows and fractured reflections made him feel both boundless and claustrophobic.

He strengthened the block on his psychic senses.

JR14's metal limbs clung to Azazel's shoulder, the spider-like AI turning his red-and-gold body to survey their surroundings. A faint whir signaled he was analyzing the area. "Environmental parameters indicate an 84% risk of immediate detection if we proceed in this direction. Conclusion: The direct path is statistically unwise. Suggest optimizing stealth through evasive patterns."

Azazel's mouth curved into a grin as he whispered back, "Noted. That's what we'll do, then." Taking in the surroundings, he adjusted his psychic energy to blend in with the surroundings. Hopefully, he wouldn't stand out since he let go of his invisibility shield to save energy. With each step, he kept alert as his gaze swept over the corridors, every muscle tuned to potential threats. The crystal walls reflected distorted versions of him and JR14—flickers of movement that vanished as quickly as they appeared, creating a chilling spectral mirage.

With every step, he sensed her—Toni. The thread was faint, but familiar. The psychic echo he'd first touched of her at FiPan, and then again on the Ozevroc ship, remained locked in his mind. Her unique signal tugged him in a specific direction.

"I sense the woman is close," he whispered to JR14. He narrowed his focus to the psychic trace. Her energy threads wove through the corridors like a shimmering web, pulling him deeper into the ship's heart.

JR14's wings flicked open before retracting. "Survival probability is now at 54.3% if you continue this course. Recommendation: revise our approach to ensure continued existence." JR14's tone was blunt.

Azazel's brow lifted. "Are you suggesting we abandon the reason we're here in the first place?"

"Negative. Suggesting an alternative operation. However, a recalculated direction may yield a better outcome on the current course."

Azazel's only reply was a single, low chuckle as he continued forward.

A thrum of energy shifted around him, as if the ship's crystalline walls reacted to his physical presence. He stopped and steadied his breath, which gave him a chance to reach deep inside to mask his energy, except for the minuscule hold he had on the woman. But with the perceived outside threat, his inner demon started to struggle, trying to emerge.

Dammit! He didn't have time for this. This, what he called his inner beast, rose at the worst times and wrestled him for dominance. A flicker of unease surged as Azazel struggled with it once again.

The effort to suppress the beast took its toll, draining him mentally and physically until his hands trembled. Since he'd stepped onto this alien ship, it was harder to cage the thing clawing inside him. For some reason, being here made his inner beast stir harder. Hungry, angry, and ready to break free. That he couldn't allow—not here, not now. If he lost control, he wouldn't just destroy himself, he'd end up costing Toni her life. Her fate depended on him. And if anything happened to her because of him, he couldn't live with that.

If he was honest with himself, his greatest fear was that this uncontrollable part of him would cause unmitigated horror and destruction, and in the process, he would lose himself forever. It was a fear he'd never shared with anyone, especially not his brothers.

Throwing his shoulders back, Azazel tightened his resolve. Failure was not an option. Not for him, and not for what had to be done.

Narrowing his gaze, Azazel turned his concentration on what was in front of him. Ahead, the lights dimmed, and the corridor narrowed as the surrounding shadows stretched in distortion. Daring to snake a small thread of his psychic tendrils ahead, he caught on to marching footsteps in the distance. Sounded like it could be a contingent of the ship's guards. Too bad dulling his own psionic energy made it hard to tune in to others, which forced him to rely on JR14's non-organic abilities.

"Alert." JR14 noted in a soft hum. His wings buzzed before settling on his shoulder. "Three Krystalii on a westward trajectory in this direction. Suggest proceeding with caution. Even with your psionic safeguards in place, the probability of interception remains at 42%. Deviate from current course to avoid detection."

Azazel nodded. JR14 was right. He'd better go in a different direction. "Please analyze the best route we should take."

"Affirmative." "I will connect to the ship's schematics and analyze several outcomes to determine the best course, as well as confirming where they are containing the human woman. Stand by."

Resting his hand against the cool crystal wall, Azazel waited, perfectly still, until he sensed the guards fading away. A small bead of sweat rolled down his temple. While his general nature was to embrace silence and stillness, doing so during this dangerous situation without accessing his strong psychic senses tested his faith in his abilities. Especially since being here was the first time in his life he was alone. Even when the Akurn scientists did their separate experiments on him away from his brothers, they were only a thought away. Best of all, they had a contingency plan in place if things ever got to the point they couldn't survive whatever was being done to them. If any of them faced death, all five of them would disappear at the same time, teleporting far away from the Akurn base.

He couldn't count on anything like that here. Aboard this ship, he was alone in a hostile environment, even with his AI companion. Taking in a measured breath, Azazel forced down the tumult churning inside him until his head cleared. Finally, his inner battle was under control.

With a cleansing breath, he glanced at the bot. "JR14, have you determined the best way for us to go?"

"Affirmative," the bot replied. "I have two scenarios for your consideration. First: An efficient route through secondary maintenance corridors will reduce travel time to the female by 23.7%. This path minimizes exposure to Krystalii surveillance and increases mission success probability." JR14's wings fluttered before setting back into his exoskeleton. "Second: A detour through auxiliary ventilation shafts reduces exposure by 37% and decreases travel time by 18.4%. Recommend immediate course adjustment to optimize retrieval efficiency."

Azazel considered the possibilities. Traveling through the maintenance corridors might let them slip by any surveillance systems, but then there could be Krystalii crew members using them. Going through the ventilation shafts offered a better chance of them getting to the woman faster and with less hassle.

No contest. Faster with less hassle was better. And it would help him keep his inner beast from getting out of hand and dividing his attention.

"Okay, *kalu*." Azazel used his nickname for the bot to relieve some of the tension he carried. And maybe, just maybe, if he was less formal with the little android, it would be easier for the sentient AI to develop some human-like tendencies. "Let's go with option number two... into a ventilation system that I can fit in. Lead the way."

"Excellent choice, *ocua*. I concur." The droid's iridescent wings slid out from under their protective panels and buzzed to lift him off Azazel's shoulder. "Follow me, as I've determined the applicable system you should utilize."

Azazel tilted his head to glance at the bot. "*Ocua*? I'm not familiar with that word."

"*Ocua* is an abbreviation for 'organic command unit A' designated for optimal efficiency," replied JR14. "Your status as primary organic directive source requires precise classification for streamlined reference. 'Azazel' lacks function-specific clarity and processing efficiency. This designation, therefore, aligns with mission protocol: identification, command hierarchy, and purpose."

Azazel stifled a groan. "Let's just stick to our names, okay?"

"Understood, Azazel."

Was that a touch of impatience in the bot's tone? One could only hope.

"Reverting to original designation protocol." JR14 continued in his metallic monotone. "However, retaining *kalu* for optimal mission cohesion, as per your directive."

Azazel watched the figure of the small bot zip ahead of him. He placed each step in a calculated rhythm to keep him hidden from the sensors aboard the Krystalii ship. With a clear goal to focus on, he could push aside the volatile part of himself, now quiet deep inside where it belonged.

What more could he ask for?

Toni's awareness crawled back in waves. First, the sound of a low, mechanical hum. Then she noticed the sharp, metallic quality of the atmosphere, tinged with something acidic, like burned circuitry or hot wires. Her body felt heavy, making it hard to take a deep breath. When she tried to sit up, the restraints on her wrists and ankles bit into her skin. Blinking against the dim, shifting light, it dawned on her she was no longer on the decrepit transport ship where that hairy, six-armed freak put her. The air was colder here, more sterile. Faint reflections of light danced across the polished walls as a bluish light overhead cast fractured shadows that whirled above her like restless spirits. Her pulse quickened as she scanned the jagged room—some surfaces sleek, others razor-sharp. The walls refractured like broken glass reaching for the faintest light.

A chill crept up her spine from the icy surface beneath her. She shifted, but the firm restraints held. Their edges were oddly warm against the numbing chill of the air. Her breath fogged in the cold.

Her eyes darted to the bluish glow of the ceiling. Above her was a lattice of thin, crystalline veins that pulsated, their rhythm erratic. A slight movement in the corner of her eye made her stiffen. One of the translucent walls rippled, bending it in strange, fragmented patterns that shifted. Her stomach churned. She clenched her fists against the cuffs, but the slick edges of their glassy, unyielding grip held her tight as something moved behind her. A faint crackle sounded, as if glass splintered. She tried to turn, but her head didn't move on the hard slab. Her skin itched. An unsettling sensation of being watched tickled the back of her neck.

"Ah, the genetic source is awake at last," a deep, resonant voice said.

The grating, masculine tone sent chills racing down her spine. The voice carried an unsettling mix of curiosity and arrogant menace.

She darted her gaze to the side.

A towering figure emerged from the shadows, his jagged crystalline body catching the ambient light. Each movement he made was slow and deliberate. The various shades of blue in the massive creature's form emitted a faint, rhythmic glow. The alien exuded an unearthly presence, as though the very air around him bent to his will.

Toni's breath hitched and her eyes widened as she locked onto his gaze. His eyes—if they could even be called that—were unlike anything she'd ever seen before. Multifaceted and clear, they shimmered with an eerie, shifting light that danced between icy blue and deep indigo. Each movement of those orbs refracted into rainbows, like shards of shattered glass suspended in motion.

But it wasn't their beauty that froze her in place—it was the greasy depth they carried. Staring into those crystalline voids felt like falling into an endless frozen landscape. Something ancient... and hungry. The light within them pulsed faintly when they narrowed on her. She was sure he wasn't just watching her but dissecting her, finding her wanting. Her throat tightened. Those weren't eyes. They were weapons.

Swallowing, she took in the looming monster. He didn't wear clothes in the human sense of the word, yet his presence was anything but bare. A shimmering mantle of crystalline shards cascaded from his broad shoulders, catching the faint, flickering light and throwing it into a storm of fractured rainbows. It flowed with an unnatural elegance, as though alive, its edges razor-sharp and glinting with every subtle movement.

Bands of intricately carved crystal coiled around his wrists and chest, barbed and brutal, etched with alien symbols that hummed with power. They didn't look like adornments but rather extensions of his jagged, apatite body, fused as if they'd grown there. A crown-like structure framed his head, its spiked edges radiating an unrelenting authority, casting faint, menacing shadows against the polished walls.

The creature was both awe-inspiring and chilling with the awe-defining characteristics of the *Rakshasa* in Korea, a demonic being who opposed the gods and disrupted the natural order. He didn't just rule—he embodied omnipotence itself.

"Where?" She coughed. "Who..." Her voice cracked, making her struggle to form words. Her throat was dry, with the lingering gag marks still fresh against her chapped lips.

"I am the supreme power of the Krystalii, Lord Baelon." The crystal brute waved a careless hand around him. "As a lower form of sentience, you, a genetic subject of interest, may address me as Savant Lord." His sneer was palpable. "Human female, you are aboard my vessel, the *Nyrlith*. Your only purpose is to uncover the priceless ability your species appears to have in adapting to alien races. Not only to breed with them, but to transform your very nature into something other than your own."

Toni clenched her jaw, refusing to comment on his outlandish suggestion. The idea that she could somehow breed with his kind was laughable. Her heart pounded as his towering form moved closer, each step sending faint tremors through the floor.

Baelon tilted his head, studying her as though she were a curious specimen under a microscope. "Your silence is admirable, though inefficacious. However, I do not need you to use words to understand you." He raised a jagged hand, its reflective surface catching the faint light. For a moment, it hovered near her temple, and then a cold, invasive sensation pierced her mind.

She gasped. The world spun as he psychically invaded her thoughts. Memories flashed unbidden—her childhood, her determination to prove herself, her desperation when she was first captured. The kaleidoscope of images burned in her mind before Baelon withdrew and left her disoriented.

"Fascinating," he murmured. His crystalline form flickered with a faint glow inside. "Your mind is remarkably resilient for one of your species. Adaptable. Persistent. Traits we value."

"Why?" she croaked, forcing the words past her lips. "Why me?"

Baelon's mouth curled into something resembling a smile. "Humanity is the key to ensuring the survival of the Krystalii. Your DNA holds secrets we can use to accelerate our evolution. You, genetic source, are not just a captive. You are a cornerstone in the future of my people."

"Cornerstone?" she spat, anger overriding her fear. "I'm not some stupid experiment you can play with!"

Baelon's crystalline form flared, his glow intensifying. "You misunderstand. This is not a matter of choice for you. As of today, your very existence serves a higher purpose. Resist if you must; it changes nothing."

The ship trembled, making Baelon glance aside, his mirrored surface catching the flicker of warning lights. "Ah, it seems I am needed elsewhere." He gestured with his blocky crystalline hand to several Krystalii in various colors behind him. "Transfer her to an appropriate facility to bring her back to optimum health. She is vastly undernourished and dehydrated." He turned to her. "We must restore your frail form to the peak of vitality. This will ensure you can serve the higher purpose of the Krystalii. The only value your existence offers."

Before she could respond, Baelon turned sharply, leaving her behind in the cold, reflective chamber with his lackeys. Toni's mind raced, searching for a way out. Her gaze darted to the other crystal creatures, who watched her silently. Like hell she'd let this crystal piece-of-shit reduce her to being a pawn in some twisted game. She'd shatter his plans... even if it was the last thing she did.

CHAPTER TWO

F ollowing JR14's directions, Azazel crawled as silently as possible behind the bot through the crystalline ventilation shafts. The corridors were narrow, with barely enough room for him to move as he wriggled on his hands and knees. He'd have thought a ship of this size would have made its ventilation shafts wider for someone of his bulk to sneak around in. When he shifted his weight, it sent faint echoes around him. He clenched his jaw, hyper-aware of the sound.

JR14's wings fluttered as he paused at an intersection ahead, scanning for movement. His front metallic claws tapped lightly against the shaft's edge. "Alert: proceed with caution. Probability of Krystalii proximity within the next 15 meters is 48.2 percent. I advise a temporary halt to reassess movement patterns."

Azazel exhaled quietly, squirming as dampness coated his back.

"Okay." He wiped the sweat from his brow. "But we can't stop every few steps, JR14. Her trail is getting fainter."

The bot turned, and his pale-blue eyes focused on Azazel.

"Acknowledged. However, haste may cause premature detection, which would decrease retrieval probability by 72 percent."

"Sometimes, logic needs to bend to instinct, *kalu*." Azazel gave a faint smirk, using the nickname to temper his frustration. He motioned for JR14 to proceed.

JR14 tilted his body, as if contemplating Azazel's words. "Instinct remains an unquantifiable variable. However, your survival rate has improved by 14 percent in past scenarios involving improvisation. Proceed."

Following the small spider-bot, Azazel pressed forward, weaving through the labyrinthine ducts. Once, Azazel froze when the hum of energy intensified around them. Voices, sharp and alien, echoed faintly. He pressed his back against the heated wall of the shaft and motioned for JR14 to cease movement.

Through a small slat in the shaft's panel, he watched two Krystalii guards pass below.

Their crystalline bodies differed, one bearing an opalescent sheen and the other with clear crystals. Their bodies refracted the light like prisms, casting eerie rainbows along the walls. One guard paused, leaning its head to the side as though it sensed something.

Azazel held his breath, his grip tightening on the edge of the shaft. He tamped down his psychic senses into an impenetrable cage within him.

JR14 whispered, his tone devoid of emotion. "Detection remains unlikely if you continue to suppress psionic output."

"Noted, JR14," he whispered back, not bothering to argue he'd already done that.

After several heavy heartbeats, the guards moved on.

Azazel expelled a silent breath of relief. "Alright, let's keep moving."

At last, the shaft he crawled through opened into a larger space. Peering through the mesh covering the opening, he spied some kind of large chamber, filled with crystalline... machines? Furniture? He wasn't sure what he was looking at, but he sensed the room was empty. But there... yes. He picked up the woman's psychic signature. Closing his eyes, he expanded his ability to glean as much about her as he could. What he got back was a strong-willed individual... human and feminine.

Her full name breezed across his mind—Antonia Soo-Min Choi. Toni. A tantalizing sense of her femininity washed over him. The same feeling he got when he first touched her essence on FiPan. Yes, this was the woman he had been sent to find.

Lowering himself into the room, he made sure his short-heeled boots landed without a sound. Glancing around the clinical, sterile environment, he took in the smooth crystal walls. In the center of the room was a raised platform surrounded by alien instruments. A faint psychic residue lingered on that slab, unmistakably human. No doubt this was where the Krystalii had held Toni.

Unfortunately, she wasn't there anymore.

Azazel strode to the platform and brushed his hand over its smooth surface. The psychic trail was faint, scattered, as if someone had deliberately masked it. His chest tightened. "Damn it. We're too late."

JR14 landed on his shoulder, his sharp limbs clicking against the fabric of his shirt. "Observation: confirm human female was held on this platform. Residual heat signatures and biological markers establish this factor. Conclusion: Primary data suggests recent relocation."

Azazel's jaw clenched. "Any idea where they took her?"

JR14's sensors whirred, his sky-blue eyes pulsating in a light orange. "Scanning for exit vectors. This may take several moments."

Azazel stepped back, clenching his hands into fists, forcing himself to remain calm. Losing his temper wouldn't help. At least his inner beast remained quiet. "Hurry, *kalu*. The longer we stay in one place, the more it increases our chance of being discovered. And I have a feeling we don't have much time."

As he waited for JR14 to finish his communication with the ship's computer, Azazel let his hand rest on the platform again, his thoughts racing. Whoever had taken her hadn't hurt her, but he could easily sense her irritation all the same.

Then something caught his attention. He whipped around and faced the doorway, sensing a shift in the room's energy. The energy wasn't hostile, but deliberate—calm yet purposeful. The crystalline walls shimmered, refracting light in soft ripples before a figure glided into the room.

The newcomer's form was slender—a male crystalline figure bathed in aquamarine and silver that glistened in the sterile light. Shimmering white eyes locked onto Azazel's with a mix of curiosity and resolve. As he sauntered closer, his movements remained fluid and non-threatening.

Azazel tensed, and his psychic protections flared. He had to force himself to rein them in before his tension caused his inner beast to wake from its slumber.

JR14 skittered to his side, wings flexing as the small bot raised his voice. "Alert. Unknown entity. Probability of engagement escalating. Suggest immediate inquiry or preemptive action."

Azazel swallowed the urge to snort at JR14's unhelpful observation.

The crystalline figure raised both hands, a gesture that Azazel took as one of peace. "There's no need for hostility." "My name is Vaeloryx, and I believe we share a common goal."

Azazel's gaze narrowed, his stance unyielding. How did the alien sneak up on him and JR14 like that? "How did you know I was here?"

Vaeloryx's radiant eyes softened. "Your efforts may be effective against Baelon's Elites, however, the ship itself is alive in its own way. Your every step, your every breath ripple through the ship's crystalline lattice. I've trained myself to sense those ripples—an ability the Elite enforcers lack."

Azazel straightened and crossed his arms, studying the creature with narrowed eyes. "How convenient."

"I assure you, it is not without cost," Vaeloryx replied. "The process is cumbersome, but necessary to survive in this oppressive environment." The crystal being took a short step forward, and the mirrors and glass on his body refracted the light into faint prisms across the walls. "I am the leader of the Auracite Resistance here on the *Nyrlith*. We are a collective who oppose Lord Baelon's tyranny and the destruction he brings to our people and other dimensions."

"Definition: Auracite," JR14 intoned. "A mythical crystalline material among the Krystalii that symbolizes purity, strength, and light."

Azazel glanced at him over his shoulder with a raised eyebrow.

"I have ascertained some of this ship's linguistic logs." JR14 answered Azazel's silent question. "However, I'm working to get into the sensitive *Nyrlith* operations."

Azazel didn't comment on what the bot said. He clenched his hands into fists and faced the alien. "I'm guessing you haven't alerted the guards about us."

Vaeloryx stopped a few paces away, his luminous gaze steady. "When we discovered Baelon had taken a human female, we focused on the reason he would do that. It became clear his intent was to advance Krystalii genetics by using her DNA to speed up creating more of his mindless minions. Once that happens, any chance we have to overthrow his tyranny will end before it begins." Vaeloryx's translucent chest shimmered as he took a breath. "This must not be allowed to happen. Our priority is to take that opportunity away from Baelon at all costs. To do that, we will help you take her away from him and then get both of you off this ship. Combining our efforts, I'm convinced we can and will achieve our shared goal."

Azazel's jaw tightened. The last thing he wanted to do was to get involved in some kind of rebellion. Obviously, he'd have a greater chance of success if he had inside help. It wasn't reasonable to think he should take on an entire alien race alone.

JR14 broke the silence. "Analysis suggests aligning with the resistance increases mission success probability to 64.8 percent. However, risk factors remain high. Recommend careful consideration."

Azazel's lips curved into a thin smile. "Appreciate the optimism, JR14." He shifted his focus back to Vaeloryx. "Why should I trust you? You're one of them."

The Krystalii's gaze was steady. "As a show of good faith, I will share with you what we know about her thus far. They have moved her to the highest-security area. The experiments on her have not yet begun because she is suffering from malnutrition and dehydration. Baelon will not start any experiments on her until she has been provided with food, water, and rest to bring her to optimal health. I assure you, that reprieve won't last long. We don't have much time to retrieve her before she is forced to undergo his harsh treatments."

The light in Vaeloryx's eyes dimmed, as if burdened by what he said next. "I've lived all my life with what Baelon does to those who defy him. Doing nothing has cost me friends, family... those I care most about. So, my friends and I have vowed to make a difference in this dimension. We view this as our only chance to fight for our very right to exist." His expression set. "You and I are not so different in that desire. Are we, Azazel?"

Azazel froze. "How do you know my name?"

A slight, playful grin creased Vaeloryx's clear lips. "Word travels quickly, even across dimensions. The *Adamou* are not unknown to us. Your arrival stirred more than just the energy of this ship."

The tension in the room thickened as Azazel weighed his options. His instincts told him Vaeloryx was sincere, but trusting anyone in this place—especially a Krystalii—felt like stepping into a minefield blindfolded. When he replied, he kept his tone low and firm. "I will agree to work with you. However, just so we're clear, my priority is getting Toni and myself off this ship, not confronting Baelon. If there's even a hint that you're playing me, Vaeloryx, I'll dismantle your resistance before Baelon gets the chance to." He meant every single word. Even if he didn't know how he'd do that.

Yet.

Vaeloryx's crystalline face shifted, and the hard line of his lips softened as he gave him an understanding nod. "Agreed. So, we'd better not waste any more precious time. If you allow, I will create a temporary coating over your psionic abilities without being intrusive, to increase your camouflage abilities. Will that be alright with you?"

Azazel hesitated. "If I feel you violating my genetic makeup, I will retaliate." He braced himself when his internal demon stirred, threatening to wake up. It took everything he had to keep it at bay while maintaining the psychic concealment he'd put in place to keep anyone from knowing the beast was there.

"I assure you, delving into anything deeper in an organic alien would be abhorrent to me." Vaeloryx held up a hand. "I offer no offense."

Azazel couldn't help the grin. He couldn't agree more. "None taken."

Without another word, Azazel sensed a warmth envelop him, like walking into a room with a higher temperature. He breathed a sigh of relief as it settled around him. The Krystalii was true to his word and didn't violate him internally.

JR14 fluttered back onto Azazel's shoulder, his mechanical limbs clicking in rhythm. "Observation: partnership formed. Must now proceed with outlined objectives."

"Good." Vaeloryx turned to lead the way. "If you would follow me, I will take you to a haven in order for us to develop a successful plan of action."

Azazel followed without a word. For better or worse, the Krystalii resistance had gained a couple of unlikely allies.

Azazel trailed behind Vaeloryx, his footsteps soundless against the crystalline floor, as the passages of the *Nyrlith* thrummed with a low, steady pulse. The smooth walls they passed were lively with shifting crystalline colors of green, blue, pink, and even midnight black.

JR14 kept a steady perch on his shoulder. His red-and-gold metallic forelimbs gave small clicks as he scanned their surroundings.

Azazel had so many questions it was hard to focus on just one. The silence between the three of them stretched.

Vaeloryx stopped at an unremarkable section of the wall. He raised one translucent aquamarine hand, his movements deliberate as the crystalline surface of the wall rippled and parted, revealing a narrow corridor lit by a swirling pale light.

"This way." The Krystalii's voice was low and steady.

Azazel hesitated, his instincts prickling. He didn't dare psychically reach out to Vaeloryx, so he had to rely on conversation to get a better understanding. "I admit I'm still nervous about all of this. How do I know you're not leading me into a trap?" *Like the alien would admit it if that was the case,* he thought.

Vaeloryx turned, and his bright-ivory eyes met Azazel's gaze. "If I were, I would not have taken you this far. Trust me, *Adamou*."

"Observation," JR14 responded. "Probability of survival increases when surrounded by individuals invested in mutual success."

Azazel glanced at the bot.

"However," the droid continued in his dry monotone, "trust remains a statistically unreliable factor."

Well, wasn't that the literal truth?

Gritting his teeth, Azazel followed the Krystalii and kept his senses sharp. The air here felt different—denser, quieter. As they moved farther in, the corridor opened into a vast chamber. The space was unlike the sterile, lifeless halls of the *Nyrlith* he'd seen so far. Crystalline structures in a rainbow of colors jutted from the ground like trees, their surfaces etched with intricate designs that pulsed with energy. A group of Krystalii stood in the center, their bodies in a variety of translucent shades.

One stepped forward, a shorter Krystalii with a feminine-shaped body of deep emerald that glistened under the pale light. "Well, look at you, Vaeloryx. I see you've located the outsider." Her voice was sharp, almost accusatory, as her glittering gaze fixed on Azazel.

"Yes, this is Azazel," Vaeloryx stated in a smooth voice. "The organic individual who appeared on our sensors. He too seeks the human woman Baelon has taken. I have verified his mission aligns with ours."

The female's emerald gaze flicked to JR14. Her crystalline form moved in a subtle shift. "And the construct?"

JR14's wings flicked out and buzzed before sliding back into their protected panel under his back. "Designation: JR14. Function: support unit. Current objective: ensure survival of biological entity." For the first time, the bot's voice came out sharp and unrelenting.

Azazel smirked, one corner of his mouth lifting. "This construct aligns perfectly with my purpose."

Another Krystalii, taller and slender with a male shaped body of pale amber, stepped close. His voice was softer, tinged with curiosity. "Organic called Azazel, are you agreeable to work with us?"

"I will do my best," Azazel said in an even tone, his arms crossed. "If you're as eager to stop Baelon as Vaeloryx claims, I believe we can help each other. But my priority is to rescue the human woman, whose name is Toni, from him."

The emerald Krystalii let out a faint hum, her tone skeptical.

"And what happens once you have her? Will you abandon us to fight Baelon alone?"

Azazel's jaw tightened, but before he could respond, Vaeloryx stepped between them.

"Enough, Laytrii. Once the female is removed from Baelon's control, that will force him and his scientists to divert their attention to her recovery, and that distraction will give us the opening we need to execute our primary objective. A rare chance to stop Baelon forever."

Laytrii's gaze lingered on Azazel for a moment before she stepped back, her crystalline body refracting the chamber's light. "All right, I concede to your suggestion, Vaeloryx. I guess we'd better evaluate the best way to retrieve this human female. What have you surmised thus far?"

Vaeloryx turned to the group, his posture commanding but calm.

"Since Baelon's private sector is near the Nexus Core, we can use that to our advantage." His steady stare met Azazel's. "The Nexus Core is how Baelon became the undisputed dictator of the Krystalii. It magnifies his already powerful psionic abilities to override anyone else's. If his attention is focused on you, we can slip in and disrupt the core to not only weaken Baelon, but also the ship's defenses. That should cause him to divide his forces." He looked at Azazel. "That hopefully will give you the opening you need to complete the recovery of the human and afford you the probability of leaving the *Nyrlith*."

Azazel kept his tone even.

"And how do you propose we do that?"

An opal Krystalii, his form sleek and angular, nodded.

"There's a private deck near Baelon's residence that houses his personal fleet of ships. You can take one of the small ones to escape."

Azazel frowned. He'd never piloted a spaceship before. Even when they planned to escape the Akurns—who created him and his brothers—in a small space shuttle, he never had a chance to travel in it. He'd teleported them far into the future instead.

Vaeloryx must've sensed Azazel's unease. "Most of those ships are self-navigating. All you have to do is use your construct—" He pointed to JR14. "—to interface with it and put in the coordinates for your escape."

Azazel's grin wasn't humorous. "So, let me make sure I understand. For this to work, I'm going in as a distraction to give you a chance to sabotage the Nexus Core?"

Vaeloryx's smirk matched Azazel's. "Ah, well, that's one way of putting it. However, dividing Baelon's forces between us gives you a better chance to rescue the woman and escape—an advantage you would not have on your own."

"Laytrii and I will lead a team to the Nexus Core and

Kyrix will go with you to help you free the female. Once that is done, he'll guide you to Baelon's private space dock. There he'll help you determine which ship is the best for you to take."

Azazel glanced at JR14, whose multifaceted eyes shone with a faint orange light.

"What is your analysis of this, JR14?"

JR14 tilted, his body giving off a low whir.

"Probability of success: 47.3 percent."

"Comforting," Azazel muttered. *Why bother asking?*

JR14's announcement earned a faint chuckle from Vaeloryx. "Your companion is blunt but correct. Baelon's Elites will sense our movements once we put this in motion. Now, with that in mind, shall we proceed?"

Azazel's gaze swept over the gathered Krystalii. They were a ragtag group, and their colorful crystalline bodies bore faint cracks and imperfections—a testament to their struggle. He forced himself to unclench his fists held behind his back. "I believe this sounds promising, but I'd prefer we sit down and plan each detail further." It was a chance to consider the plan's viability. And, if it fell apart, at least he'd give himself an opportunity to come up with a Plan B beforehand.

With a nod, Vaeloryx gestured to a cluster of low, crystalline structures that formed a rough semicircle behind him.

"Agreed. No reason for us not to be comfortable while we do so." The surfaces shimmered with a warm glow that cast delicate patterns on the chamber floor.

Azazel studied the crystalline seats. He let loose an inaudible sigh. Exhaustion wracked him, making it hard to move, and he'd like nothing better than to sit down and take a breather. But it looked like Vaeloryx wanted to jump into this planning session right away. So, taking time out wasn't on the menu.

Not like he had a choice, no matter how low his energy was. He'd used a lot of power to teleport to the *Nyrlith*. And even if he was at full strength, the psychic restraints embedded within the vessel were stronger than he'd first assumed.

Gazing around the austere environment, he grimaced as he lowered himself onto the seat of a crystalline formation. Its smooth surface contoured around his frame and was surprisingly comfortable. JR14 stayed perched on his shoulder, and his metallic limbs shifted as he settled.

"Before we start, I must warn you about something," Vaeloryx said, his voice smooth as he took his seat. "You must refrain from using your psionic energy, especially your telepathic abilities, as much as possible." The aquamarine crystals along his cheeks lit into a soft silver.

"Because Lord Baelon has unfettered access to everyone's thoughts by using the Nexus Core, it gives him the ability to crush all attempts at rebellion, big or small."

Azazel's eyebrows rose. "Then how do you communicate with each other without him knowing?"

Vaeloryx turned until the side of his chest was visible to Azazel. Embedded there, where a human heart might be, a faint, silver glow flared to life.

"This device is called a Resonant Node. It allows me to communicate with others without using telepathy." A resonant hum echoed in the chamber as his voice emerged. He nodded to his companions behind Azazel. "We all have one that neither the Elites nor Lord Baelon are aware of." His words came out in a resonant hum. "Efficient, isn't it?"

Azazel studied the star-shaped device inside the Krystalii's chest. "I'm sure it's efficient, but it doesn't appear subtle." It reminded him of the walkie-talkies the humans used before cell phones.

The hum shifted, a faint ripple of sound that reminded Azazel of amusement.

"Subtlety is a luxury, *Adamou*. Not a necessity."

"Analysis: device functionality operates on vibrational frequencies. Probability of interception by Baelon's Elites: 23.8 percent if utilized in high-risk areas." JR14's front claws clicked with each enunciated word.

Vaeloryx inclined his head.

"True, but its range and encryption ensure that only those I choose to communicate with can interpret the resonances."

Azazel frowned.

"So, what's stopping Baelon from hearing you right now?"

Vaeloryx's reply came through the node. "Because these devices are not made of any type of crystalline structure. Its natural lattice absorbs and diffuses the frequencies in random sequences. Only a node attuned to mine can receive the signal. Also, we have the same material embedded in this chamber. It's the reason I brought you here, to shield us from his prying senses."

Azazel's mouth twisted as he thought. "That's good to know. But what happens once we leave here?" He gestured to the silver light blinking under the Krystalii's crystal chest. "And how will that work for me?" He leaned back. "I doubt you can embed that within my body the same way yours does."

Vaeloryx extended a small oval box of what appeared to be made of a dull material, like metallic plastic. One end of it beeped with a steady white light.

"This is a Sub-Node. With it, you can communicate with me directly, no matter where you are within *Nyrlith*."

With a wary eye, Azazel studied the unit as Vaeloryx dropped it onto his open palm. The faint vibrations from it brushed against his skin like a heartbeat.

"How do I use it?" He brought it up to his face, squinting as he turned it over.

"If you will allow?" Vaeloryx stood in front of Azazel with a pointed finger. "I assure you, this will be a minor intrusion as I convey instructions on the Sub-Node." The tip of his finger had a pale glow.

Azazel stared at the twinkling light on the box before slightly nodding. He'd used the same technique when he wanted to give his brothers the necessary information the quickest way.

After a light touch against Azazel's temple, Vaeloryx moved back to his seat.

Azazel blinked as the knowledge of the Sub-Resonant Node filled his mind. A faint hum from the node on Vaeloryx's chest caught his attention.

"Speak, test to see how it carries your voice. Even if you whisper."

Azazel studied the flickering light, now a soft yellow at the Sub-Node's edge. The thing felt alien, unnatural, but strangely familiar. He glanced at his Krystalii host. "Does it broadcast my speech and not my thoughts?"

The corners of Vaeloryx's clear lips curled with a mischievous grin. "It does not transmit telepathically." His tone came out steady as it resonated through the device in Azazel's hand. "Only what you vocalize. But I must caution you that long transmissions increase the risk of detection."

Azazel pursed his lips as he studied the node as Vaeloryx spoke through it. Using the knowledge the Krystalii had just given him, he flipped a switch on the other side to turn it off.

"Thank you. This will be very helpful." After giving the device one last look to make sure it stayed off, he slipped it into the side pocket of the loose trousers he wore.

"Now, let us address our basic collaborative strategy." The glow in Vaeloryx's eyes met Azazel's stare with quiet conviction. "Earlier, I said that the closer we get to Baelon's private sector, the tighter the ship's defenses will become."

Azazel leaned forward, resting his forearms on his knees.

"Okay, so how do we do this without setting off the ship's alarms?"

Vaeloryx's crystalline body shifted. "As I've stated before, the Nexus Core lies next to Baelon's private chambers, where the human prisoner is held. Once you enter where she is kept, it will alert the security systems. Kyrix will help you keep the Elites busy, giving us enough time to slip into the Nexus Core compound. Once we disable the core, it will force the ship to divert energy from all unnecessary security systems to make repairs. Once that happens, it will give you the chance to obtain the human female.

"And if the core doesn't go down?" Azazel tapped his forefinger on his lower lip.

"Then we then will use a secondary approach." Vaeloryx seemed unfazed by the skepticism. "Since Laytrii and I will be the ones at the core, we can feign an attack on a nearby secondary propulsion array to help draw the Elites away even more. If executed correctly, this will also buy you enough time to extract the human and escape."

Azazel leaned back and draped his arms across the back of the couch.

"That might work."

"The only way we can be successful in battle is open communication to outline strategy and adaptability," Vaeloryx continued. "Efficient communication will maximize our chances."

"Observation," JR14 interjected, his voice clinical as ever. "Joint probability calculations suggest a 63.2 percent increase in mission success with coordinated efforts. However, residual risk factors remain high in either scenario."

"Encouraging," Azazel stated. "And once I have Toni, Kyrix will take us where we need to go?"

Vaeloryx gestured toward the opalescent Kyrix, who'd remained silent until now.

"Yes, most of my duties are in Baelon's private sector." He inclined his head, his voice soft but steady. "If that part of the plan has to be abandoned, we will regroup and head back here to determine our next steps with the others."

Azazel frowned in consideration. His mind raced. The plan wasn't perfect—far from it. But at least it was a first step. There wasn't time to come up with something else. He had to get Toni out of Baelon's grip before the Krystalii started those experiments on her. And working with the rebellious aliens was far better than working alone. He straightened, his gaze sharp as it locked onto Vaeloryx.

With a terse nod, he agreed.

"Then let us do everything we can to ensure this plan works. Because failure isn't an option for either of us."

Vaeloryx inclined his head in agreement, his translucent aquamarine features unreadable.

"Just so. Let us begin."

Toni's knees buckled when she was popped into a crystalline cage by an unseen force. The frigid air clung to her skin like a damp chill, sapping the heat from her body with each passing second. She shivered and exhaled, her breath coming out in thin, white wisps. Trying to keep warm, she hugged her arms around herself as the translucent walls around her flickered to life, casting eerie, fractured shadows across the smooth floor.

The room was vast yet suffocating. Towering walls were faceted like the inside of a hollowed-out geode. A pulsing, irregular, blue-green dimness illuminated the space. The only thing that the diffused glow provided was a feeble light across the walls, pale and unnatural. It offered no comfort—no heat—just a dead light that settled over her like a shroud.

Toni rubbed her arms, but the chill clung tighter, seeping into her bones as if warmth had no place on this alien ship. She sucked in a sharp breath, searching for a trace of something familiar—a metallic tang, a hint of ozone—but the air carried no scent. It came across as artificial, manufactured, like everything else about this stupid, bizarre place.

Swallowing with a dry throat, she did her best to ignore how her tongue lay heavy and scratchy as sandpaper in her mouth. She licked her cracked lips, but that didn't help. She hadn't had water in what seemed like days, making every cell in her body scream for hydration. To make things worse, the acid in her stomach twisted with hunger. Looking around, she shivered. Every moment stretched, and the oppressive silence amplified the sensations burning inside her. She pressed her palms against one of the crystalline walls. The hard material was smooth, cool, and unyielding.

Inhuman.

A sharp sound echoed, breaking the silence. A part of the wall slid open, and the hulking figure of Lord Baelon sauntered in. The wall solidified behind him. The apatite-blue crystals composing his body clinked with each movement.

He stopped a few feet from her, his fists on his hips.

Toni stumbled backward until her shoulders met the icy surface of the crystalline wall. The cold bit through her thin shirt, but she pressed harder against it. She tensed as her breathing turned shallow. Her only thought was to get as far from the towering figure as she could.

Baelon's multifaceted eyes glinted in the dim light as he raised his crystalline hand. With a subtle movement, the walls of her cage shimmered. The glow changed from its blue-green to a red-yellow, a warmer, faint hue. The oppressive cold eased enough to make the pervasive chill melt away. She sighed at the welcome warmth.

"Human physiology is distastefully delicate." Baelon's voice resonated like glass shattering on a hard floor. "But I will not allow such trivial limitations to compromise your value."

She wanted to spout a scathing retort, but forming the words was beyond her. Her dry throat burned, causing her tongue to swell. Thought she lacked the strength for a contemptuous retort, she could still manage a good glare. Maybe that would distract the walking-chandelier from noticing her trembling knees.

Baelon gestured again, and a faint mist formed within the cage. It swirled like an ethereal tornado, condensing into a small, crystalline vessel that hovered just within her reach. It shimmered with liquid—a pale lavender substance that refracted the light like a mirrored lilac flower.

"Drink." Baelon's tone left no room for argument. "You require hydration, and this will suffice until your condition stabilizes."

Toni hesitated, her gaze darting between the goblet and the angular alien figure before her. Was it a trick? Another form of manipulation? It was hard to decide, between her parched throat and spinning head.

"Is this how you're going to kill me?" she croaked. Wow, look at her with the gift of gab after all. Even if her intended scorn came out as a hoarse whisper.

Baelon tilted his head, his expression impassive. His crystalline form flickered in various blue hues. "You misunderstand." His tone was tinged with condescension. "This is not an offer. It is a necessity. Your continued survival ensures the fulfillment of my purpose. Therefore, if you refuse, I will have no choice but to force it upon you. And I assure you—" he sneered. "—you will not enjoy the experience."

The pulsating light within the crystalline walls intensified, as if the ship itself urged her to comply. Unable to fight off the mounting pressure, her legs gave out. She sank to the ground, clutching her stomach as it twisted in hollow pain.

With blurry vision, she extended a trembling hand for the chalice. The liquid inside sloshed as she brought it to her lips. The first sip felt strange, cool and weightless like water but with an odd, electric sharpness that tingled against her tongue. It slid down her throat, quenching the fire and spreading warmth through her chest. Her body absorbed it, as though hungry for what it offered.

Baelon remained silent, his crystalline form glowing a deeper sapphire, as if in satisfaction. "I believe adaptation is your species' most valuable trait," he murmured. "We must preserve this attribute."

Too bad the liquid didn't erase the chill in her veins. Or somehow take away the oppressive weight of the cage. She wiped her mouth with the back of her hand and glowered at him. "You think this changes anything?" she rasped, her voice gaining strength. "You can't just... fix me and then expect me to lie down and let you experiment on me."

Baelon's crystalline lips curled into a thin, unnerving smile. "I expect nothing from you but existence, human. It is in your nature to resist. That will not change the inevitability of your purpose."

With that, he vanished, leaving her alone in the dim, pulsing glow of her new prison. The gnawing pit in her stomach turned to acid. "I swear to God this isn't over," Toni whispered, her voice now steady.

First things first. She'd finish the stuff shards-for-brains gave her. Then she'd figure out how to get out of this mess. Whatever twisted plans Baelon had in mind for her, he could shove them into the deepest void of space. Nothing was going to happen to this lady.

No way in hell.

Azazel followed Vaeloryx through the labyrinthine corridors of Baelon's private sector, keeping his focus razor-sharp on his surroundings. Because he had to keep his psychic talents hidden, he'd forced himself to rely on his five senses.

Along with his trusty AI companion resting on his shoulders.

Since he couldn't use his psionic powers, Azazel created something to defend himself with. Before they left the protected chamber, he used his powers to make a katana, identical to the one he'd had on Earth. He kept the blade in the scabbard attached to the sash wrapped around his waist.

He moved behind the gemstone male through the low light of the crystalline corridor, his every step deliberate and silent.

JR14 clung to his shoulder, the faint hum of his wings the only sound he made.

Behind him, Laytrii and Kyrix moved with silent stealth. Their crystalline forms shifted in hues of emerald and opal.

Around them, the walls pulsed in ominous shades—deep purples and bruised blues—that cast eerie, flickering shadows.

Azazel clenched his fists, keeping his mind sharp on everything around him. The nerves in his body screamed caution the farther they headed into Baelon's private sector. Thank the goddess his inner beast remained still.

"We are close to the Nexus Core," Vaeloryx murmured. The aquamarine crystals and mirrors on his body had a faint glow. "Prepare yourselves. Once we disrupt it, this area will destabilize."

Azazel nodded, his jaw set. "Let's hope this diversion works. We can't afford to be pinned down here."

Something about how easy it was to get to Baelon's private sector didn't seem right. There weren't any guards. Nor did the rebels have a problem gaining entrance. What kind of maniacal dictator left himself open like that?

Either the guy was an intense egomaniac who never doubted his hold on his subjects—or

this was all a trap. But what he couldn't figure out was, if it was a trap, why go through all this? Wouldn't it be easier to either hold Azazel... or kill him?

Keeping his eyes open, he continued to follow Vaeloryx down the elaborate crystalline doorway toward the end of the hall.

"Observation," JR14 interjected. "Probability of encounter with hostile forces has increased to 79.6 percent. I advise implementing tactical readiness."

"Noted," Azazel muttered. So, there *were* guards. But why hadn't they come to stop the intruders? Once again, he puzzled over the notion that Baelon didn't have a huge contingency of troops controlling this sensitive area. Another question popped up. If it was this easy to get here, why hadn't Vaeloryx and his crew done this a long time ago? Lips thinned, he brushed his hand over the hilt of the blade strapped to his side.

Vaeloryx stopped at a crystalline console embedded in the wall, its surface etched with shifting glyphs. He placed his hand on it, and the glyphs flared to life. "Laytrii, cover the rear," he commanded. "Kyrix, assist me with the override."

With a low hum, the door rippled and slid apart, revealing the heart of what Baelon kept in his private sanctum. The core chamber was vast, its walls lined with intricate crystalline conduits that pulsed with blinding energy. At the center stood a towering structure of translucent glass and shifting light.

That had to be the Nexus Core they'd told him about. It thrummed with raw energy, its vibrations resonating deep in Azazel's chest.

Laytrii moved into position, her emerald body refracting the dim light. "We're exposed here," she hissed. "So, we'd better make it quick. Kyrix will take you to the place where Baelon is holding the human female. Once you're in, it'll sound off the alarms." Her grin was infectious. "And that'll give us a chance to take this damn thing out."

Azazel glanced at the opal male before scanning the corridor, keeping his senses on high alert. "Okay, which way?" He grimaced as the air grew heavier, charged with a subtle vibration that set his nerves on edge. "Wait." He held up his hand. "JR14, are you picking up anything unusual?"

JR14's bulbous eyes flickered as he inspected around them. "Anomalous energy signature detected. Hostile entities approaching from the eastern corridor."

"Son of a *lilit*," Azazel hissed. The guards' approach didn't surprise him. What shocked him was there weren't more guards loitering around inside. *Ezeru*, he didn't like any of this. With a smooth and deliberate move, he drew his blade. Its edges mirrored the gleam from the crystal corridor. "Change of plans. If you disrupt the core first, it'll give me a better chance to get Toni."

Vaeloryx's expression hardened. "That's not what we agreed on," he hissed. After a silent beat, his clear crystal lips creased into a frown.

"But... fine. Looks like I don't have a choice." He turned to his Krystalii companions. "Laytrii, Kyrix, begin the disruption."

The two Krystalii nodded and moved to opposite sides of the chamber.

Laytrii's emerald form shimmered as she extended her arms, sending a wave of energy into the conduits.

Kyrix followed suit, his opalescent body emitting a bright glow as he channeled his power into the core.

The room shuddered as the hum escalated into a deafening roar.

Azazel's eyes narrowed as he felt the shift in the ship's energy.

JR14's voice cut through the chaos. "Alert: Elite enforcers' response imminent."

Dammit! He should have left when he had the chance.

Positioning himself between the console and the approaching threat, Azazel focused.

The first of Baelon's enforcers appeared, towering crystalline figures of brown agate with chiseled edges and an aura of palpable menace. They charged without hesitation, and the crystals on their bodies glinted like blades.

He met their attack head-on. His blade clashed against an Elite's arm with a resounding crack. Sparks flew as he parried a second strike from another, his movements fluid and precise.

"Laytrii, Kyrix, get ready," Vaeloryx commanded, his voice cold and steady.

Laytrii unleashed a burst of energy into the console, making her bright-green body flare. "Keep them off us, *Adamou*!" she called.

"I'm trying!" Azazel growled as he drove his blade into an enforcer's chest.

The crystalline body shattered, and shards scattered across the floor.

He stiffened, his breaths coming out labored. Good to know the Krystalii were susceptible to physical attacks. But it was puzzling why they didn't just use their psychic powers to hold him back.

No time to ponder. Another guard attacked, replacing his downed comrade.

Outside the room, an echoing clatter of glass footsteps sounded, telling him more Elites were on their way.

"Core override complete," Vaeloryx announced in a calm tone. "The system will collapse. Now is your chance to grab the female. Go!" His last word came out in a growl when two Elites converged on him.

Laytrii battled next to him, keeping the descending forces busy.

Azazel nodded, stepping back as the corridor trembled.

The walls flickered, their mirrored glow dimmed.

"This way!" Kyrix barked, motioning for him and JR14 to follow.

Alarms blared, and their piercing wail echoed through the unstable halls.

Azazel's heart pounded as they entered Baelon's private chamber next to the Nexus Core.

A massive doorway loomed ahead. Intricate patterns around it pulsated with a faint light.

"She's in there," Kyrix slapped his hand next to the door. "Retrieve her and then go through the only open hallway inside—it leads to his private ship dock. Your construct should be able to guide you to one you can operate." The opal Krystalii glanced over his shoulder, his breaths coming out short before turning back to him. "I'm afraid you're on your own from here. I've got to go back and help the others divert the guards headed this way. If you can't get a ship, head back to the rendezvous point." The door rippled and parted, revealing an inner sanctum.

"Understood." Azazel slipped his katana back into its sheath. "JR14 has the coordinates of the docked ships. If things don't turn out like we planned, we'll meet you there as soon as it's safe to do so."

Kyrix nodded, his iridescent features unreadable before he turned and ran back the way they'd come without another word.

Walking through the open doorway, Azazel was met with stifling air. Heavy with the scent of minerals mixed with an underlying metallic layer. The room was lavish in its starkness, its walls adorned with jagged crystal formations that glowed with a faint violet light. At one corner, a figure sat against the crystalline wall—a woman.

He froze. Her very essence hit him like a blow. Even in this alien environment, she appeared otherworldly. Her dark hair framed her delicate face, her skin luminous under the faint light. Thank the goddess, she appeared unharmed. His breath caught. The more he studied her, the stronger something deep inside him shifted. He swallowed as he scanned her strong-yet-soft features. This was a woman with a magnetic presence.

Toni.

"Verified: organic female human," JR14's voice broke through his thoughts, his words a distant whir. "Vital signs stable."

Azazel didn't waste any time racing toward her.

Her eyes widened, and a faint moan escaped her lips. And in that brief moment, their gazes met. Those eyes, a deep and startling shade of cornflower blue, locked onto his.

The world paused.

Inexplicable warmth flooded his chest, a sensation he'd never experienced before.

"Who…" She stared at him, her voice trembling but steady. "Who are you?"

"Trust me," Azazel said, his voice gentler than he expected. "I'm your way out."

The sound of distant footsteps shattered the moment.

Vaeloryx's voice echoed through the Sub-Node dangling from the sash wrapped around his waist. "Azazel, the enforcers are closing in. You must leave now."

Azazel didn't hesitate. He scooped Toni into his arms, making her squeal as she wrapped her arms around his neck. He held her close, her slight weight easy to handle as he headed toward the open door. "JR14, prepare for extraction."

"Affirmative," the bot replied, and his wings buzzed in a steady rhythm.

Azazel sprinted through an open doorway and headed left. If he wasn't mistaken, it was where Kyrix had told him to go. At least he hoped so. He struggled to pay attention to where he was going. It was hard to shake the image of Toni's mesmerizing eyes—the way they pierced through him—that ignited something deep and primal inside him. So much so that his inner beast twitched with interest.

Son-of-a-*lilit*! Last thing he needed was this added distraction. He didn't have time to moon over a woman he hadn't even introduced himself to yet. Ignoring his instinctual reaction to her, he redoubled his efforts and concentrated on putting one foot in front of the other.

The ship trembled around them, the room's defenses faltering under the strain of the destabilized core.

Azazel tightened his grip on Toni and raced down the chamber. The sound of chaos and conflict grew louder around them with each step.

When Lord Ronald-McDictator vanished, the only thing for Toni to do was finish the liquid stuff he had given her. After she swallowed the last sip, her heavy eyes demanded some downtime. And before she knew it, she was out like a light.

She jolted awake as the platform beneath her shuddered. Her head pounded, and she touched the side of her face and tried to wade through the thick fog churning inside her brain. Glancing around through blurry eyes, she noticed the light had changed to a violet color that bathed the crystalline room. It pulsed erratically, throwing distorted shadows across the walls. *Son of a bitch!* The damn place better stop wavering around or she'd spew.

With a moan, she covered her stomach with her palm and sat up, leaning against the mirrored wall. Something caught her attention, making her look around. What was that? Her pulse quickened.

A loud crack split the air, and the heavy chamber doors slid open.

Toni froze. Her breath hitched as a figure rushed through the threshold, his silhouette sharp against the flickering light.

Holy God! No way was that Baelon.

With an unbelieving stare, she took in the man standing a few feet away. He was all hard lines and silent intensity. A man who didn't need to speak to make the room bend around his will. She watched him the way prey watches a predator—fascinated and wary, but unable to look away. His long dark hair, pulled back in a thick braid, leaving a strong scruffy jawline clear, high cheekbones, and mahogany-brown eyes that stared at her with timeless purpose. His face could have been chiseled by a master sculptor—sharp angles, powerful lines, and a quiet intensity that dared her to look away. The slight edges of a scar above his left brow only enhanced the rugged potency of his features.

She sucked in a breath and scanned what he wore. A loose, tunic-style shirt in a neutral color covered flowing trousers held together by a wide, black sash wrapped around his trim waist. And, if she wasn't mistaken, snuggled in that sash was an honest-to-god katana.

For a split second, Toni's breath caught. She couldn't have envisioned a more-compelling heroic figure in one of her movies if she tried. This man was impossibly striking, a vision of something fierce and noble that didn't belong in the nightmarish reality she found herself stuck in.

Suspicion reared its ugly head. Toni's heart thrummed harder. Baelon was a master manipulator. This man—this apparition of a "rescuer"—could be another one of his cruel games. How else could she explain it? As if her idea of a perfect man just happened to stride through the door to rescue her. The guy radiated undeniable confidence. A living embodiment of every fantasy her personal leading man would be. Her throat tightened as she sat ramrod straight, fighting to stay calm.

"Who..." She swallowed to keep the trembling out of her tone. "Who are you?"

"Trust me." He said in a gentle tone. "I'm your way out."

Yeah, right. Like she was stupid enough to buy that shit show.

Clattering footsteps from outside the room echoed.

"Azazel, the enforcers are closing in. You must leave now."

Was that strange voice coming from some kind of... beeper attached to the sash on his trim waist? And... Azazel? What kind of name was that?

Next thing she knew, his brawny arms swept her up and held her close. With a sharp shriek, she wrapped her arms around his firm neck and hung on as he raced out of the room the same way he came in.

"JR14, prepare for extraction."

"Affirmative," came an answer from a red-gold spider buzzing next to her. A flying spider? No, wait. It looked metallic. And it talked. *Must be some kind of alien robot.*

The ship trembled, causing the man to stumble.

She gasped and hung on tighter. Fortunately, he never faltered. Shouts and the sounds of pursuit echoed from behind them, making it clear they were being chased. It stood to reason it had to be Baelon's flunkies.

And on cue, a sharp, blaring alarm echoed down the corridor, growing louder.

The man she assumed was Azazel muttered a curse under his breath in a strange language.

Adjusting his hold on her, he shifted her weight and held her close to his wide chest.

She gasped and his masculine scent blanketed her with tantalizing warmth, a heady mix of spice and earth that ignited her senses, leaving her yearning for more.

"JR14, what's their position? And can we still make it to Baelon's hangar?"

The small, spider-like machine continued to buzz beside them. His red-and-gold body glinted in the dim light.

"Elites have detected energy fluctuations in this sector and cut off all access to the space dock. Probability of pursuit in that direction has increased to 92.4 percent. Suggest continued extraction in a different direction." His voice was mechanical and unemotional.

Toni groaned at the obvious statement.

"What... what is that thing?" She pointed to the red-gold spider-thingy.

"JR14 is my AI companion," Azazel stated, speeding down the corridor. His steps were quick but controlled, each movement smooth despite her added weight. "Introductions later. Right now, we have to get away from Baelon's enforcers."

"Where are we going?" Like she had any suggestions.

"Someplace safer than here," Azazel said.

Oh, great, she thought. *Someplace safer. Obviously a man of few words.*

The hallway turned narrow and pulsated with a weak light. Toni glanced over Azazel's shoulder. She squinted and caught sight of movement—shards of light that resolved into sharp, crystalline forms. Her stomach tightened. "They're coming," she whispered. She cleared her throat, trying to stop her voice from trembling.

Azazel didn't look back. "I know."

JR14 flew before them, and his short metallic claws in the front clicked as he zipped through the air.

"Suggestion: deploy secondary plan. Corridor ahead leads to a ventilation access point. Narrow passageways will hinder Elites' mobility."

Azazel's grip on her shifted as he picked up speed. "Will it buy us enough time?"

"Probability of success: 68.7 percent," JR14 replied. "Recommendation: extreme caution."

"Caution?" Toni muttered with a weak smirk. "Darn, what a great idea."

Azazel didn't answer. Instead, he veered to the left and dashed into a dimly lit passageway.

Holy cow, this corridor was even narrower than the one they'd been in. Toni swallowed her bout of claustrophobia as the hated crystalline walls pressed in.

Behind them, the sound of pursuit grew louder. Heavy footfalls and alien voices shouting commands.

Toni's fingers curled into the fabric of his shirt. "They're getting closer."

Azazel's jaw clenched. "Not for long."

Ahead, JR14 paused at the edge of what looked like a sheer drop. The small AI turned back, his soft blue eyes focused on Azazel.

"Access point located. Ventilation shaft is ten meters below. Maneuverability required."

"Great," Azazel muttered. "Hold on, Toni."

"Hold on to what?" She didn't have time to wonder how he knew her name. Questions for him died as he leaped into the shaft without hesitation.

Toni screeched as the air rushed past them, cool and sharp as they fell. Her heart pounded, and her eyes widened with fear in the darkness.

Azazel twisted midair, his movements precise, as he grabbed a crystal outcropping. His grip steadied them for a moment before he swung into a narrow opening on the side of the shaft.

She gasped, her pulse racing.

"Are you insane? Who do you think you are? Tom Cruise doing his own stunts?" In real life, she never dreamed anyone would or could do something so reckless without extensive planning. Not even the craziest stuntman in the business would attempt to do anything like that until he and his crew planned everything down to the nth degree.

"No," Azazel said in a flat tone. "Just experienced."

Experienced? In what? If this guy claimed he did this sort of thing all the time, he couldn't be real. He had to be something the sparkle-tyrant dreamed up from her mind.

JR14 landed on Azazel's shoulder with a soft flutter of his wings. "Pursuers have paused at the shaft's edge. Likelihood of continued pursuit: 41.2 percent. Recommendation: immediate removal from this area."

Azazel adjusted his grip on Toni.

She watched his gaze sweep across the cramped space. At least there was more light here.

"Where does this lead?" he asked his AI companion.

"To a secondary junction near the resistance's safe zone," JR14 said. "Probability of our continued safety increases in that direction."

Azazel didn't say a word. He moved, his steps sure despite the cramped conditions.

Toni felt every jolt, every shift, and couldn't help but marvel at how he carried her without breaking into a sweat. Damn superhero holding her wasn't even breathing hard. "I don't know who you are," she kept her voice low. "But... thank you." Even if he was some kind of decoy from the Krystalii, it didn't hurt to let him think she was buying into this whole charade.

He glanced down at her, his expression unreadable. "We will have a clarifying discussion when it is safe to do so."

"Can't wait," she mumbled.

Behind them, the faint echoes of the enforcers' pursuit faded into silence.

For the first time, Toni took a deep breath and sagged against Azazel's chest. Whatever this madness was, at least she was free of the blue-boulders' grip—for now. And it was all because of the man holding her. Maybe later she'd get a chance to figure things out.

To decide if she was in the arms of a possible betrayer or not.

CHAPTER THREE

Finally. The man holding Toni put her on her own two feet. It took a moment for the room to stop spinning, but soon enough, she crept behind him. Staying close to his powerful body, she moaned when a smidgen of his warmth touched her. Taking a fearful look behind her, she shivered and folded her arms across her chest, hoping to ward off the relentless chill.

She might be grateful he'd put her down, but the keen loss of his body heat made her shiver. Damn, she sure missed that human heater. She studied the firm muscles of his back, and the mesmerizing swing of his ankle-length silky braid tied at the nape of his neck. Wait, what kind of man grew his hair that long? And, if she wasn't mistaken, the exposed tips of his ears had a slight point.

She considered the rest of him. The almond-shaped of his eyes gave him the look of an ideal Asian elf. Yeah, a muscular stuntman from Hong Kong who'd fit nicely on the set of any Lord of the Rings franchise. He even had a sexy accent to go along with the exotic vibe.

Shaking herself out of her musings, she glanced around and noticed the faint hum of the ship buzzing in the background. The strange sound rose and fell like a hypnotic chant.

Okay, enough walking behind a man like some kind of damsel in distress from an old silent movie. Gritting her teeth to keep them from chattering, she trotted to Azazel's side and studied his attractive profile. Shimmers of the violet lights around them highlighted his sharp features.

"We're lost, aren't we?" She grimaced at the impatient, whiny tone of her voice. She sounded like a petulant child. But dammit, she couldn't help it. At least she didn't demand to know if they were there yet.

Azazel glanced at her, his expression tight, his almond-shaped eyes narrowed. "We're not lost."

"Oh yeah? Because this hallway looks exactly like the last four we've been down." She gestured at the glittering, translucent walls. "I declare, walking around this sparkly-doom fun house is like a place you can check out any time you like but you can never leave." Kudos to the classic rock band Eagles for an astute description of the wandering shit show she was in.

JR14, perched on Azazel's shoulder, flicked one of his metallic front legs. "Clarification: Sub-Node failure has resulted in temporary navigational impairment. Probability of current route leading to rendezvous point: 16.8 percent."

Azazel's scowl deepened as he stopped and glared at the spider-droid. "And you couldn't have mentioned that sooner?"

JR14 clicked his forelegs in what Toni swore sounded like a condescending rhythm. "Organic impatience noted. Suggested course correction: Utilize map matrix manual override."

"Which I couldn't do while I carried her." Azazel countered in a low tone.

Toni bristled. "Well, good thing you're not carrying me now, eh?" She'd be darned if she took the blame for them getting lost. "So, go ahead. Nothing's stopping you from playing with whatever toys you've got up your sleeve, now is there?"

He turned, his towering figure seeming to fill the narrow space.

She sucked in a breath as his nearness did all sorts of uncomfortable things inside her. Especially to her lady parts, now paying close attention. Crossing her arms to cover her hard nipples, she glowered and stared back. For a moment, his eyes burned into hers with an unspoken challenge in their depths.

"You could barely stand."

Azazel's soft words caressed her like velvet wrapped around steel.

"Much less run with the speed necessary to escape that stronghold."

He stepped closer, and his tantalizing scent teased her nose.

"I assure you, I will do my best to take you to a place where we can escape the Krystalii. Shall we continue?"

Her cheeks flushed, a mix of anger and embarrassment for acting like one of those spoiled divas she had to work with. "Of course," she muttered, looking away. Great, trust her to let the great bitch of the galaxy named Antonia Soo-min Choi out. Way to alienate the hunky guy trying to save her.

Azazel's slight smile warmed before he turned and moved forward again, his long strides steady, his thick braid swinging back and forth.

Toni couldn't help getting lost in the play of his backside muscles under his loose trousers once again. The simple power in his every movement was sensual and primal as hell.

No. *Focus, you friggin' floozie.* He could still be a trap, just like everything else on this asinine ship.

When she followed Azazel around a corner, she skidded to a stop to avoid running into him.

They'd hit a dead end.

A large door dominated the space, its surface etched with strange, shimmering symbols.

The faint hum around them grew louder.

Azazel hesitated, his hand resting on the hilt of his katana. "JR14, what's behind that door?"

"Unknown," the AI replied. "However, energy readings are consistent with Krystalii life-support systems."

"Well, that sounds just sound peachy." she stated in a dry tone, standing next to him. She rubbed her arms, trying to ward off the chill that made her skin pebble. Did it just get colder here, or was she imagining things?

Azazel paused before the crystalline door. His hand hovered above the glowing surface as he studied it with narrowed eyes. An eternity passed before he placed his palm against it. He closed his eyes as if listening to something only he could hear.

Toni stepped closer, a tight grip on her upper arms. "What are you doing?"

"One moment, please," he murmured, his voice low and distant. The faint light from the door pulsed in rhythm with his touch.

She frowned when a crease formed between his brows. "Okay, this is officially weird. What's going on? Are you... feeling something?"

Azazel's eyes opened, their usual sharpness softened by a distant glaze. "Krystalii signatures. They're here... but not fully."

Toni tilted her head and planted her palms on her hips. "What does that mean?" *Damn man was as exasperating as hell.*

"It means their presence is fragmented," JR14 interjected from Azazel's shoulder. His tiny sky-blue eyes glimmered as he looked at her. "Localized energy fluctuations suggest incomplete materialization. Hypothesis: these signatures may represent partially transitioned entities—neither fully in this dimension nor the next."

She blinked, turning to the spider-like AI. "Wait, what? You're saying there are half-ghost crystal aliens behind that door?"

"Clarification: not ghosts. Dimensional overlap. Probability of successful materialization upon interaction: 73.5 percent."

"Great." Toni rolled her eyes. "So, we could be walking into a room full of invisible aliens that could pop out at any second. Fantastic."

Azazel's hand dropped to his side, and his fingers brushed the hilt of his katana. He whispered, his voice steady. "We'll know for sure once we're inside. Stay close."

"Oh, don't worry," she muttered. "You couldn't get rid of me if you tried. Just think of me as your personal shadow—clingier than a wet piece of gum stuck on the bottom of your shoe." To make her point, she grabbed the loose material of his tunic. Just to make sure he didn't go far. "So, tell me. Are you psychic on top of everything else?"

Azazel's lips quirked with the faintest hint of a smile. "What would you do if I said yes?"

She snorted. "Reconsider all my life choices."

JR14's mechanical voice clicked in. "Advisory: recommend minimal hesitation. Delayed action may provoke spontaneous materialization of adversarial forces."

Azazel gave a small nod to the AI, his gaze steady as he looked at Toni. "You ready?"

She swallowed hard to steel herself. "I guess as ready as I'll ever be." She shrugged with a ghost of a smile. "Just don't start levitating like Dr. Strange. I don't think I could handle that." At least Azazel didn't wear a creepy cape like that Marvel character did.

He pushed the door open and stepped inside.

She kept a tight grip on his shirt and stayed as close to him as she could without tripping them both. The eerie cobalt-blue color of the room made her blink as the unsettling pulse of the crystalline walls matched the tension squeezing her chest. The air inside was colder, causing her to shiver harder. *Dammit!* Why wasn't there a single cozy space in this hellish nightmare? She moved even closer to Azazel. Her visible breath hitched as her eyes adjusted.

Rows upon rows of crystalline pods lined the walls, each with a low light that undulated in an erratic rhythm. Inside, indistinct humanoid shapes floated, their crystalline forms distorted by the refracted light.

"Oh my God, what the hell is that?" Toni whispered as she released her rescuer's tunic and grabbed his lower arm.

"Krystalii incubation chambers." Azazel's voice was grim.

Her stomach turned. "You mean... baby monsters?" *Oh God.* Flashes of the movie *Alien* passed before her eyes. Just what they needed.

The muscles in his chiseled jaw tightened. "That's an adequate a description as any."

A sudden clang echoed from somewhere behind them, sharp and metallic.

He stiffened.

She released him as he tightened his grip on the katana at his side. Her pulse skyrocketed.

"JR14?" Azazel whispered.

"Pursuers have resumed movement. Likelihood of detection within this sector: 78.3 percent."

"Well," Toni muttered. "I wouldn't bet against them in Vegas with those odds."

Azazel shot her a look, his voice calm but firm. "Stay close."

"Oh, don't worry 'bout that, Captain Obvious." Her heart hammered as they moved through the room, weaving between the eerie pods. "But I warn you, if something tries to grab me, I'm tripping you and running the other way." She'd like nothing better than to trust him, but the hard, icy knot of suspicion in her chest refused to go away.

Now might not be the best time to ask, but she couldn't help herself. "Where did you come from, and why are you helping me?" She gnawed on her bottom lip to stop her chin from wobbling. Great, her shivers were taking over. "What's in it for you?"

Azazel paused and turned to face her. For a moment, the sharp planes of his face softened. "I'm here because it's the right thing for me to do."

Well, wasn't that just a dandy non-answer? She'd like to believe him. Really, she did. Maybe living in LA and working in the movie business made her distrustful of everyone, but trust was a luxury she couldn't afford. Not here, and certainly not yet.

Another clang rang out, closer this time.

He grabbed her arm, pulling her behind him as he drew his katana in one smooth motion.

The blade gleamed in the dim light, a promise of both protection and danger.

"Stay behind me." His voice was low but commanding.

Toni swallowed hard, her heart pounding as she did as he asked. She might be skeptical as all get-out concerning him, but she wasn't stupid. Even if he was sent to betray her, hiding behind his hard, muscular, warm body was as good a place as any.

Now if only she could quell the spark of something deep inside her that urged her to trust him. No way. That stupid something could just shut the hell up.

Azazel tightened his grip on the hilt of his katana as they moved through the incubation room. The faint hum of the crystalline walls matched the steady pulse of his frustration. Toni's sharp remarks and her reluctance to trust him grated on him. Son-of-a-*lilit*! What he wouldn't give to stop everything and address the growing mistrust creeping between them. It'd make things so much easier. Maybe it'd help calm her the constant shivers.

Perched next to him on his shoulder, JR14 clicked his front metallic claws.

"Observation: subject human female named Toni exhibits recurring signs of mistrust toward primary organic. Probability of this hindering cooperative efforts: 72.3 percent." His voice came out cool and analytical.

Azazel's jaw tightened. Great, his unemotional bot picked up on the apprehension she harbored about him. With his gaze fixed ahead, he muttered, "Thank you for the insight, JR14." Tack that info onto the expanding list of problems making this rescue damn near impossible.

The pods lining the walls cast eerie shadows, and their contents flickered like ghostly specters. Behind him, Toni's teeth chattered.

Her breathing was shallow, her steps hesitant as she trailed behind him.

He stopped and faced her. His lips flattened as he studied the blue hue on her full lips.

She skidded to a halt and stood there, shivering, her jaw quivering and her arms wrapped around her waist.

Damn it! He'd better do something. This damn place was as cold as a refrigerator. "Here, put this on—" He whipped his tunic off and handed it to her. "—or you'll freeze to death." He'd rather conjure up a warm jacket with soft insulating fur, but he didn't dare use his psychic powers. That would be a sure way to get caught by the Krystalii.

Toni clutched the fabric close to her chest as she watched him with wide eyes.

"Won't... don't you need it? W-won't you be c-c-cold?" Her voice caught.

Moving close to her, he tilted her chin up and looked into her cornflower-blue eyes. He couldn't resist feeling her soft skin, but the brief touch served a more important purpose: it allowed him to send her a drift of warmth to overcome the onset of hypothermia in a way that wouldn't alert the Krystalii. "You don't have to worry about me." He took the material from her clenched fists and pulled it over her head.

It was so big on her that the sleeves covered her hands, and the hem went to her knees.

"I'm used to the cold." Plus, he could regulate the temperature of his body to keep himself warm. He sent another brush of warmth her way. "Now, don't fall behind," he admonished before he turned around.

"Aye-aye, mon Capitaine," she muttered.

At least the quiver was gone from her voice. But Azazel couldn't help but catch the stress in her tone as she masked her fear with sarcasm. He smiled as the tension in his shoulders relaxed. Sarcasm he could deal with.

She reminded him of his younger brother, Arakiba, who did his damnedest to irritate him with his vast arsenal of sardonic nonsense all the time. It was how his brother dealt with fear or when he was unsure of something. That experience allowed him to relate to Toni using it.

And he respected her strength and her refusal to crumble under the weight of the madness she found herself in. He grimaced. It gnawed on him that she expected him to betray her. If only he could enter her mind to show her the real person he was. If he could do that, it might ease some of her worries. Too bad that wasn't a good idea on this ship with so many psychically strong Krystalii. They'd have no trouble picking up the energy he'd have to use.

Not for the first time, he questioned how humans relied just on conversation to communicate with each other. It was one of his least favorite ways to relate his intent since speaking didn't only involve words, it also required the right body language and tonal nuances. By itself, it was fraught with inadequacies and misunderstandings.

But, for now, he'd better focus on finding them a safe harbor or somehow get the Sub-Node to work again. And communicate with her the best he could with what he had. "JR14?" he whispered. "Where's the nearest exit?"

The spider-like AI scuttled ahead, and the radiant orange in his multi-faceted eyes scanned the room.

"Proximity analysis indicates a corridor at the far end of this chamber. However, activity levels suggest a high probability of Elite patrols within adjacent pathways."

"Fantastic," Toni muttered from behind him. "So we're either stuck in here with the pods of doom or we play hide-and-seek with crystal bad guys. Great options."

Azazel glanced over his shoulder with a slight smile. "*Hebat*, I am sure we will uncover another probability."

Her eyes narrowed, and she crossed her arms. "Oh well, in that case, I've got nothing to worry 'bout." She tapped her forefinger against her chin. "I'll just ignore the fact that I'm trapped in an alien ship with a guy who talks like he stepped out of *The Epic of Gilgamesh*. What does that word even mean?"

For a moment, the corner of his mouth twitched, but he suppressed the wide grin that threatened to burst free. "It translates to 'Lady of the Skies.' I am impressed you know your ancient Babylonian history." While he wasn't from that civilization, it amused him when he discovered how much that culture had taken from the alien Akurns.

"Yeah, well, watching *Ancient Aliens* has its perks." She gestured to the rows of pods. "Let's talk about these things, okay? Are they going to... hatch or something?"

"Unlikely," JR14 interjected. "Current energy readings show dormancy. Activation requires specific external stimuli."

Azazel exhaled. Back to the key problem, getting out of here. They needed to reach either the rendezvous point or, if lucky, the shipping dock to grab a spaceship. "Let's not take a chance that we do something to wake them up. If we move quickly, they won't become a problem."

Trusting Toni would follow him, he turned and walked ahead of her. He heard the silence as she hesitated, but soon her footsteps echoed against the crystalline floor behind him. It was easy to sense her eyes on him, as if she was trying to decipher whether he was her savior or her doom. Her unspoken doubt weighed on him. He swallowed a sigh.

JR14 clicked his limbs, his voice cutting through the tense silence. "Alert: Proximity sensors detect movement within 30 meters. Suggest evasive maneuvers."

Azazel spun and scanned the chamber, searching through the low light.

The faint shadows of the pods shifted, the hum of the ship growing louder.

His grip on the katana hilt tightened as he turned to Toni. "Stay close behind me," he ordered, his voice low.

"No argument from me," she muttered, stepping closer. Her tension radiated off her in sharp waves, like static before a storm.

The sound of crystalline footsteps echoed through the chamber, growing louder with each passing second.

Azazel's senses sharpened, his mind calculating their next move. They couldn't afford to fight here—not surrounded by dormant Krystalii pods. One wrong move, and the entire room could come awake. "JR14," he said, his tone clipped. "Options."

"Recommendation: Proceed to the ventilation shaft located five meters ahead. It provides a direct route to an unmonitored sector."

Azazel glanced at the far wall, where a faint outline of a vent was visible. "Can you open it?"

"Affirmative." The AI's iridescent wings fluttered out as he zipped forward with mechanical precision.

Toni grabbed his arm, her nails digging into his skin. "What happens if we don't fit in it?"

He met her gaze, his expression calm despite the tension crackling around them. "We will."

Her lips parted as if to argue, but before she could, a sharp, metallic clang echoed behind them.

Azazel turned sharply, his katana raised as the first shadowy, Elites appeared at the chamber's entrance. "Go!" he barked in a harsh whisper, pushing her toward the vent JR14 was connected to.

Toni scrambled toward the bot, her movements clumsy, but didn't hesitate.

Azazel followed close behind, his blade glinting in the dim light as he kept his body between her and the advancing Elites. "JR14, hurry!" he snapped as he reached the vent.

The AI's eyes flickered from their orange color to pale blue. "Access complete. Proceed."

Azazel shoved Toni through the opening before sliding in after her. The narrow space was just wide enough for his shoulders, but he hurried, the sound of the Elites' pursuit echoing behind them.

JR14 buzzed ahead as the cover closed with a click behind them. "Keep moving," he said to Toni. "I'm right behind you."

Her breath came in sharp gasps as her hands scraped against the smooth walls of the shaft. "No worries. But I sure hope you know what you're doing."

Azazel's lips pressed into a thin line. "So do I."

Behind them, the sound of pursuit faded.

Still, Azazel's tension didn't ease until they reached an end that opened to a dimly lit corridor. At least it was away from the incubation room. Avoiding the Elites wouldn't last long. They'd soon trace the shaft and discover where it led.

"Let's go through there to find another way." He scooted around Toni to kick the crystal mesh off the opening, and they dropped to the floor inside. He went first, then caught her as she fell in after him.

JR14 resumed his place on Azazel's shoulder.

Once they were all inside, Azazel straightened with his katana in hand and scanned their surroundings. "This looks good—for now. Any Krystalii here, JR14?"

"Negative, area clear of hostiles. Advisory: this status is temporary and may shift without notice."

Toni leaned against the wall, her chest heaving and her hand over her heart. "You know, you both suck at giving pep talks."

Azazel turned to her, his expression softening. "At least we're both still alive. That should count for something."

Her gaze lingered on him for a moment, and the strained lines bracketing her mouth softened. "Yeah, well, you're right. Thanks," she muttered, looking away as a faint blush colored her cheeks.

He nodded, his resolve to get her to safety hardening. She needed to be somewhere where she wasn't under constant threat. "Okay, JR14." He glanced at the bot on his shoulder. "Any suggestions on where we go from here?"

Toni followed Azazel deeper into the dim corridor, her nerves strung so tight, she was afraid the slightest nudge would set her off. Her pulse hammered from the narrow escape, and the memory of the suspended Krystalii shimmering in those large glass beakers wouldn't go away. To make matters worse, every step through the metal-infused crystal passage amplified the tension between her and Azazel. She couldn't let herself get paralyzed by fear. But it was hard to decide which threat was greater—the army of crystal soldiers or the mysterious man himself.

Her fingers grazed the wall, smooth in some areas and splintered in others. She stole a glance at Azazel. His broad shoulders and confident stride exuded calm, but the energy coming off him reminded her of a sharp, coiled serpent barely held in check. *Damn,* she'd give anything to trust him. He'd saved her twice now. But how could she trust anyone or anything in this crazy place?

It was hard to shake the feeling that Baelon had sent Azazel to her. What better way to observe how she reacted when confronted with life-threatening danger than having her ideal man work with her to gain her trust? Really, the guy was a sexy mix of Jason Momoa with the mysterious sensuality of Keanu Reeves. She doubted her experience around those kinds of men prepared her for the likes of Azazel.

Especially here.

The man in question slowed and glanced at JR14. "Where to next?" His voice was low but firm.

"Immediate area secure," JR14 replied, his spider-like form crouched on Azazel's shoulder. "Next access point is a central node chamber, 300 meters east."

Toni's stomach twisted. "Central node chamber? That sounds important. And we know important means guarded." *Oh God. Were they going into another teeny, cramped shaft?*

Azazel looked at her, his dark gaze clear. "Yes, but it also means we have a chance to find a ship to escape in. Or, at the very least, discover a way to disable this ship's ability to track us." He shrugged.

Damn. She sucked in a breath. Even that simple gesture was done with the grace of a dancer. Or an expert in some kind of martial arts.

"Either way, it gives us a better chance of survival."

"Yeah, well. I'm sure miracles happen all the time," Toni muttered, crossing her arms. "I hope you have a Plan B if things don't work out."

He didn't blink. "I assure you, that won't be necessary."

She blinked in return. For the first time, she was positive he was lying to her. The spider-bot on his shoulder also glared at her with its two sky-blue, multi-faceted orbs. No help there. Her throat tightened. "Well... that's spectacular. Good thing we have nothing to worry about, then."

Before she could say anything else, a low rumble vibrated through the walls.

JR14 clicked his frontal claws, his mechanical voice sharp. "Warning: proximity sensors detecting Krystalii convergence on multiple levels."

Azazel's jaw clenched. "They're triangulating our position."

Heat rose in her chest, clogging her throat. "Why?" She croaked. "What did we do—"

"We didn't do anything," he interrupted. "The Krystalii think like a hive. Once one knows, they all know."

"Well... bully for them. Freakin' cheaters." Her sarcasm felt hollow as the vibrations grew stronger. "So, got any ideas?"

"Yeah. Run."

He grabbed her wrist and, with a gentle yank, raced ahead.

The twisting, maze-like corridor made her dizzy. Around her, the crystalline walls gleamed as if they were alive and watched every movement as they raced through them.

The sound of their pursuers grew louder, the clinking of glass-like footsteps echoing closer every second.

Toni struggled to keep up, her breath ragged. "Azazel, they're getting closer!"

"Don't worry," he said in a clipped voice. "We'll make it."

Her legs burned and her heart pounded, but she didn't dare slow down. Not that she could while the man had a tight grip on her wrist. A part of her wanted to yank free and curl into a ball into a corner and let the nightmares run by. But the memory of those glinting, faceless soldiers burned into her mind. At least Azazel's tight grip grounded her in this endless chaos.

"Here!" he barked, releasing her wrist as he shoved open a door that led into a dark chamber.

Toni stumbled through the door behind him. When she straightened, she gasped.

They were in a vast room filled with strange, crystalline machinery in a multitude of colors. Each pulsed with faint, rhythmic lights in random patterns.

He moved to the center and waved a hand over the strange console. "JR14, can you disable their tracking signals?" he asked in his soothing voice.

"Working." The AI fluttered down to the control table. One of his thin legs jabbed into the crystal material, causing the yellow glass to glow.

She bent with her hands planted on her thighs to catch her breath, her chest heaving. Gulping, she looked up. "Do you know what you're doing?"

"Let's find out." Azazel's hands flexed on the hilt of his katana as his gaze fixated on the door.

The rumble outside grew louder. The Krystalii were here.

"Signal interference activated. Pursuit delayed." JR14 chirped.

Azazel exhaled, his shoulders relaxing. "Good. That buys us—"

A deafening crash cut him off as the door splintered open, shards of crystal scattering like shrapnel.

Three Krystalii Elite guards stepped through. Their clear angular forms gleamed in the dim light.

Toni's blood ran cold. "Azazel..."

He stepped in front of her, his katana gleaming as he shifted into a fighting stance. "Stay behind me."

Her throat tightened as the Elites advanced, their movements unnervingly smooth and synchronized. She had a wild idea that the raw power emanating from them pulsated with alien energy that reached out, trying to grab her.

Azazel didn't wait. He surged forward, and his blade sliced through the air with precision.

The first Elite shattered under his strike, shards blowing apart like a chandelier crashing to the hard floor. The other two adapted, their movements faster, more deliberate.

Her heart raced as she pressed herself against the wall. She had to help, to do something. But what could she do? Her gaze darted around the room, searching for anything—something—that could give them an edge.

She glimpsed a glowing panel near the far wall. Its symbols flickered like a heartbeat. She didn't know what it did, but it looked important.

"Toni!" Azazel's shout snapped. "Get out of here!"

"No!" She bolted toward the panel, her fear drowned out by a surge of determination. If she couldn't fight, she'd find a different way to help.

"What are you doing?" Azazel yelled. His voice was tinged with panic as he parried another strike.

"Just keep them busy!" she shouted as her fingers flew over the panel. Hoping for a miracle, she pressed the meaningless symbols.

With a roar, machinery sprang to life, shaking the room.

When the surrounding lights flared, the Krystalii stumbled and hesitated.

"Toni!" Azazel demanded, his katana slicing through another Elite. "What did you do?"

"I don't know!" she admitted, her voice shaking. "But it's working!"

Before she could say anything else, a sharp, searing pain shot through her chest. She gasped as her vision blurred. She collapsed to her knees.

"Toni!" His voice was distant, frantic.

Her breath hitched as she crumpled to the cold floor. The world around her spun, a chaotic whirlwind of light and shadow. The sounds of battle echoed in her ears—Azazel's sharp grunts, the crystalline shattering of another alien Elite, the hum of machinery pulsing through the chamber like a threatening heartbeat.

Her fingers twitched, brushing against the bottom of the smooth console she'd been working on moments ago. Pain radiated from her chest, sharp and unrelenting. Not that she'd let that stop her. She had to finish what she started. For some weird reason, the console had responded to her touch, to her desperation. She wasn't sure how or why, but damn if she'd let the effort go to waste.

"Toni!" Azazel's voice sliced through the haze, sharp and commanding. His boots slammed against the floor as he moved toward her, his katana flashing as it caught the light. "Stay with me."

"I'm fine." Toni gasped, doing her best to swallow the trembling in her voice. She forced herself to sit up, rubbing her eyes to clear away the blur. Even with the dangerous tilt to the room, she focused on Azazel.

"You don't look fine," he observed in a quiet tone. "Can you move?"

She braced her hands against the floor, her arms shaking as she pushed to stand. "Yes, just give me a minute." With a grunt, she staggered to her feet, her legs wobbling beneath her.

Azazel gripped her arm to help her.

Every nerve in her body screamed, demanding she sit down. Not gonna happen. No way would this girl let that crystal-creep Baelon get his hands on her again. Clenching her teeth, she pulled herself up to the control panel, slapping the surface to steady herself. Narrowing her eyes, she struggled to focus on the glowing symbols.

The sound of stomping crystal feet told her more guards had found them.

"Just keep those freaky crystal assholes away from me," she demanded as Azazel released her. She didn't look at him, instead focusing on the console. "Come on," she muttered, her fingers skimming over the alien interface. "Whatever you are, whatever you did before—I dare ya. Do it again."

The lights on the console flickered, pulsing at an erratic pace under her touch. A low hum built in the air, growing louder, deeper, until it vibrated in her bones.

The Krystalii soldiers paused, their crystalline bodies twitching as if sensing the shift in energy.

Azazel seized the moment, cutting through the nearest Elite with a precise strike. Shards rained down around him as he spun to face the others, his braid whipping through the air. His naked, masculine torso shone in the low light.

"What are you doing?" he called out, glancing at her over his shoulder.

Toni jerked her head away to stop from ogling the impressive sight of the man's imposing physique. *Damn, girl. Get hold of yourself. Pay attention. Life-and-death situation here.* "Improvising." She croaked and forced her fingers to move faster. At first, nothing happened, but then the symbols shifted and aligned under her hands. She didn't understand it, not fully, but instinct guided her—like solving a puzzle she didn't know she could solve.

The hum reached a crescendo and shook the chamber.

The remaining Elites faltered, their movements disjointed.

Azazel didn't hesitate, cutting through one with a swift, decisive blow before turning to the last. "Whatever you're doing, keep doing it!" he shouted. With one high-powered swing, his katana met another Elite's weapon in a clash that sent sparks flying.

"Of course, Commander Chaos!" she snapped, her voice raw. Sweat dripped down her temple as she pressed her hand against the blinking surface.

While she worked on the alien console at a frantic pace, JR14 buzzed by her head and landed on a nearby surface. He observed her movements with keen, luminous orange eyes. His metallic limbs twitched as he turned his attention to the console's response to her touch.

"Observation," he intoned, his voice precise and clinical. "Human female's interaction with the console exhibits an anomalous pattern of resonance alignment. Hypothesis: her bioelectric field synchronizes with the interface at a molecular level. Likelihood of this being a random occurrence: statistically negligible."

She glanced at him but didn't stop her fingers from flying across the console. "What in the hell does that mean?"

JR14 tilted his small metallic head. The orbs of his eyes turned from orange to sky blue. "Clarification: your physiology appears uniquely compatible with this technology. Probable cause: genetic markers or latent psychic potential currently unidentified. Further study required."

She had no respose to that shitload of crazy. "Holy cow. Now's not the time for scientific research, Mr. Wizard!" Toni snapped, her voice strained. "Just let me know if I'm about to blow us all up, 'k?"

"Probability of detonation: low," JR14 replied, unperturbed. "Probability of successful activation: increasing. Suggest continuation of current actions."

Azazel dispatched another Krystalii, then spared a brief glance at JR14. "Can you simplify that assessment?"

JR14's legs clicked in a way that Toni suspected was how he displayed exasperation. "Simplification: the human female is the key."

A symbol lit up under her hands, catching her attention. The blazing crimson light erupted in a surge of energy.

The Elites froze mid-motion, their crystalline forms cracking as if struck by an unseen force.

Azazel leaped back, shielding his eyes as a shockwave rippled through the chamber.

The light faded as quickly as it came, leaving an eerie silence.

She slumped against the console, her chest heaving. Her vision swam, but she forced herself to look up.

The Elites were gone, nothing but glittering shards scattered across the floor.

Azazel turned to her, his katana still raised, his expression unreadable. "Are you all right?" His soft voice was hesitant.

Toni managed a shaky nod. "I think..." She swallowed. "I guess so. Did... did I do that?"

His gaze flicked to the console, then back to her. "Yes, whatever you did worked." He stepped closer, his hand hovering near her arm as if unsure whether to touch her. "Are you hurt in any way?"

JR14 flew up to land on Azazel's shoulder. His glowing sky-blue eyes scanned Toni as she leaned against the console, her chest heaving. The tiny spider-like droid tilted his metallic head. "Observation: subject Toni exhibits no critical injuries. Superficial abrasions and minor contusions detected. Bio-signals remain within acceptable human parameters. Conclusion: the subject is physically fine."

She raised an eyebrow, still catching her breath. "Gee, nice supportive bedside manner, Doctor Gizmo."

JR14's iridescent wings twitched before sliding inside his exoskeleton. "Statement: emotional reassurance is not within my programming."

"I guess what you're saying is, I'll live." She grimaced. Live, yes. Not suffer any consequences, no. She swore every part of her body screamed in protest. Even breathing was a chore. But she refused to let it show. "So, what do we do now?"

Azazel's jaw tightened as he glanced around. "We'd better move. What happened here must've alerted every Krystalii where we are. It wouldn't surprise me if reinforcements are on their way."

JR14 clicked his claws as the luminescent blue of his eyes flickered in rapid succession. "Observation: current energy discharge levels have triggered proximity alerts across at least three adjacent sectors. Confirm Krystalii reinforcements will arrive within two minutes." The bot swiveled his head toward Toni, scanning her again before turning back to Azazel. "Recommendation: immediate relocation to minimize encounter risk. Pathway analysis is underway. Suggest avoiding primary corridors to evade patrol convergence."

Azazel nodded, his grip tightening on his katana. "Can you determine an adequate way for us to depart, JR14?"

Toni couldn't help her wide grin. Darn man talked like a history professor she had in college. Except Azazel had the sexiest accent to go with his killer body.

JR14's iridescent wings gave a faint hum as he processed. "Observation: secondary ventilation shaft located thirty meters northwest. Probability of route being unmonitored: 68.2 percent."

"Another vent?" She groaned. "Wonderful. Yippee Ki-Yay."

"Disclosure: survival rarely aligns with preference," JR14 replied with his normal bluntness. "Initiating route guidance."

"Well, when you put it that way," Toni muttered, pushing off the console with a wince. Her body protested like an eighty-year-old's. "At least we're consistent." She flipped her hand in Azazel's direction. "Okay, lead on, Rescue Ranger. Take us to the next disaster."

Azazel's lips quirked into the faintest hint of a smile. "We are still free, no?"

She aimed a pathetic glare his way. "Listen. Do me a favor and don't quit your day job. Your and your droid's talent as motivational speakers suck."

Sheathing his katana with a sharp click, he offered her his hand. "Come on, *hebat*. Let's find a way out of this room."

She hesitated, her eyes locking with his. There was something in his gaze that made her relax. Something steady and unyielding she'd give anything to trust. Maybe she'd allow that trust to grow when death wasn't lurking like a door-to-door salesperson refusing to leave the porch. With a sigh, she accepted his hold. "Fine. But if I die running around this stupid ship, I'm making it my afterlife mission to haunt you."

Azazel's smile widened, just a fraction. "I wouldn't have it any other way."

CHAPTER FOUR

Azazel couldn't believe the Sub-Resonant Node still wasn't working. There had to be a better way to meet up with Vaeloryx and his ragtag band of misfits in that safe room. This wasn't the first time his inability to teleport himself and Toni with his psychic powers had frustrated the hell out of him. It'd make things much easier.

"JR14—" He turned to the bot on his shoulder. "—if we continue on this route, will it lead us to the rebels' refuge?"

JR14's iridescent wings buzzed as he adjusted his position on Azazel's shoulder. His metallic claws clicked against Azazel's bare skin.

It wasn't uncomfortable, except for a little tickle when the bot's "nervous tick" kicked in. Especially since he wasn't wearing a shirt. He had to admit, he rather enjoyed going around bare-chested. He loved how Toni kept giving him side-glances under her lashes when she thought he wasn't looking, as if he wouldn't notice her stealing lingering peeks at him.

The only problem was, whenever she glanced at him like that, he had to remind himself not to throw his shoulders back and preen like a proud peacock. While he normally didn't enjoy people staring at him, he rather liked it when she did.

"Negative, Azazel." JR14's voice, crisp and mechanical, held a hint of wryness that jerked him out of his musings. "Vaeloryx's sanctuary is located 87.3 kilometers away from this route's trajectory. Alterations to our trajectory are needed to ensure efficiency." The bot paused, and his ochre-colored optics flickered. "However, if your organic sentimentality dictates you do not adhere to my specifications, we can continue on our current path."

"Check him out." Toni snorted, crossing her arms. "Organic sentimentality. I think you're being chastised."

Azazel might agree, but they had more pressing matters. "I think it's best we follow your advice, JR14." He addressed the small droid on his shoulder. "It's better if we go your way, even if it costs us time." Eying Toni, he watched her lips twist into a grimace. She must've hurt herself more than she let on. "It'll give us a chance to catch our breath. And, if we're lucky, we'll figure a way off this ship without the Krystalii knowing."

"Yeah." Toni agreed as she leaned against the crystal wall, her arms still crossed. "I'm all for taking time to stop running around this ship like crazy people." She gave a brief chuckle. "Besides, I could use a break."

On that, Azazel agreed. He didn't like how pale she was. "Have you finished analyzing the quickest and safest route to Vaeloryx's refuge from here?" he asked his AI companion.

JR14's optics flickered, changing from dark orange to a light-pumpkin color. "Analyzing." The bot's front claws clicked in a soothing rhythm. "Unconfirmed. The energy fields in this sector disrupt precise navigation. However, I have developed coordinates that will align with a 63.4 percent probability of intersecting the rebels' approximate location."

Azazel clenched his jaw. "Can you narrow those options down?"

"Organic impatience is counterproductive. Additional data required..."

If Azazel wasn't mistaken, JR14's tone carried a hint of exasperation. Talk about impatience. Looks like the droid was learning emotional reactions after all. "I'm afraid we don't have time for additional data, *kalu*." He laced his tone with a soothing cadence. "We cannot wait for perfection. Please finalize the best direct route."

Toni stepped toward him and firmly gripped his arm.

His breath caught as the pleasure at her touch tightened something low inside him. How could her innocent touch be so provocative?

"Who is this Vaeloryx rebel you keep talking about? More importantly, is he willing to help us?" She worried her bottom lip. "Or will we walk into a Krystalii trap?"

Azazel covered her hand with his. He couldn't resist the lure of caressing her back. The sensual sensation of holding his skin to hers deepened. "I thought the same thing when I first met him." He squeezed her hand. "But he and his fellow rebels aren't like the other Krystalii. They are determined to not only stop the invasion but want to overthrow Baelon. Without their help, we don't stand a chance of escaping."

She tilted her head, which caused her silky hair to swish across her shoulders. "That doesn't explain how you can trust him."

The intelligence in her bright blue eyes was piercing, as if searching for sincerity in whatever he said.

"I feel he hates Baelon more than he hates us," Azazel replied. With reluctance, he let her go and stepped back. "And right now, that's enough for me." His skin where she'd held him broke out in chill bumps, as if mourning the loss of her warmth.

"Path selected," JR14 interjected. "Probability of success increased to 71.2 percent. Proceeding requires entering an auxiliary maintenance shaft twenty-three meters ahead."

"Well—" Toni shrugged with a grin. "—at least it's not another dusty, claustrophobic ventilation tunnel."

"Yeah, thank the goddess for small favors." Azazel agreed. "Okay, JR14, lead the way."

She fell into step beside him as the spider-bot flew in front. "I have to admit I'm still concerned," she whispered. "Trusting a Krystalii seems like a reckless thing to do."

"Sometimes relying on instinct is the only thing you can depend on," Azazel replied. A memory of him accidentally teleporting his three brothers seven thousand years into the future was a prime example. He'd only been trying to take them to a waiting spaceship in a hangar across a courtyard under attack. But instead, he transported them far into the future—and ended up in the right place at the right time. It turned out doing something so unexpected saved the day. Even if it wasn't what he meant to do.

Out of the corner of his eye, he watched Toni's lips twitch into a reluctant smile as she kept pace with him. Trying not to be obvious, he observed her.

She had a slight limp but otherwise didn't let on if she was in any pain.

A spark of pride flared as he watched her.

Everything she'd endured could've broken her—but it hadn't. She wasn't just surviving, she was fighting back and reclaiming every piece of herself.

After what seemed like an endless amount of time, the corridor ahead narrowed into a dark, crystalline hallway. Just wide enough for them to pass in a single file.

Azazel crouched and gestured to make sure Toni followed as JR14 scanned the area in front of them. Thankfully, she tiptoed with quiet steps behind him in the oppressive stillness.

Before they reached the end of the shaft, JR14's voice buzzed in Azazel's ear.

"Energy signatures detected ahead. Non-hostile alignment. Likely match for Vaeloryx's faction is 95.2 percent."

Azazel exhaled, relief tempered by caution. He didn't know how, but it looked like they had made it. Turning to Toni, he said in a firm but quiet voice. "Stay close. Hopefully, we're in the right place."

She shrugged. "We'll be shit out of luck if we aren't." Her eyes met his with surprising intensity. "And then we won't have to worry 'bout anything since we'll probably be dead."

He nodded. No argument there. "I'm afraid you're right." He took the lead, and the air shimmered when he and Toni passed through an invisible barrier. The familiar crystalline walls glowed with a softer, warmer light.

Figures emerged from the shadows—rebel Krystalii with fractured, dulled surfaces. Their forms were less imposing than the gleaming soldiers they'd evaded.

Vaeloryx stepped forward. His rough aquamarine-and-silver crystal body was now marked with new ragged scars. His deep, resonant voice filled the chamber. "Azazel. We lost hope you'd find us when the Sub-Node failed to work."

Azazel squared his shoulders, his gaze steady as he watched Laytrii and Kyrix along with several other Krystalii joining their group. "I'm not sure why it stopped working, but we'd better fix it or create another way to communicate."

Vaeloryx's gaze shifted to Toni, his crystalline face unreadable. "I see you've liberated the human female."

"Yes, this is Toni." Azazel introduced her. He decided not to tell the Krystalii what Toni did in that strange chamber to paralyze the Krystalii. It might've been a fluke, or it might be something they should keep to themselves. "She's been through a lot, and I would appreciate it if you could provide a place for her to rest and receive some sustenance to refresh her."

Toni stiffened beside him, and her breath hitched.

At least she didn't pull away or argue.

Vaeloryx inclined his head slowly. "Baelon has already programmed the *Nyrlith* to provide the nutrient fare for a human." He gestured with his crystal hand to an empty part of the room.

A shimmering light of iridescent colors formed into a comfortable-looking wide pad, complete with thick covers and plump pillows.

"You both may take your rest here."

He turned his attention to the voice behind him. It was a citrine-yellow Krystalii, whose serene expression made Azazel's eyebrows rise. What a surprise to see a crystal being with an eager, welcoming expression like that.

"This is Tharion," Vaeloryx introduced the male. "He will see to your every need while we work together."

Tharion grinned, making his clear, butter-colored eyes sparkle. "I am so very honored to assist you while you're here. Anything I can do—" he informed them with his hands clasped together over his chest. "—anything at all, don't hesitate to ask."

"Oh, for the galaxy's sake!" An azure-blue Krystalii female tapped her foot and scowled. "We don't have time to babysit these organic creatures, Thar. We've got a dicktatar to eliminate!"

Toni snickered next to him. "Dick-tatar," she mumbled with a grin.

"Saphirae, enough." Vaeloryx slashed his hand through the air. "We should take this time to prepare. Since we weren't successful in dismantling the Nexus Core, we must go back and try again."

"Barely made it out in time." Laytrii grumbled.

Vaeloryx didn't acknowledge her comment. "After the humans have regained their strength, we'll determine our next steps."

Azazel nodded in agreement. Even though he could keep going, he doubted Toni had the same stamina he had. "Yes, that would be perfect. Thank you." He put a hand over his heart and gave Tharion a slight bow, never taking his eyes from him.

"Oh good!" Tharion clapped his hands with a wide smile. The tinkling sound of his applause had a musical tone. "We've created a place for you to sit and partake of the substance Baelon programmed into the ship's database. Just follow me, and I'll get you some right away."

With a smile, Azazel took Toni's hand and followed the yellow Krystalii, with JR14 staying glued to his shoulder. For the first time since setting foot on the Krystalii mothership, he allowed himself a sliver of hope.

Even his inner beast rumbled in silent agreement.

Toni sat cross-legged on the pad Vaeloryx had made for her and Azazel. She sipped from the goblet Tharion had given her, filled with lavender liquid. Settling back on the seat, she gave a hum of approval. *Darn thing was surprisingly comfortable.* She leaned back with a grateful sigh while Azazel spoke with their hosts. It didn't take a genius to figure out the Krystalii had powerful psychic abilities, but she never dreamed they could conjure something out of nothing, like this comfy couch.

What would that be like? To do or create anything out of nothing? Or go anywhere on a whim? She'd produced several movies with similar themes, but the heroes in those stories usually didn't end up with a happy-ever-after ending. The main storyline had the hero overwhelmed by their powers and turning into unfeeling monsters, the kind who didn't care if they hurt or murdered those who got in their way. She grimaced. Just look at Lord "frosty facet" Baelon. Now there was a poster boy for a person who had a god complex, forcing his will on others and killing anyone who stood between him and whatever his objectives were.

Maybe wishing she had that kind of potential wasn't such a good thing after all.

Dropping that morbid thought, she pressed against the cushiony backrest and glanced around. Thankfully, the rebel hideaway was warmer than the rest of the ship she'd been on. But the air still carried a metallic chill that rattled her bones. Azazel, with JR14, carried on with their plans as the Krystalii sat in a loose circle on the pad with them. Light danced across their crystalline forms, giving her a surreal impression that the aliens were made of fractured stars.

"I'm afraid I have some disturbing news I must share before you retire," Vaeloryx said in a louder tone.

The breathtaking colors of his aquamarine-and-silver scarred body somehow radiated a calm authority.

He tapped a jagged hand against a console that appeared in front of him, and a holographic display flickered to life. He indicated a map of what he called the galactic seat of the Federation Consortium. He called it the chancellor's palace, an immense space station shaped like an elegant, sprawling city that orbited the planet Zerin.

"Baelon has made his move. The dimensional invasion has begun. His forces have concentrated on the planet Zerin and at the chancellor's palace. The Elites are dismantling the Federation's government as we speak."

Toni's breath hitched. She pressed a hand to her chest, her heart hammering against her ribs so hard it squeezed the air from her throat. She gripped the chalice hard enough that some of the liquid swished over the rim.

Vaeloryx continued.

"Added to that, the first wave of his fleet has already deployed to most of the secured strategic outposts across the galaxy."

Azazel lifted the goblet he held to his mouth and drained its contents. His expression remained impassive.

Toni's stomach churned at the image the Krystalii projected. She wasn't a soldier or a strategist, but even she could see the Consortium didn't stand a chance if Baelon's forces gained total control. She glanced at Azazel. He'd put the goblet on the floor next to him and studied the hologram with quiet intensity. His eyebrows slanted into a deep furrow.

"Do you know what Baelon's endgame is?"

Azazel's voice might be calm and measured, but Toni watched his jaw clench and his eyes narrow.

Vaeloryx's gaze darkened, making the silver color darken to a dull gray. The rest of his crystalline face remained unreadable. "Control. He seeks to absorb the Consortium's genetic and psychic resources. What the general population of the Krystalii is unaware of is that our birth cycle is weakening and has been for several millennia. This is why Lord Baelon's prime directive has been an obsessive need to capture a human to use your species' adaptability. He feels this is the key to reversing our decline. Therefore, he intends to harvest the material he deems necessary. At any cost."

Toni shivered and crossed her arms. *Time to join the conversation instead of sitting on my ass while my* species *is on the chopping block.* "Harvest necessary material? You mean... my people?" Her voice came out sharper than she intended. "He's planning on harvesting humans from Earth?"

"Yes," Vaeloryx answered. "As I have stated, he has a particular interest in your species. In addition to being adaptable to producing young for an alien race, it's your resilience, your psychic potential that is notable. All of which makes Baelon view humans as a threat as well as a resource." His shrug was stilted and unnatural. "He sees no difference."

Toni's hands clenched as a wave of anger surged through her. No one had the right to reduce someone to a resource. "Why not start here, then?" She waved at the planet Zerin and the chancellor's orbiting palace on the hologram. "Why not go straight to Earth and gobble all the humans up?" She snorted. "It's not like we could fight against him."

"Earth may be the endgame," a bulky-Krystalii announced in a rough, gravelly voice.

The voice came from an imposing male made of obsidian crystals standing off to the side. His glossy black crystals carried glowing, violet iridescent streaks, which made him quite intimidating.

"But Baelon is astute enough to take out the biggest threat to his invasion first. That way, all the other systems in this dimension will fall in line with whatever he wants."

"That's correct, Kaelith." Vaeloryx made a halting gesture with his palm up. "However, we need to allow the organics some time to re-energize before we discuss what to do next."

The sneer on the inky Krystalii's face made Toni's face heat.

"Organics." The brute snorted. "Creatures with no power or strength. I don't see the value of bringing them into our group. What do they have to offer besides needing us to waste time as we take care of them? We'd do better on our own."

"Yes, well, about that." Azazel looked at his hands before glancing back at the Krystalii. "I have certain, ah, talents that align with yours."

Toni had drained her own cup and now frowned at Azazel's announcement. *What did that mean? How could he possibly be like the Krystalii?* Her eyes widened. *Wait. He never denied being a psychic when she teased him about it. Had she been right all along? Did that mean he was some kind of plant from shards-for-brains Baelon?* She straightened and put her own goblet on the floor. A surge of unease sent acid burning up her throat. Trying to go unnoticed, she scooted away from Azazel.

She didn't get too far before he put his arm around her waist. "*Hebat,*" his voice caressed in a soothing tone. "Whatever has put that fear in your eyes, I assure you it's not what you think."

Toni jerked in his hold and turned to him.

"Yeah? Isn't that what people say when they're hiding something?"

Azazel straightened, his back ramrod steel. The slight upward tip of his ears darkened.

"Antonia—" He held his opposite hand up. "—I am not the villain here. My priority was to rescue you and take you back to Earth." He glanced at the still and silent Krystalii. "But now things are much more dire."

He turned his attention back to her.

Toni's heart raced at the pleading in his mahogany-colored eyes.

"However, you are correct that I purposefully held a part of myself from you. And it's time I confess that I'm something more than what I appear."

Toni's pulse hammered as she glared at Azazel. "All right, what do you mean by something more?"

His shoulders straightened, and his face tightened under her scrutiny. He looked at her as if weighing the best thing to say. After a quick glance at the Krystalii, he exhaled, then he spoke in a soft, but steady tone. "I'm like them, Toni." He nodded toward the Krystalii rebels. "I have psychic abilities like they do."

Toni blinked. Her head felt light as a chilly wave of disbelief washed over her.

"Psychic?" Her voice cracked. "Like reading minds and all?" She gulped. "Moving things with just a thought?" She clenched her fists at her sides, knuckles white. "And you didn't even consider that was something I should know about?"

He glanced away from her with thinned lips.

"It was never my intention to hide anything from you." Throwing his shoulders back, Azazel continued. "Believe me, I want nothing more than to share with you who I really am." He waved a hand around him. "Ever since I came aboard, I've had to suppress my psychic abilities to keep the Krystalii from finding me." His grin was self-deprecating. "And since we've met, all we've done is run around this ship to avoid getting caught."

Toni rubbed her arms and hung her head. *Fair enough.* She looked up at him.

"Okay, but we sure could've used some extra mojo a couple of times back there." She gave a nervous chuckle.

JR14 chimed in, his metallic voice precise and matter-of-fact.

"Clarification: Azazel's psychic capabilities are substantial, ranging from telekinesis to telepathic resonance. He applied those abilities when the Federation Consortium tasked him with locating and extracting you."

Toni's jaw dropped. "They sent you to find me?" She paused, her mind reeling. "Only because I'm... a target for Baelon?"

"No." Azazel frowned. "I mean, yes, you and those other women who were taken from the exchange. All of you were more important than you realize, Toni. Your resilience, intelligence, and adaptability are everything Baelon seeks to exploit. I... I couldn't let that happen to you."

She frowned as an alarming thought occurred to her.

"Have you been reading my mind all this time?" *Jen-Jang*! She thought in Korean. *Did he know she mistrusted him?*

A flicker of hurt crossed his face, but he looked straight into her eyes. "Of course not. I assure you, I avoid invading anyone's privacy without being invited." He shuddered. "I consider that no better than violating someone physically."

Vaeloryx leaned forward, and his crystalline form glinted under the dim light.

"With Lord Baelon remaining unaware of Azazel's presence, his abilities may be our greatest asset," he said in a measured tone. "Let us go forward in establishing trust between us. Without it, this mission will fail before it begins."

Toni's gaze darted between Azazel and Vaeloryx as her heart pounded. *Ah, moment of truth.* Though doubt clawed at her, she couldn't look away from Azazel. Something in the depth of his gaze—raw, unguarded—held her spellbound. Beneath the sobering darkness in his eyes, a quiet sincerity glimmered. A flicker of vulnerability, so real it pushed her fear aside and gave her room to reconsider. With a sigh, she slumped against the pad.

Taking in a lungful of air, she looked up at him and exhaled.

"Okay, fine." She flipped her hair behind her. "But if you so much as think of going anywhere near my mind, I'll figure out how to make your fancy-schmancy psychic brain regret it."

Azazel's lips twitched into a faint smile. "I wouldn't expect anything less."

That smile made her tense shoulders relax. That is, until her eyes caught on the glorious display of his naked, muscled chest right next to her. The warmth from his body reached out to her, making her tingle all over.

Lifting her chin up to meet his eyes, she gave him a mischievous smirk. *The only way she could continue to work with him was if he'd put a damn shirt on.* He had no right to prance around and distract her all the time. "I may be tired, but do you think we can find some clothes to put on before we do anything else?"

It wasn't like they were in some kind of rom-com where the leading hunky man ran around half naked all the time. This was more like a high-stakes sci-fi thriller, and darn if she'd let the well-built leading actor get in the way of the main plot of this screenplay.

After all, a girl's gotta keep her priorities straight.

Clothes. The woman wanted clothes. Azazel glanced at his bare chest. His ability to regulate his own body temperature made him forget he only wore loose pants and boots. The katana and sub-node strapped to the sash on his waist didn't count.

She shivered and rubbed her arms. "You gotta admit, it's freezing in here."

"Oh, I can help you with that!" Tharion snapped his fingers. "Follow me, darlings." He turned with a sway of his trim hips to the opposite side of the chamber. "I've been dying for ages for someone to try these on." He looked over his shoulder and glared at his crystal companions. "The naysayers here have no sense of what decent invaders should clothe themselves in before going into battle." He huffed. "These heathens ignore the nuances of psychological combat that give an added edge to any conflict."

"Only primitive creatures require coverings over their inefficient bodies." Kaelith's gravelly voice echoed in the large room. "That, at least, is something I can agree with Lord Baelon on."

"Oh, posh!" Tharion waved a dismissive hand. "You are a primordial brute who doesn't have an iota of sense of civilization. Or what civilized people should wear." He stood in front of Toni and looped his arm through hers, hauling her to her feet. "Trust me"—he patted her hand—"you're gonna love this!" He snuggled up to her and giggled.

Azazel's eyebrows lifted when she giggled back. It was light, unguarded—an amazing, carefree sound. He watched them with a sense of unease, their heads together in whispered conversation. Her leaning toward the citrine Krystalii like he was her best friend unsettled Azazel. What the hell could they be talking about?

"I assume what Tharion provides will meet with your approval." Vaeloryx stood next to him with his hands behind his back. "He is quite talented with the visual arts. I'm sure he won't choose something that would make you uncomfortable."

Uncomfortable? Azazel glanced at him before turning back to watch Toni and Tharion disappear through an open doorway. Maybe it would be prudent to have a say in whatever those two concocted for him.

"You may be right, but I'd still better go with them to see what they have in mind. Hey, Toni!" Without a backward glance at the tall aquamarine Krystalii, he sprinted after her.

"Wait up." He skidded to a stop and froze when he took in the supply area almost as wide as the outer chamber. Stacks of clothes sat beside weapons he couldn't identify. And the rest looked like alien junk—or maybe tools? He couldn't tell. Half the stuff buzzed or blinked when he got too close, and none of it made any damn sense. "What is this place?" he whispered.

"This is the Vault of Forgotten Worlds."

Azazel startled when Vaeloryx spoke behind him. He'd been so caught up in the unusual sight of so many things crammed into one place. Vault of Forgotten Worlds. What a fitting name. The room was a cavernous expanse, and its glinting crystalline walls were filled with spider veins that pulsed in time with the ship's energy flow. From floor to ceiling, shelves carved from the same shimmering material were stacked with artifacts that gleamed under the pale, flickering light. To add to the strangeness, a low hum vibrated through the air, tapping against his temples.

In the center of the room stood a massive circular platform, its surface etched with intricate patterns he couldn't decipher. Objects hovered above its surface, suspended by some invisible force—blades, orbs, and small devices that radiated an alien energy he knew not to touch.

Toni moved ahead, her footsteps hesitant. She paused before a rack holding what appeared to be uniforms, running her fingers over the smooth, metallic fabric.

"It's like armor," she murmured, glancing at him. "But... if I didn't know any better, I'd swear they were alive."

Azazel gave her a brief nod, but his attention was fixed on a nearby shelf where several weapons hummed in faint tones. He cast a wary glance at Vaeloryx, whose aquamarine crystalline form reflected the soft glow of the vault.

"Our ancestors attuned everything in here to the *Nyrlith*," Vaeloryx explained, his voice steady but firm. "Tools, clothing, weapons—it's all designed to resonate with our energy. Your organic forms may find it... unpredictable."

Azazel frowned. "Unpredictable how?"

Vaeloryx's crystalline face tilted, the gesture unreadable. "Anything here could amplify your abilities—or destroy you. It depends entirely on your will."

Azazel studied Toni, chatting with Tharion as they pulled out swaths of material and clothing. "Are you saying we can use anything in here that conforms to our unique signatures?"

"Yes."

Interesting. "And is it possible those items could *hide* our presence?"

The ridge above Vaeloryx's eyes furrowed. "I suppose so." His answer came out slowly. "No one has taken the time to test anything in here. To be honest, the proximity to this place is why we set up our headquarters here. Our people have forgotten its existence for thousands of years. None of the Krystalii has an interest in a collection of curiosities from alien races we've already conquered."

"Observation," JR14 interjected. "The neglect of such a repository indicates a severe lapse in resource optimization. Thousands of years of untested alien technology could provide significant tactical advantages if analyzed and adapted in a concise, methodical manner."

"That is a valid suggestion, *kalu*." Azazel said, turning to Vaeloryx. "While Toni and I uncover suitable clothing and weapons to use, why don't you have one of your people take a look around here to see if there is anything you can use to help sabotage the Nexus Core?"

The crystal male's humanistic smirk matched the droll look in his silver eyes as he glanced at Tharion chatting with Toni. "Yes. I agree with your valid suggestion."

CHAPTER FIVE

F or the first time since waking up in this godforsaken hellhole, Toni breathed a sigh of genuine relief. She'd been cold for so long, she was pretty sure her bones had frostbite. With any luck, her teeth chattering in a castanet impression had taken their last bow.

She flexed her fingers and marveled at how the strange material of the suit she had put on responded like a second skin. The deep midnight blue fabric gleamed with a subtle incandescence, as if it generated its own light. Gold veins traced intricate patterns along her arms and torso that pulsed in rhythm with her heartbeat. When Vaeloryx explained earlier that the suit was alive—or something close to it—she had doubts. Now she shivered for an entirely different reason. The idea of wearing something alive made her throat tight. But she couldn't deny how the warmth or how perfectly it fit, as if it had been created just for her.

Glancing next to her, she studied Azazel. Now there stood the poster boy for tall, dark, and dreamy—on steroids. His suit mirrored hers, but instead of navy blue, his was a deep obsidian black, the gold accents bolder and more pronounced.

The suit highlighted his powerful physique with every movement. Hard, masculine muscles rippled under the fabric, leaving little to the imagination. Around his shoulders and chest were faint, crystalline plates that shimmered in jagged patterns, a stark contrast to the smooth texture of the rest of the suit. His already commanding presence magnified.

If she concentrated, she sensed some kind of energy coming from him. Contained, but humming with potential. She smiled, watching JR14 settle onto his normal perch on Azazel's left shoulder. The slippery-looking material didn't seem to cause the little droid any trouble. He hung on just fine. *Guess having eight legs has its advantages.*

Looking at the arms of her suit, she was once again awestruck. She hadn't known what to expect when she went into the Vault of Forgotten Worlds with Tharion earlier. But now she was glad she'd taken the chance to wear something so alien. She loved the soothing sensation of the suit against her skin. She turned to Vaeloryx, who was watching them with an unreadable expression.

"Are you sure..." She hesitated, searching for the right word. "Since these suits are... um, alive, that they won't mind us wearing them?"

"In the general sense, yes, they are sentient." Vaeloryx's crystalline body reflected shattered images in the chamber's dim light. "I find it fascinating that the suits you've chosen are ancient Krystalii creations. They were made to attune to the wearer's energy and amplify their abilities. Trust me, if they didn't want to bond with you, you would not have been able to put them on. But,"—he warned, his tone stern—"they can be unpredictable. We are not sure if they only magnify your strengths, but they might also heighten your weaknesses. I suggest you use them with caution until you are in sync."

JR14 clicked his metallic front claws, his voice analytical. "Assessment: The unpredictability factor increases mission risk by 0.47 percent. Organic recommendation: Avoid emotional instability. Current probability of catastrophic amplification: Less than moderate."

Azazel raised an eyebrow, glanced down at the bot on his shoulder, then at his suit. "Unpredictable how?"

Vaeloryx's blue-hued crystalline face hardened. "The suit reacts to your intent. If you lose focus or let your emotions overwhelm you, it may act of its own accord, amplifying what you cannot control."

Toni frowned, running a hand over the smooth fabric at her side. "Well, doesn't that sound like a lot of fun?" Sarcasm aside, it sounded like a recipe for disaster. Especially if she had to control her emotions while on a hostile alien ship. Not like she had a choice.

With a snort, she glared at everyone around the room, daring any of them to suggest this was something she couldn't handle. *Look at her career in the film industry, how she'd clawed her way up. Dealing with entitled douchebags on Earth was tougher than handling psychic alien invaders from another dimension. Thank you very much.*

"Think of it as a necessary challenge," Vaeloryx stated. "Wearing these suits will hide your psychic and physical presence from Baelon—at least for a time. Without them, Baelon would have a better chance at detecting you once you left this section of the ship."

When Azazel flexed his hands, the gold veins in his arms brightened before dimming again. "If I'm not mistaken, I believe they'll help us in a physical fight as well." His voice was thoughtful.

JR14's iridescent wings shifted from under his back panels before sliding out of sight again. "Observation: The organic man demonstrates commendable confidence in managing advanced alien technology. Probability of successful adaptation increases with continued focus and discipline. Outcome: Encouraging trajectory."

Vaeloryx inclined his head. "Precisely."

Toni glanced at Azazel, her breath catching as she watched him again. His bound dark hair around his face was tousled, as if he'd run his hands through the strands and loosened them. His muscular frame reminded her of a warrior created from some ancient myth—dangerous, regal, and heartbreakingly out of reach. Something about him stirred a part of her deep inside. Something she didn't dare name. Heat rose in her cheeks the longer she fixated on him.

Tearing her gaze away, she focused on her own suit instead. She relaxed and smiled as she stroked the material covering her stomach. It looked like the more she wore it, the more comfortable it became. "I hope it doesn't take long for us to sync with one another," she muttered under her breath. *Understatement of the year.*

"I trust you will adapt quicker than you expect," Vaeloryx said. His tone softened. "But remember, the suits are tools. They do not replace your skills or resolve."

Azazel nodded. His mahogany-brown eyes met Toni's. "I know we'll both manage just fine."

Before she responded, JR14 clicked his front limbs from his perch on Azazel's shoulder as he chimed in. "Observation: The organics have sufficient intelligence to maintain vigilance."

Toni gave the small android a wry smile. "Aw-shucks, gizmo-brain. Appreciate the vote of confidence."

Azazel's lips twitched into a one-sided grin as he shifted, the crystalline plates on his suit catching the light. "Are you okay with wearing the alien suit, Toni?"

Head thrown back, she straightened. "Oh sure. Wearing a superhero suit always helps when diving headfirst into a deadly situation. It's what I live for."

"Well now, darling, we all know the ancients didn't design this technology with you in mind," Tharion whispered, winking. "But there's a secret about it I haven't shared with you yet."

"What? Oh, goodie. Another surprise." Toni touched her throat.

Tharion's golden-yellow crystals shimmered in the dusky light of the vault when he leaned toward her. "Since the suits have allowed you to live this long, you're in no danger of them killing you." A heartfelt sigh with his golden hand over his heart. "I have to say, I'm so excited that you two are the first to work with them. It is an honor to witness how the technology of the ancients has adapted to you." He squealed, placing his hand over his mouth. "Who'd have thought it took organic aliens from another dimension to make that happen?"

"Yeah." She shuddered, then turned a glaring eye on the Krystalii. "Good thing you didn't warn us that these things might kill us before we put them on."

Now didn't that just ramp up the creepy factor? But since the freakin' suit didn't kill her, maybe she had nothing to worry about. It'd sure be great if it kept her hidden from the sparkle-tyrant. Hard to ignore Vaeloryx's warning, though. Wearing this suit might amplify something about her she wasn't aware of. *Oh well. She'd just have to make sure she didn't lose control or anything.* She snorted. *Yeah, no problem. Honing her Mr. Spock impersonation would come in handy about now. She'd just suck it up and pretend the whole situation didn't scare her shitless.*

At least she wasn't freezing any more.

Toni followed Azazel back to the rebel command chamber. Lost in thought, she watched the walls shimmer with crystalline threads. Their moving parts created a mosaic pattern that was soothing as well as mesmerizing.

When she and Azazel entered the main room, a group of the Krystalii rebels turned to face them. Most of them sat around a table made of clear crystal while others were wandering about. Some had expressions of curiosity, but others scowled.

An unfamiliar noise buzzed in her head, faint but persistent. As the weight of the Krystalii stares weighed her down, her body suddenly stood taller, her back straight. Then she felt the suit coat her mind with a layer of protection. How she knew it was the suit that blocked the sound was beyond her. But the sudden absence of the buzz made her catch her breath. Strangely, she hadn't noticed the background noise until it was gone.

"You all right, Toni?" Azazel came close enough to whisper, his voice a low, soothing caress. "You seemed startled for a moment."

"I think I just felt the suit working," she murmured. "It's keeping the Krystalii out of my head." She bit her bottom lip and glanced at the rebels. "Do you think it's protecting me from them?"

"That's possible," Azazel assured her. "I tried to do a brief scan on you to test it, but I couldn't penetrate the mental shield over your mind. Which is good, since it'll keep the Krystalii from invading your thoughts as well."

Now that was something she could get behind. Maybe she had a chance to keep Lord crystal-creepy-ass out of her head.

"I'm surprised those ancient battle suits chose you," Laytrii observed, her crystalline emerald features catching the light as she spoke. "How unusual."

Kaelith regarded them with a calculating gaze. The streaks of violet in his obsidian eyes widened.

"They may aid you, but do not trust your safety to them alone. Since the ones who created them didn't live long enough to conduct adequate tests on them, they remain unpredictable. It'd be unfortunate if they crashed just when your survival depended on them."

"Noted." Azazel's tone was smooth. "However, can we go over a few things before we retire for the night?"

On his shoulder, JR14's spider-shaped red-and-gold metallic frame gleamed in the low light. The android's iridescent wings flicked once, a lilting, mechanical sound. Azazel took his previous seat with Toni nearby.

Once everyone settled, Vaeloryx leaned forward, his angular features set in stern lines.

"Please begin, human."

Toni's mouth dried. She hoped Azazel wouldn't say anything to jeopardize their alliance.

Azazel began.

"I've been thinking about what we did before when I found Toni." He gave her a sideways glance with a serene smile. He turned back to the Krystalii. "And I believe we should repeat what we did earlier, but with a few changes."

Kaelith crossed his bulky crystalline arms. The movement made a soft, grinding sound, like stone shifting.

"What exactly do you propose?" His voice held a note of interest, but his skepticism remained clear.

"The first thing we should do is sabotage the energy core of the *Nyrlith*." Azazel put up his hand to forestall questions. "Just enough to disrupt the systems and force Baelon to divert resources to make the needed repairs."

"Disrupting the Energy Crux is all well and good, but what of Baelon's psychic network, the Nexus Core?" Saphirae's voice carried a weight of quiet authority. "Without destroying that first, his forces could stop us with very little effort."

Azazel sat back and steepled his fingers.

"That's the second part of this. Since Baelon and his Elites won't recognize my psychic signature, Toni and I will infiltrate the Nexus Core at the same time you create chaos when you take down the

Energy Crux. Your insight into the ship's systems is invaluable—"
He nodded at Vaeloryx. "—and you have a much better chance at
amplifying the disruption there than I would."

Tharion looked from Vaeloryx to Azazel.

"That sounds risky." His eyes narrowed. "And no one has mentioned the Dimensional Rift Epicenter that creates a pathway between
our dimensions. Without neutralizing that, Baelon's invasion force
can continue gathering unlimited resources from there. He'll be unstoppable if that stays open."

Toni flipped her hair behind her shoulder. That was the whole
kit and caboodle, wasn't it? Disabling the ship and the Nexus Core
wouldn't matter if they couldn't close that portal.

"That takes us to the third phase," Azazel continued. "When Toni
and I disrupt the Nexus Core at the same time you take out the Energy
Crux, it'll divide Baelon's forces even more. And once that happens,
it'll give us the perfect opportunity to sabotage the Dimensional Rift.
From what I can tell from the map you've shown us, it's by the Nexus
Core. During the chaos, Toni and I should have enough time to shut
the Rift down as well." He leaned forward, resting his elbows on his
thighs. "Once that's done, I'll contact my allies in this galaxy and ask
them to converge on the *Nyrlith* with an overwhelming force that will
prevent him from taking control back."

Toni snorted. Oh sure. Easy-peasy.

JR14 clicked his front pincers together.

"Statistical probability of success: 38 percent, factoring in current
resources and known variables," he observed. "Advice: organic male
and female should retain optimistic outlook."

Toni shot the android an amused glare.

"Wow. Way better pep talk, widget-wonder."

Azazel's full lips turned up in a half-smile, but he didn't comment.

Vaeloryx tapped his crystalline fingers on his thigh, the sound sharp and deliberate.

"Your plan carries a heavy reliance on coordination and timing. What assurance do we have that you can handle the interference at the Dimensional Rift Epicenter? And just how will you contact these allies to do as you say? I warn you, Baelon's reach far extends beyond this ship. He may have already eliminated whatever allies you think you have."

Toni stilled as doubt flared. She pressed her lips together and clamped down on the sensation. As she struggled, a warming flow from the suit delivered added strength to her mental shields, giving her a chance to breathe in a sigh of relief. Now wasn't a good time to drown in doubt.

"I assure you, that is something I am not concerned with." Azazel sat back and rubbed his scruffy jawline. "I have every confidence they are even now ready to board the *Nyrlith* at a moment's notice. Once I disable the Nexus Core, I can open an outside psychic path with them."

Kaelith leaned forward.

"And what about casualties? Your plan puts a lot of our people in harm's way." He turned to the female sitting next to him, the one Toni wasn't familiar with. The creature looked as if her body was composed of moonstone, with soft hues of blue and lavender covered by an opalescent sheen.

"Lyrentha," Kaelith continued. "Do you think your healing could handle the influx of casualties if things get out of hand?"

The female opened her mouth, then closed it as her lilac eyes narrowed. After a moment, she nodded.

"I believe I can." She swept her elegant hand to a group of rebels behind her. "There are others I can call on to aid me if necessary.

However—" She looked from Toni to Azazel. "—I am not familiar enough with your species to be of much help if something traumatic happens to you."

"That's a risk we're willing to take." Toni spoke up for the first time. Meeting Lyrentha's piercing gaze, she kept her face relaxed and squared her shoulders. "But I think we have to act as soon as possible before Baelon finds out what we're up to."

"I agree." Azazel addressed the Krystalii in his even tone. "I'm grateful we are working together to create a positive outcome. Thank you." He put his hand over his heart and gave a brief nod.

Toni's chest warmed, her heart thundering. She admired the conviction in his leadership.

For a moment, silence hung heavily in the chamber.

When Saphirae spoke, her tone remained measured.

"It is possible, that for the first time, with the help of these two—" Her crystal face smoothed as she spoke. "—the impossible is finally within our reach. We can finish what needs to be done to free our people."

Kaelith tilted his head.

"Agreed. This plan has enough merits to outweigh the potential risks."

Vaeloryx looked at his obsidian companion before nodding.

"Very well. But know this—" His gaze swept over the group, not just those at the table but all the rebels in the room. "—failure is not an option. This will be our only chance to go against Baelon and his Elites. The survival of our people depends on it. Do all of you agree?"

Another silence before several crystal heads either nodded or voiced their agreements.

Toni exhaled a silent breath. Maybe, just maybe, if everything went according to plan, they'd avoid the annihilation of their standard way of life in the Milky Way galaxy.

Vaeloryx, along with the other Krystalii, decided on the various tasks as the meeting wound down. All too soon, the rebels dispersed into separate groups and began preparations.

Toni lingered, her thoughts heavy. She turned to Azazel.

"So, be honest. What do you really think?" She narrowed her eyes. "Do we stand a chance with this crazy plan?"

"Yes, I believe so." He tilted his chin toward the Krystalii. "It helps that they see this as their last chance to stand against the tyrant ruling their lives," Azazel said in a low voice as he watched the Krystalii. "We've given them a hope I doubt they've ever experienced before."

JR14 clicked his front claws.

"Even the slightest mistake can shatter the fragile construct of hope. Recommend continuous monitoring of the Krystalii to ensure compliance."

Azazel nodded with a wry smile.

"So noted, *kalu*. That will be your assignment."

"Affirmed, *ocua*."

"Toni—" He leaned close, his voice lowered to a husky tone. "—I can tell you're exhausted. Why don't we find that quiet place to sleep?"

Toni nodded. He was right. Like a balloon losing air, she slumped in her seat. She was beyond tired. It was a stretch just to keep her eyes open. The weight of everything she'd experienced crashed through her. It looked like saving the galaxy had to be put on hold for now. Beauty sleep first.

Azazel hadn't realized how tricky it would be to explain sleep to a crystalline alien who didn't even know it existed.

The notion only began to make sense to the Krystalii when Vaeloryx brought in their healer, Lyrentha, who outlined how it worked.

Once the lecture was done, Vaeloryx offered to create a bed for them, which Azazel politely refused. He could generate a perfect sleeping pad for the two of them, much better than a creature made of glass and crystals could.

The Krystalii male led them to a semi-private room large enough for Azazel to create a comfortable pad for himself and Toni.

Speaking of Toni, her silence throughout the process worried him. Her head hung low, and her breathing was shallow. If he didn't know any better, he'd swear the woman slept where she sat.

After one last look at her, he closed his eyes and summoned a soft mattress with blankets and pillows, using as little psychic energy as possible to conserve his strength. Once that was done, he swept Toni into his arms and took her to the sleeping pad.

She startled, looking at him with unfocused eyes.

"Come, *hebat*," he coaxed. "Time for you to sleep."

With a winsome smile, she nodded and yawned. "Yeah, good idea." She lay on the bed and curled into a ball on her side, facing him.

Azazel chuckled when she fell fast asleep.

"JR14, would you keep a vigilant eye on us while we sleep?" he asked the spider-bot resting on his shoulder.

JR14 shifted his small front metallic legs with a faint click as he processed the request. His iridescent wings twitched under his back plates before he spoke.

"Affirmative," the droid replied with a hint of sarcasm as the faint blue glow of his optics brightened. "I shall ensure the perimeter remains uncompromised during your biologically mandated period of unconsciousness." The tiny spider-bot skittered down Azazel's arm and flew to rest on a nearby crystal tower. There, he adjusted his position to get a full view of the surroundings, his back against the wall. He tapped his front claws against the polished surface.

"You may sleep undisturbed," JR14 added, turning his gleaming red-and-gold body toward Azazel. "Though I am perplexed why you require my surveillance when your psychic field is already attuned to this environment. Should anything occur here, I calculate a 96.7 percent probability you would already be aware of it."

Trust the darn android's penchant for overanalyzing.

"Just in case, JR14, I'd feel better with your added monitoring."

JR14's front limbs twitched.

Azazel interpreted that as a bot shrug.

"As you wish. But when you awaken, I expect acknowledgment for maintaining the highest standard of vigilance. Anything less would be, in my estimation, unjust."

With that announcement, JR14 settled into his watchful stance.

"Rest well, Azazel, along with the human female Antonia. I shall guard your serenity with unparalleled efficiency."

Azazel chuckled. "Thank you, my friend."

From his perch, JR14 muttered, "Calling me your friend will not improve your survival odds. However, your designation is noted."

Letting the bot have the last word, Azazel crawled into the bed with Toni. He decided to keep the suit on and nestled beside her, pulling the light comforter over them. Wrapping an arm around her waist, he brought her close and inhaled her sweet scent. His nose twitched as he imagined that her musky aroma was a combination of amber wrapped in a slight bouquet of jasmine, which was ridiculous since she couldn't be wearing any perfume.

Maybe the suit she wore amplified who she was on a basic level. While he didn't consider the garment in any way sentient like the Krystalii suggested, he could appreciate how it adapted effortlessly to his bodily needs. It was a marvel of ingenuity. The suit didn't just regulate his internal body temperature. It handled all his basic needs, like nutrition and elimination of waste, without alerting the wearer, extracting nutrients and water from existing atmosphere to fuel his body and removing waste on a microscopic level. *What an excellent tool it would be when going into any long-term endeavor, like exploration.*

Or battle.

He only wished he'd thought of creating something like this for himself and his brothers to use when they were slaves of the Akurns.

But the suit was the least of his concerns. While analyzing it would be a worthwhile venture, what he'd rather do was analyze the strong, undeniable attraction he felt for Toni. He adored her sharp wit and unadulterated ability to see things in a surprisingly different way. Oh, he could have entered her consciousness without her knowing to uncover whatever he wanted about her. The anticipation of letting it all unfold naturally kept him in suspense.

To uncover what her interests were, how she grew up, and what mattered most to her would be a tantalizing experience. Why, for instance, did she leave Earth to join the alien exchange? That had to mean she didn't have a man in her life. If so, why not? She had to be one of the most attractive women he'd ever seen.

Not that he overindulged in feminine company like some of his brothers did. While he explored various aspects of his sexuality, it wasn't something he focused on. So much had happened in the seven thousand years since he arrived in the future. He'd been eager to uncover it all, especially humanity's growth and evolution. What began as curiosity had become a deep passion for history. Especially the arts, which included writings and the priceless paintings and sculptures created throughout the centuries.

Azazel yawned so hard his jaw cracked. Enough lying here wishing things were different. Closing his eyes, he focused his psychic energy to slumber...to be at rest. In the ensuing quiet, the hum of the ship faded until it became the gentle rhythm of waves lapping against a distant shore. It took him a moment to recognize he was no longer on the *Nyrlith*. At least not mentally.

Azazel exhaled and embraced the strands of a *Dreamwalk* his subconscious must have created. Opening his eyes, he saw the woman of his dreams in the distance, shimmering into existence. Her soft edges slowly sharpened into reality the closer she came. Standing in front of him, she watched him with her head tilted, her full lips pursed as if ready to ask him something.

Even though he hadn't intended to create this experience, he had no problem taking control of the situation. He held out his hand. "Come with me, Toni," he reassured her when her beautiful blue eyes widened. "I want to take you somewhere—somewhere safe and beautiful so we can spend time getting to know one another."

Toni glanced at his outstretched hand, her brow furrowed.

Azazel waited until she reached out. When their hands touched, a flare zapped through him. The feeling reminded him of those sparklers he watched the humans play with during their national holiday. The background flickered, bending and melting away as if reality itself dissolved into a pool of liquid light. He pulled her close, and she gasped as the world reformed around them.

When the image coalesced, they stood on the veranda of a beach house situated in a lush, organic landscape. Soft golden sand stretched in either direction, meeting a turquoise sea that glistened beneath a yellow sun just beginning to set. The air was warm, caressing them with a silken breeze. It brought with it a faint, briny scent of the ocean mixed with the sweet aroma of blooming beach pea flowers from a nearby vine that curled up the house's wooden beams.

The house itself was an open, airy structure with walls of polished driftwood and large glass panels that invited the outside in. Gauzy curtains fluttered in the gentle wind, and the interior glowed with the amber light of the setting sun. Inside, a plush, cream-colored sofa nestled near a low table adorned with fresh fruit and flowers. The soft melody of wind chimes danced on the breeze, their sound mingling with the distant call of seabirds.

Toni's breath caught, her eyes wide as she turned in a slow circle, taking it all in. "Azazel... this is..." Her voice trailed off. "What is this?" She shook her head. "This doesn't look like we're on the *Nyrlith*."

His grip on her hand tightened, and he gave her a soft smile. "I assure you, we are still on the Krystalii ship," he explained. "But this is a place I crafted in our dreams for us to get to know one another better. This—" He waved his other hand. "—is called a *Dreamwalk*. It's a private sanctuary that exists only in our minds."

Toni let go of his hand and stepped off the edge of the veranda, watching her bare feet sink into the giving sand. "This feels... real," she murmured, bending to let the grains slip through her fingers. "The sand, the air... even the smell of the ocean." She stood and took a deep breath.

It was then he noticed she wasn't wearing the battle suit. Instead, she had on a blue two-piece bikini that matched the color of her eyes. Wrapped around her trim waist was a multi-colored gossamer sarong.

Clearing his throat, Azazel focused on her face instead of her glorious body. "It's real because you and I share a bond." He joined her at the railing. "It's as real as reality can be." He ran a finger in a light caress over the top of her hand. "It's real because you're here to share it with me."

She turned to face him, her expression soft as her eyes searched his. "You did this... for me?"

"For us." He reached out and brushed a strand of her hair behind her ear. "I..." He cleared his throat. "I'm drawn to you in a way I've never experienced with anyone before. And I was hoping—" He took her hand and brought it to his mouth. "—you would feel the same way. That you'd like to get to know me better, too." He kissed her soft skin, never taking his eyes from hers.

The blue of Toni's eyes darkened as her pupils widened, swallowing the color until the only bit of blue remaining was a sliver around her black pupils. Her sensuous lips curved into a sultry grin. Grasping his hand covering hers, she stepped closer until the warmth from her body coated his. "I'm glad you want to get to know me better," she murmured in a throaty tone. "And that you created such a romantic place to do so." She whispered the words against the base of his neck.

Azazel closed his eyes, trying to control the dark, hidden part of himself that demanded freedom. His body clamored and burned with a feverish, urgent ache to claim the woman in his arms. His inner beast stirred awake, fueling the relentless carnal hunger pounding through his skull. Every inch of his body thrummed with a raw, aching need. His only solace was how her curves fit into his body's hard angles and planes, as if she belonged there. The inner beast clawed at the cage Azazel kept it in. It thrashed against the restraints with a howl of unrelenting fury, desperate to break free.

Taking a fortifying breath, Azazel let her scent and feel of her body against his wash over him, helping him regain control once again. He glanced out at the horizon and watched the sun as it painted streaks of pink and orange across the sky. "I'm grateful you like it." He nuzzled the top of her head. The feel and scent of her calmed the beast. It crouched in a watchful silence.

Toni's soft laughter came across as a light, harmonized sound that complemented the wind chimes. She reached for his hand and laced her fingers with his. "So, how do we get to know one another, Azazel?" Her grin was mischievous. "Where do you want to start?"

He gazed at her, the vibrant colors of the dream world reflecting in her eyes. "I can think of a couple of ways." He challenged her with a grin, tilting his chin up. He wasn't sure if he was challenging her... or the savage part of himself he struggled to keep on a short, brutal leash.

Toni couldn't remember the last time she'd enjoyed spending time with a man as much as she did with Azazel. And on a private beach she could have sworn was real. But the man—wow, here was a man with a curious mixture of innocence combined with a world-weary outlook on life.

When he explained his upbringing, she understood most of what he said, but it was hard for her to imagine how he grew up. Created thousands of years ago by alien scientists called the Akurn, as a brute slave in southern Africa to mine for gold. His history was as foreign to her as a low-budget B-movie becoming a serious Oscar contender.

What truly blew her mind was that, rather than becoming mindless labor drones, he and his brothers developed powerful psychic abilities. An unintended consequence of the Earthborn DNA woven into their creation.

"Wait." She raised her hand. "Are you telling me that humans were the ones with psychic powers and not the aliens?" Her nose wrinkled. *Boy, did Hollywood get that wrong.* She grasped a grape and plopped it into her mouth. The implications were staggering. *Think of the storylines she could produce for her next movie project.* After a quick glance at the bountiful picnic Azazel had provided on a wide blanket, she chose a bruschetta slice smothered in a savory herb mushroom sauce.

Azazel nodded.

"Yes. From what I understand, none of the other *Adamou*— what the Akurns called us— had psychic abilities unless they included hominoid DNA from Earth." He glanced at the setting sun resting on the horizon, giving the ocean a golden glow. "My brothers and I hid our psychic talents from the scientists when we were young. It wasn't until later that we learned the truth: the last batch of slaves hadn't been destroyed. They'd been sealed away. Their powers were so overwhelming that the Akurns, with all their advanced technology, feared they didn't have enough power to destroy them."

Chuckling, he glanced at her and leaned back on his hands, crossing his ankles on the soft beach blanket. "Which sort of happened to them, anyway. See, what the scientists on Earth were doing, combining Akurn DNA with any other specie's was illegal. When the ruling party of the Akurns discovered what they'd done, they sentenced the whole complex to be destroyed." He frowned. "I was trying to teleport myself and three of my brothers to a nearby spaceship where our brother, Adapa, was already on board. It was a ship we'd prepared to escape. But before we could, the Akurns attacked the compound, raining down high-powered laser fire all around us. In the chaos, I did get us to the waiting ship—but landed us seven thousand years in the future instead." With a sigh, he sat up cross-legged, resting his elbows on his thighs. "Since then, I've gone over and over on what I had to be thinking to make that kind of mistake." He rubbed his temple. "All I remember was the desperate rush to reach the ship—nothing else mattered but getting my brothers and myself to that safe place. As the world burned in raging flames barreling toward us, my only thought was to get to Adapa because he desperately needed us." He chuckled. "I didn't know those words would anchor the jump, taking us to the future where his need for us was even greater."

Toni didn't need to be a psychic to recognize a man riddled with guilt. She scooted closer to him and placed her hand on his firm thigh. "Didn't you say that you and your brothers saved Earth from being destroyed by the Akurns? Why do you feel guilty about that?" She squeezed his leg to comfort him while popping another juicy purple grape into her mouth.

When he zeroed in on her hand, she jerked it away, curling her fingers into an embarrassed grip.

"Oh, I'm so sorry. I shouldn't have…"

"No—" Azazel looked up at her, and the mahogany color of his eyes darkened. "—I like it when you touch me." He took her fist and brought it to his mouth and kissed her knuckles. "In fact, I prefer it."

Her face flushed, and heat crawled up her throat and cheeks. Not one to deny her emotions, she nodded.

"So do I." She swallowed the grape. "But why do you feel guilty about what you did?" She leaned closer to him. "Didn't it turn out for the best?"

Now his steady gaze focused on her mouth when she spoke. "Yes, but my eldest brother, Adapa, almost died because we were separated from him for so long." He glanced at her and tilted his head. "Since the five of us were created together, we're permanently linked. If we end up in different, ah, dimensions, we cannot survive apart for very long. My reckless action almost killed him." The last sentence came out in an anguished whisper.

Well, shit. That confession just pissed her off. Didn't his family recognize the heavy guilt he suffered from? Some freakin' psychics they were. Letting Azazel endure such a heavy burden that only got deeper the longer he carried it. *Once she got those idiots in a room, she'd give them a piece of her mind with both barrels.*

"Okay, listen here." She scooted close enough their knees touched. Grasping his hands in hers, she leaned in. "My mother stressed to me that if guilt means extending worry about what you've done, it doesn't do any good nor does it help. The only thing you should do is strive to not do such a thing again. So, tell me, Mister It's-all-my-fault, did you deliberately mean to kill your brother by separating from him for over seven thousand years?"

Azazel's eyebrows furrowed. "What? No!"

"I said—" Toni hesitated, her heart tapping a nervous rhythm against her ribs. Then, before she could overthink it, she did the one thing she'd never done before. With a quick *hmmm* under her breath, she took matters into her own hands and scooted onto his lap. She wrapped her legs around his trim waist to settle dangerously close to his groin. With bold intent, she linked her arms around his thick neck, clasping her opposite wrist. If it was the last thing she did, she'd make the stubborn ass pay attention to something other than his self-imposed guilt. "—was it your intention to kill Adapa by disappearing into the far future without him?"

Azazel's lips thinned into a straight line. "That's absurd. I'd never do that!" He jerked back and gazed at her with wild eyes. "How could you even suggest..."

Toni caressed his cheek. "I'm not the one suggesting such a thing. You are."

His mouth dropped open.

She was glad she was sitting on his lap when slight tremors racked his body. It told her he at least considered the point she was trying to make.

"I..." He swallowed hard, his Adam's apple bobbing. "You..." He closed his eyes.

She waited.

"You... are right." He placed his forehead against hers and sighed.

His glorious chest rose and fell against hers. Her nipples tightened. Even though her skin was covered, her breasts were ultra-sensitive. His hold on her shoulders loosened, which gave her a chance to rest her head against him and snuggle.

"There's something else I'd like you to consider." She roamed her fingers over the firm hills of his solid pecs. "Maybe destiny intended you to be there, exactly when it was most critical. I don't think you had a choice at all." The last words came out in a soft whisper.

Azazel's breathing evened out.

"And maybe..." She dared. "Just maybe, we're both here because this is where we're supposed to be. Together." She put her finger under his scruffy chin and turned his head to face her. With measured slowness, she leaned in and covered his tempting lips with her own.

"Antonia."

Azazel breathed her name. The sound tore something deep and raw inside him as she pulled away. Her precious kiss—*gods, that kiss*—wasn't just lips meeting lips. It claimed a piece of him he didn't even know he dared to share. A slice of previously denied peace. A flicker of hope instead of guilt.

Even though they were in a psychic *Dreamwalk*, she was as real to him as the terrible dark loneliness he'd endured all his life. As it receded, the snarling beast he carried deep inside stayed tranquil and still for once. If he didn't know better, that was a sure sign this woman was the missing half of his soul. One that even his inner demon craved.

"Azazel," Toni whispered back. She grabbed the back of his head in a tight grip before seizing his mouth again with hers.

Flames of electricity shot through him, tiny licks that brought him alive. A trembling ache started low, creating a tension that cried out for her. The background faded away. His only reality was her soft hands roaming over his near-naked body, over the swimsuit he wore. Nothing in his life—no moment of triumph or pain—had prepared him for the wildfire she ignited in him. It wasn't anything as simple as want... or lust. It was an all-consuming need that built with every caress.

Exploring her kiss with his eager lips and tongue, his unsteady hand traveled over the tempting plumpness of her breast, which was covered by the minuscule triangle of cloth of her bathing suit. He had no trouble pushing this aside to clasp her trembling mound. Drifting his mouth to the corner of hers, he moved to the flowing curve of her chin, down to the vulnerable line of her throat. Ancient words tumbled out of his mouth, words that were lost in the annals of time. In the back of his mind, a part of him urged caution, warning him he was moving too fast. But inflamed emotions took over, filling him with a clamoring need that made the practical thought disappear in a mere whisper.

Immersed in the unfamiliar sexual sensations bombarding him, he swept his tongue over the pulse in her neck. With a teasing nip, he scraped his teeth over the spot. He sucked in a breath as white-hot pleasure that bordered on pain consumed him. He cupped her swollen breast before teasing the puckered skin of her nipple with a brief pinch. For a split-second, he swore the feeling was a mix of the two of them merging into one. Their souls connecting on a level he'd never dreamed was possible.

Damn, even his inner beast rumbled with carnal anticipation, stalking inside him. If he wasn't mistaken, the "other" demanded satisfaction with the female in his arms.

Azazel's heartbeat pounded inside his head. And, since that inner beast was cooperating, he had the freedom to relish the sensations happening between him and Toni. He closed his eyes and surrendered. He moved his mouth up her throat to her chin and nibbled before conquering her lips again as he massaged her breast. The very air around him shifted until all outside sensations fell away. Except for her... for Toni. The dewy silk of her skin, the satin curtain of her dark hair draped over his hand as he cradled the base of her skull.

She clung to him as her need and hunger joined his.

Her dark, erotic images fueled his desire, building a fire in his blood.

"Wait." Toni jerked her lips from his with a strangled moan.

Opening his eyes, he watched her troubled expression as she tilted her head and scooted away from him. Mentally as well as physically.

She drew in a slow breath and faltered. "I don't... I mean, I do...but..." Her blue gaze was unfocused. "I'm just having a hard time with how fast things are happening here," she confessed in a soft, but unconvincing, tone.

His inner beast grumbled. Not strong enough to cloud his mind, but strong enough for Azazel to clamp down on it to keep it from trying to reach out to Toni's mind. "Tell me," he whispered, keeping his tone open and soothing. He leaned back, mourning the distance as he let his hand fall from her full breast. He licked his lips, savoring her flavor as he did his best to collect himself. To give her some space even though she didn't move from his lap.

Toni's crystal-blue eyes darted around before focusing on the radiant sun setting in the distance. "I make it a point to try to be honest with myself." She took a deep breath before her gaze swung back to him. "And to be honest with those I get involved with."

Azazel stilled when she said, "get involved". He gave a brief nod to encourage her to continue.

"Usually, I let things develop naturally."

Toni's slight grin and colored cheeks told him her confession embarrassed her.

"Dissecting a relationship has never been on my agenda." She waved a hand between them. "But the strong feelings I have for you are, um, hard to take in." Grasping his hand resting on her knee, she gave him a beseeching look. "And I admit it scares the hell out of me." She bit her bottom lip.

Azazel fought the urge to pull her back into his arms. With sheer control, he concentrated on releasing the tension between his shoulders. Thankfully, the beast remained subdued, so he didn't have to fight on that front. He squeezed her hand back. "Believe me, you're not the only one scared." If they were being honest here, she would have to know she wasn't the only one with those fears. He looked into her eyes and confessed a personal secret he'd never told anyone before. "I've been alone all my life. I've never allowed anyone to get too close, terrified that if they did, they'd reject me." Especially that hidden part of himself he'd vowed to never show anyone.

Toni's eyes bulged before she sputtered a burst of laughter. "*Heol!*" She exclaimed in Korean. "If nothing else, the fact that you actually admitted that just proves you are exactly who you claim to be—an alien guy from the past with just enough humanity to be delightfully awkward." Chuckling, she wiped a tear from her eye. "Or you're gay." She looked him up and down. "Which you're not, are you?"

His grin turned sultry. "I can guarantee with one hundred percent certainty I am only attracted to the opposite sex." He pulled her close with half-lidded eyes, leaning close enough to continue where they left off. Before his lips met hers, an incessant ping tapped at his consciousness.

Dammit!

What he wouldn't give to ignore it. But if he did, it not only wouldn't go away, but it would also get worse.

With a frustrated huff, he straightened and increased the distance from her. "I'm so sorry, *hebat*. But I'm afraid our time here is coming to an end. JR14 is trying to get my attention, so I must finish this pleasant *Dreamwalk*. Please prepare yourself to be awakened."

Toni rested her head on his upper chest, where her deep sigh resonated through his skin. "Okay, but can we do this again?" She twirled a finger around one of his hardened nipples. "Maybe in real life?"

Azazel kissed the lustrous hair on the top of her head. It was all he could do to keep his volatile inner self in check. Damn beast was becoming more of a problem than ever before. It didn't agree with the separation and vibrated inside him with rage. He shuddered. No telling what would happen if he lost control, even in this *Dreamwalk*. His only recourse was to make sure his inner self knew he and Toni would get together again. And in such a way, they'd have enough time to explore each other.

After a tense moment, his inner beast snorted and faded into the background. Smiling with relief, he took Toni's cheeks between his hands and stared into her alluring eyes.

"That, my love, is something I can guarantee will happen."

CHAPTER SIX

M ^{*y love?*}

The whispered words echoed clear and strong the moment Toni opened her eyes. She groaned and rubbed her face. Ooh-whee—was that a dream or what? She could swear her toes still had beach sand stuck between them.

My love.

Azazel's deep, rumbling tone reverberated through her mind. Was that really him? No, no—it had to be a dream. She exhaled and flopped her hand down beside her, heart pounding like crazy. Damn, it had been a while since a dream hit her like that. She giggled. Look at her, turned inside-out like a teenager experiencing her first real kiss. Scratch that—her first so-called real kiss hadn't come close to feeling like *that.*

And that tense expression Azazel had in the dream? Erotic and slow-burning. Her breath caught just thinking about it. Unreal or not, she couldn't resist sneaking a peek at the actual man behind the fantasy. She turned to where she'd last seen him, hoping to catch him asleep so she could gawk at him all she wanted without getting caught.

Only... he wasn't there.

Toni sat up, running her hand over the soft mattress where he'd been. The light blanket felt cool. He'd been gone for a while.

"Shit!" She scrambled off the platform, arms windmilling to keep from face-planting on the smooth crystal floor. Jeez, could she be any more of a klutz?

A strange thought pricked the back of her mind. Maybe the alien suit she wore was still acclimating to her, making her motor skills go on the fritz. She blinked. Where the hell had *that* idea come from?

She ran her hands down the sleek fabric of the suit as it adjusted against her skin. A subtle hum of energy buzzed beneath the surface. This wasn't just clothing. It was alive, somehow. Aware. She couldn't shake the feeling that it studied her. "Okay, my friend," she muttered, patting her stomach. "We've got this. You and me."

Sure, talking to her outfit felt a little silly, but hey—when in Rome. Shoulders squared, she stepped out of the sleeping alcove into the large chamber where Azazel and the rebels were gathered around an oval crystal table, murmuring in low voices. She took the moment to study the literal man of her dreams.

Azazel stood tall, hands clasped behind his back, his profile calm and non-threatening.

Her gaze drifted down his body—compact, firm muscles showcased in his form-fitting suit—then back up to his face. Masculine. Chiseled jaw dusted with stubble. High cheekbones under almond-shaped eyes. His features hinted at a mixed heritage, not unlike her own. Her bright-blue eyes—thanks to her white American grandfather who stayed in Korea after the war—were usually the only clue to her mixed background.

But Azazel's ears? Those slight pointy tips were sexy as hell. She'd always been a sucker for Vulcans and elves.

"Yes," Azazel said, turning to Vaeloryx. "We can begin as soon as Toni is ready."

"Begin what?" Toni slipped up beside him. She caught a flicker of heat from his eyes and she grinned. "Just fill me in on the plan."

Vaeloryx waved a hand over the table, activating a holographic schematic of the *Nyrlith*. "As we discussed earlier, we'll start by disabling the Energy Crux, then you'll disrupt the Nexus Core's psychic network. Once we hit both fronts, it should force Baelon's Elites to split in response." He gestured toward the map.

Toni had no clue what she was looking at—schematics weren't her thing—but she nodded and pretended to follow.

"There's been a change of plans. Instead of the two of you attacking the Dimensional Rift, Kaelith and I will do so." Vaeloryx continued. "That will give you the chance to find a ship to escape in."

Kaelith grinned and rammed his knuckles into his open palm. "Been waiting forever to crush some of them Elites."

He reminded her of The Thing from the *Fantastic Four* movies. All about the clobberin'.

Vaeloryx expanded the projection to show a vast, cathedral-like room of mirrors and glass. In the center hovered a clear, multi-faceted crystal.

Toni leaned in for a better look. That was some high-tech doohickey they were hijacking. If she didn't know any better, she'd have thought they were looking at the actual place.

"To help with that," Saphirae added, "I'll broadcast a temporary bypass to mask the Nexus Core's defenses. And you—" She looked at Toni. "—can slip in with this while Azazel guards the entrance." She handed over a strange, crystalline device glowing with soft blue light.

"This shard is a dampening rig," Saphirae said, its rods casting dancing patterns across the room. "Don't drop it."

Toni turned it over, gasping as it pulsed faintly in her hands. "This thing feels... weird."

"It's grown, not built. That's how it generates the signals we need to disrupt Baelon's reach. It'll sync with your suit—helping you focus on what you want it to do. But I warn you, if your thoughts scatter, so will the signal."

Toni let out a shaky breath. "Okay. So, uh, where do I stick this thing?"

Saphirae pointed at a section of the holographic conduit stretching upward. "Here. Attach the rig using the magnetized clamps—once it locks on, it'll emit an interference that will jam the Krystalii's psychic signals."

Oh sure. Like she'd done this a million times. She gave a resigned nod.

"The device acts like a magnet," Saphirae added. "Stick it anywhere on your suit until you're ready to use it."

Toni nodded again, then slapped the shard to the small of her back. It clung comfortably in place. Lightweight. Barely noticeable. She glanced at Azazel, who watched her with a soft, unreadable smile.

JR14's sky-blue eyes remained steady on her from his shoulder perch.

Azazel appeared so calm. So maddeningly composed. She narrowed her eyes. One day, she'd pull that look from him for real—that taut, ravenous expression etched with the kind of desire that haunted her from that dream. Yep, number one on her bucket list once this was all over.

"We'll only have a limited amount of time to strike at the Dimensional Rift Epicenter once you two complete your task," Vaeloryx said grimly. "In order to facilitate that and for you to do some real damage to the Nexus Core, your construct—" He nodded at JR14 sitting on Azazel's shoulder. "—will infiltrate a back door we've downloaded specs into his system that will give him the directions he needs to plant decoys inside. Once that's done, it'll increase the chaos throughout the ship, giving us a better chance of hiding while we shut down that Dimensional Rift." He looked around at the group. "Remember, that's the key to ending this nightmare for good. If we don't cut that off, nothing else we do matters."

"Yeah, 'cause...kablooey!" Tharion spread his hands in a cartoon explosion. "Lord Baelon will have no trouble turning us all into space molecules."

Toni folded her arms. "Awesome. If we all get blasted into cosmic dust, someone better film it so we can get a heartfelt slow-mo scene when the image fades to black."

After Tharion's oh-so-encouraging description, Toni hung back while the rest of the group finished coordinating their plan.

Vaeloryx, along with Kaelith and Saphirae, would head to the Energy Crux, the ship's energy room, while she and Azazel went to the nearby space dock to secure a ship.

Hopefully, the mass confusion would make it hard for Baelon to coordinate with his creepy, spark-throwing interdimensional minions and prevent him from getting any more replacements.

Vaeloryx designated which rebels would be left behind to coordinate the overall effort and monitor their progress through the Resonant and Sub-Resonant Nodes. Once the plan was finalized as much as it could be, there was a lull in the conversation.

"I think we should call this 'Operation Twinkle Demolition'." Toni jumped in. When she got a round of blank stares, she shrugged. "What? Every covert operation should have a name." When the stares didn't change, she put her hands on her hips. "Geez, even back in World War II, they had Operation Paperclip to recruit Germans for the Allies. Giving this crazy plan a name is the least we can do."

The only one to offer a comment was JR14. "Statistical analysis indicates 'Operation Twinkle Demolition' has a 52 percent success rate, which I have rounded up because of organic inconsistencies."

Azazel and the Krystalii remained silent, unimpressed by her lame attempt at humor.

Spoilsports, Toni thought. *Oh well. No accounting for tastes.* With a toss of her head, she let out an indignant huff before following Azazel down a corridor. *All right,* she thought, *as far as she was concerned, Operation Twinkle Demolition had officially begun.* She stayed close behind the handsome hero, and her heart hammered in rhythm with the soft thrum of the ship's systems.

JR14 clung to Azazel's shoulder, his spindly legs flexing every few seconds.

Ahead of them, the rebels—Vaeloryx, Kaelith, and Saphirae—moved with disciplined precision. Their crystalline forms reflected under the eerie inner glow of the ship.

Toni studied them.

Vaeloryx led the others, his angular features set in a determined grimace.

Kaelith, ever the vigilant commander, scanned their surroundings, his sharp-eyed gaze darting from shadow to shadow.

Saphirae walked beside him, gripping a compact device wired with luminous crystal veins and a layered tech so advanced, Toni wouldn't be surprised if it thought for itself.

Toni might not understand how the thing worked, but she trusted the engineer's quiet certainty more than succumbing to her own fears.

All of this was odd, though. *If the Krystalii rebels had all this tech before meeting us, why didn't they use it?* She found it hard to believe that only Azazel had the unusual psychic mojo to pull that part of this off. Her lips tightened. *First chance she got, she'd talk to Azazel about her concerns in private.*

"Almost there," Azazel murmured. "How are you holding up?" His voice was low but steady.

Some kind of soothing presence brushed against her, reassuring and grounding. It was strange. Ever since that dream, she swore she somehow had a connection with him. "I'm trying not to think how all this could go sideways," Toni whispered back, her voice tight. She tightened her grip on the dampening rig she'd moved from her lower back to her side. "You?"

"Focused." Azazel's lips twitched as if he was trying to smother a grin. "But if I had a choice, I'd rather be back on that beach with you."

Toni stopped dead in her tracks, her mouth gaping like a codfish's. "I..." She stared at Azazel. "You... we..." *Great. She suffered from a bad case of word vomit.*

"Come along, *hebat*." Azazel put a light grip on her elbow and propelled her forward. "I'll feed you some more grapes on that beach later. Right now, we've got to be somewhere else."

Unable to sort through his outrageous statement, she followed along, sputtering as she let him lead her around like a lost puppy looking for his momma. *That wasn't a dream created by my lust-fueled mind? Holy shit!* She glanced at Azazel's handsome profile. *He... they...*

"Antonia," Azazel whispered. "Let's concentrate on getting this done, okay?"

Oh sure, get the dangerous thing done first. How am I supposed to do that after he'd dropped that stupid bombshell? Men.

A warning flickered in her peripheral vision and diverted her attention. The suit gave her a warning zap that made Toni's pulse spike.

"Movement up ahead." Azazel announced, confirming what she already knew. "Two Elites coming this way."

"I see them," Vaeloryx's smooth voice cut in, crisp and authoritative. "Kaelith, handle it."

With a wide grin, Kaelith nodded once and rushed ahead of them. His bulky crystalline arms morphed into sleek blades.

Before Toni figured out what he was doing, Kaelith's lithe figure dissolved into a blur, moving faster than she could follow with her eyes.

The guards never stood a chance.

By the time she heard the thud of shattering crystal, Kaelith was back, his blades reforming into hands as if nothing had happened.

"Clear," he said around his huge smile, satisfaction lacing his voice.

Azazel gave a sharp nod. "Thank you. Let's move."

The group pressed on, the air growing heavier as they neared the core.

Something buzzed and pushed against Toni's mind, a reminder of Baelon's oppressive psychic presence that saturated the ship. The suit warmed up. It must be helping to dampen whatever was attacking her, but some of the oppressive sensations continued to seep in. It made her think of how the air felt when a storm threatened to break.

When they reached the Energy Crux chamber, Toni's breath caught.

The massive, glowing center loomed before them, a pulsating mass of light and crystalline tendrils that radiated power trapped in a hollow, transparent tube.

It was both beautiful and electrifying as she watched the unimaginable power radiating in a contained space.

"Here's where we separate," Vaeloryx announced. "We'll take care of the Energy Crux while the two of you head to the Nexus Core." He nodded his aquamarine head to a hallway on the left. "Tharion will guide you through your Sub-Node." His clear eyes landed on Toni before darting back to Azazel. "As you Earthers say, good luck."

"Yeah... meet you on the flip side." Toni gave him a two-fingered salute.

"Hurry, then, there isn't much time," Vaeloryx warned, his tone clipped. "I suspect Baelon's Elites are sending more sentries our way."

Azazel's presence brushed against Toni's mind as his soft voice whispered, *"Ready?"*

Her eyes widened. She nodded. *How did he do that?* Not wanting to delve into that possibility, her gaze darted around the chamber, trying to uncover any threats. *Like she could do something if anything attacked.*

JR14 wiggled on Azazel's shoulder as if to steady himself.

A sudden pulse of energy slammed into Toni's mind, making her stagger. She gasped, clutching her head as the suit's shields flared in response.

Azazel was beside her in an instant, his hand steadying her shoulder. "Baelon knows we're here," he said, his voice grim. "We're out of time."

The chamber shuddered as an alarm blared. Crimson lights bathed the hallway. The sound of stampeding footsteps echoed through the corridor.

"They're coming," Kaelith growled, his blades forming once again where his hands were. "Saphirae, Vaeloryx... into the engine room now!"

With that command, the three Krystalii rushed into the blazing chamber, leaving Toni and Azazel alone in the hallway with JR14.

Azazel grabbed Toni's hand, pulling her toward the exit on the left. "Let's go!"

Sprinting alongside the man holding her in an iron grip, they raced down the corridor as the sound of pursuing forces grew louder. Toni's heart pounded as she struggled to keep up, her mind racing. The suit's shields held strong, but the psychic pressure was unmistakable and relentless.

"Turn left!" Tharion's voice barked from the Sub-Node clipped on Azazel's waist.

With a quick turn, Azazel darted into a narrower passage.

They rounded the corner, and a group of Elites blocked their path.

The air crackled with psychic energy as the crystalline soldiers advanced, their forms radiating menace.

"I'll handle them." Azazel stepped forward. His psychic energy surged, colliding with the Elites in a visible wave of power. "Go!"

"Azazel—" Toni began, but he cut her off with a sharp look.

"Go! Use the dampening rig like Saphirae showed you! Trust me, I've got this."

"Go!" Tharion's disembodied shout from the sub-node repeated Azazel's command. "Be sure to keep the dampening rig out of the Elites' hands!" His frantic voice echoed loud and clear.

A sense of déjà vu tightened her chest as she Azazel take his katana from the harness on his back and leap to fight the Elite guards blocking their path.

The ear-piercing shrill of the ship's alarms in the background turned into a blaring taunt.

Toni held her breath as she watched Azazel battle the Elites in a coordinated frenzy, then they disappeared in a cloud of crystalline dust.

She took a step forward with her hand outstretched, but Azazel's voice echoed in her head.

I'm fine! Even though he spoke to her mentally, she'd have to be an idiot to miss the tension in his tone. *Take JR14 with you. He'll help you place the dampening rig in the right place.* She hesitated, but jumped when he shouted, *GO!*

"All right, already. Sheesh." Toni groused out loud and glanced over her shoulder, then looked around her. "Now, where's that freakin' bug?"

"Comparing me to an air-breathing arthropod is neither conducive nor correct."

JR14's red-and-gold body gleamed in the reflective light of the hallway as he zipped toward her in a zigzag pattern before settling on her left shoulder. "Suggestion: I am open to giving you further instructions if this concept is confusing for you."

"Not today, widget-wonder." She grimaced. "Instead, why don't you make yourself useful and point me to the Nexus Core so I can put a bee in their bonnet?"

"Antonia."

If Toni wasn't mistaken, the spider-bot's tone was brimming with impatience. *Lookie there, the little droid was finally loosening up.*

"Again, with an insect reference." His iridescent wings fluttered out before retracting. "Information: aboard this inter-dimensional vessel, there are no organic..."

She sighed. *Damn, Azazel had to have the patience of a saint to deal with this little guy. Good thing JR14 was as cute as a... well, bug.* "Please desist this unnecessary line of conversation, JR14. It is imperative we complete our assignment to disrupt the Nexus Core." *See, she could talk all nerd-like with the best of them when she put her mind to it.*

"Affirmative," the bot answered. "Directions: Proceed forward, and I will instruct you when to change course."

When the piercing alarm continued to wail, she put her hands over her ears. "I don't suppose you can do something about that stupid alarm, could you?"

The suit she wore heated at the neck before spreading down her arms. A sense of serene quiet filled her. It took a moment before she realized the annoying sound had stopped. Breathing a sigh of relief, she shook her hands to rid them of the tickling sensation, as if they'd fallen asleep. "Thanks, JR14."

"Clarification," JR14 said from her shoulder. "I did not rectify the alarm system of the Krystalii ship. Opinion: Concentrate on the mission. Investigate the reason for the silence at a more opportune time."

Well, he had a point. With a frown, Toni pulled the dampening rig from her waist and clutched it in a tight grip. She had a sneaking suspicion that her suit had something to do with modifying the sound. But JR14 was right. Now wasn't the time to figure it out.

Sprinting down the low-lit corridor, she let the hum of the Krystalii ship, vibrating through the soles of her boots, calm her. Each step she took created a light echo in the hollow hallway that looked like it was made of a fusion of crystal and metal.

JR14 shifted, and his claws gripped her shoulder to keep steady. His iridescent wings flicked open for a moment before snapping shut again. "Left turn ahead. Then proceed twenty meters to the bulkhead entrance," he instructed, his voice crisp and precise.

Toni nodded, panting. "Got it, bug-brain."

"Correction: I am JR14. That identifier is neither accurate nor amusing. As I have already stated, I am not an organic construct."

She chuckled despite the knot of tension tightening in her insides. "Brother, you need to work on your sense of humor."

"Humor is inefficient."

Ha! She'd argue that if there were time, but she had arrived where she was supposed to be. As she got close, the doorway hissed open. Peeking inside, she verified all was clear. At least as far as she could tell. She slid inside, and the door whooshed closed behind her.

"Think there's a lock on this thing to keep everyone out?" She glanced at the door, then at JR14.

His bulbous head looked up at her, and a low glow of soft blue in his round eyes shifted to a brick red.

"Information not available." JR14 responded.

Damn. Oh, well. Nothing to do about that. She'd work with what she had.

Ahead of her, the Nexus Core chamber stretched in an intricate web of glowing conduits and crystalline spires that pulsed with blue-and-violet energy. It was eerily beautiful, like standing inside a living geode.

"Okay, where do I put this thing?" Toni lifted the dampening rig for the bot to see.

"Proceed to the central column. Rotate the device counterclockwise and align the magnetic clamps with the primary conductor rods. Failure to align will cause immediate electrocution."

Toni swallowed hard. "Yeah, good. No pressure."

Taking another careful look around, she took cautious steps towards the core. Clutching the dampening rig in a sweaty grip, she aligned it as the bot instructed. Her heart pounded when sparks danced and flickered along the conduits.

JR14 lifted off her shoulder to hover beside her, his claws flexing.

Dang bot acted as if he was nervous or something.

Toni held on to the dampening rig then positioned it until it clicked. Yeah, it stuck!

"Clamps engaged," JR14 confirmed. "Next phase is to activate the pulse disruptor. In three—" He stopped.

"What?" Toni hissed, glancing at the bot when it stopped talking. When the droid pointed one of his claws behind her, panic flared. She turned and froze.

Clear crystal figures stepped through the open archway. Elite guards. Their transparent, glass-like bodies refracted the ambient light, casting rainbows across the chamber. They moved in unison with predatory grace, surrounding her in seconds.

"This is an unfavorable situation that presents significant challenges."

Trust JR14 to state the obvious.

"The great and mighty Lord Baelon has allowed you to come this far," one Elite said in a deep, resonant hum. "But we order you to cease all movement."

JR14 shifted, making her look at him. His claws clicked as his eyes turned burnt orange. "Analysis complete. Structural instability detected in Krystalii guards," he whispered low.

Hopefully the goons hadn't heard him.

"Breach confirmed. The Nexus Core system is no longer stable. Suggest targeting weakened areas to neutralize threat."

"I'm not attacking them," Toni growled under her breath. She tightened her grip on the rig still attached to the column. Her pulse thundered in her ears as the guards closed in.

As one, they took a unified step toward her.

A wild idea hit her. She suddenly knew how to stop them. Stupid scheme or not, it was now or never. Wincing, she shouted, "Hasta la vista, baby!" and slammed her hand down on the activator.

The chamber exploded in a blinding, colorless light.

Leaving Toni might not have been the smartest thing Azazel ever did, but he'd be damned if he let these Elites get close to her. To make matters worse, these guys felt different from the ones he'd battled before.

Deep inside, he focused his inner strength to teleport him and the guards to a different location away from her. A surprising well of unknown power rose within him, taking over like a giant fist that grabbed all five of them. When the instantaneous teleportation stopped, he landed mid-step and staggered, freezing. Eyes wide, his breath caught as he stared into the annoying mug of his younger brother, Arakiba. *This wasn't where he meant to go...*

The look of concern in Arakiba's gray eyes made Azazel frown.

"You okay, bro?" Arakiba's blond eyebrows rose, furrowing his forehead.

"Back up and give him some room, Ba." His other brother, Asmodel, pulled at the black T-shirt Arakiba wore. "He hit his head pretty hard."

Azazel frowned. *He hit his head?* That didn't sound right. The last thing he remembered was battling... battling? Who in the *ezeru* would he have to fight? With a jerk, he looked at his empty hand. Wasn't he holding some kind of sword? The word *katana* floated by, but he couldn't grasp what that meant. Rising to rest on his elbows, he glanced around. He didn't recognize the room, which was odd. Especially when the background was hazy.

"Where am I?" He did his best to clear a dry throat.

"We're visiting Adapa's home in San Francisco." The second eldest brother, Abalim, crossed his arms with a scowl. "When you tripped, you bashed your head on the corner of the table there." He nodded his dark head at the oval coffee table next to the plush sectional couch he was lying on.

Azazel's eyebrows rose. "Excuse me?" Other people may suffer occasional clumsiness, but not him. He never stumbled on anything, even as a child. His natural athletic abilities, combined with his keen psychic sense, would've safeguarded him against anything as simple as tripping. This constant struggle to keep his inner demon from gaining control made him extra careful, perhaps more so than necessary, but he would never risk losing dominance. No need to let the unwanted passenger in his head gain power.

Arakiba whooped and slapped his knee. "Funniest damn thing I'd ever seen! You planted face-first on the ground, out cold like a snowman in a blizzard." He wiped a tear from his eye. "And the look on your face just before you splatted on the rug..." He kissed his fingers. "Priceless!"

That statement made Azazel's frown deepen. He swung his legs over to sit upright. Taking a quick internal assessment, he verified there was no pain. If he'd fallen like his brothers said, he'd at least have a massive headache, and he would be dizzy and nauseous. But there was nothing. The only symptom he suffered from was confusion, along with a heavy dose of frustration. Nothing here seemed right. His eyes narrowed. They were lying to him.

And they never lied to each other.

"Why are we here?" He glanced around, his chest tightening at the unfamiliar place. When a sudden memory struck him, he stood with his hands tightened into fists. "What about the invasion?" Looking around, he sucked in a breath. "Where's Toni? Have the Krystalii taken over?"

"Krystalii? Toni?" Asmodel flipped his long brown hair over his shoulder and scratched the side of his jaw. "Who in the world are you talking about?"

"He doesn't know what he's saying," Abalim waved a hand, as if dismissing Azazel. "Some delusion created by the bump in his head." His brother took a menacing step toward him, stalking him like an enemy. His head lowered as his dark eyes squinted at him. "Maybe we should give him something to let him sleep. We can't let an injury like that go untreated."

Now the beast inside Azazel roused awake. Not yet conscious, but alert enough to put him on guard.

"I don't need to sleep. I know exactly what I'm saying." He faced the other three. Narrowing his eyes, he studied the three men. "What happened with the Krystalii?" He put his hands on his hips. "And where is Toni?"

"There's no such thing as a Krystalii, bro." Arakiba shrugged. The sneer twisting his grinning lips put Azazel on edge. "And never heard of some guy named Tony." He glanced at Asmodel standing next to Abalim. "Looks like he's a little cray-cray. Dude doesn't know what he's talking about."

For the first time since he woke up, a sense of calm came over him. The beast inside grumbled, but for now kept a vigilant watch in the background. It was then that Azazel recognized where and what he was dealing with.

Clasping his hands in front of him, he gave his brothers a respectful nod. "Well played, Lord Baelon. But I assure you, I know you created this construct from images in my mind. They aren't real."

The image of his brother Arakiba clapped his hands before morphing into the crystal-blue form of the Krystalii autocrat, Lord Baelon. The background changed as well. Now he was in a chamber that pulsed with crystalline light emanating from every surface. It was as if the walls were alive, glimmering with alien purple-and-blue-hued facets that reflected his own distorted image back at him. The air carried a biting chill that had a metallic taste, sharp enough to feel like a warning. There wasn't any visible door or entryway, only endless crystalline patterns flowing like frozen rivers across the walls, ceiling, and floor.

He tested his limbs. Resistance. A cage—not physical, but psychic. Tendrils of crystalline energy formed a lattice around him, translucent and crackling with electric blue light. When he probed the bonds, they pushed against his thoughts with a sharp, needling force. What was worse, he could feel them feeding off his energy. A trap. When he tried to move, he ended up with invisible tendrils of psychic energy snaking around his body, squeezing him with icy pressure. Each strand vibrated, resonating with the crystalline hum of the chamber, like a living program fabricated to sap his strength and suppress his abilities.

"You should've known better than to challenge me in my domain, you flesh-born wretch." Lord Baelon's crystalline form refracted the chamber's light into eerie rainbows.

His body gleamed with cruel elegance, but Azazel's sharp eyes caught something. The faintest cracks webbed Baelon's glass-like skin, and his movements seemed less fluid than before, his steps almost... hesitant.

He radiated sharp angles and jagged edges, his form sculpted from deep blue apatite, with veins of silver and deep indigo threaded through his crystalline skin. His eyes, deeply set within his face were twin pools of multifaceted fire, and they narrowed as he studied Azazel.

Azazel exhaled, keeping himself centered. Surprisingly, his inner demon remained still and quiet. "Obviously, I didn't know better," he stated aloud in a patronizing tone that cut through the hum in the room. "Because your arrogant intentions are flawed." He tilted his head, his calm gaze fixed on Baelon. "It appears your plans are ineffective in achieving your goal."

Baelon's smile twisted, and his mirrored eyes compressed into fine slits. "You flatter yourself. You are nothing but an echo of dust. I find your words as empty as the so-called rebellion you've joined with those traitors aboard this ship. I will break all of you without reservation." His voice carried a resonant echo that sounded from everywhere at once. "You are a caged, flesh-bound animal. Broken."

The tendrils around Azazel tightened, bruising his ribs. He didn't allow his expression to falter. Instead, he focused inwardly. The pain was a distraction, a crude tool. He tilted his head, unruffled. "Broken? Hardly." He flexed his mind again, not to escape but to test. The bonds strained under his touch, like taut wires stretched thin, as if ready to fray. *Might be breakable, then.*

Baelon's expression flickered. The light within his body dimmed before flaring again. A tremor ran through him—brief but telling.

Azazel noted it, tucking the observation away. "You're weakening," he stated with a steady tone. He cocked his head when a thought came to him from a novel he'd read not so long ago. If he remembered correctly, the aliens attacking Earth in that story didn't take into account the natural countermeasures the planet carried. H.G. Wells might've been on to something when he wrote *War of the Worlds*.

"I suspect this dimension doesn't suit you, does it?" He pursed his lips and examined the crystal man with an up-and-down glance. "Your inner light is dim, Baelon. And if I'm not mistaken, a good amount of your edges have dulled. I believe this universe is eating you alive," he observed, his voice measured. "This dimension is rejecting you, isn't it? Your kind wasn't meant to stay here this long, was it?"

Baelon hissed, and the surrounding walls pulsated.

The psychic bonds around Azazel tightened and pressed into his mind. Pain lanced through his temples, but he met Baelon's eyes. The crystal dictator's crystalline face twitched—an almost imperceptible reaction, but enough for him to recognize his strike had landed.

"Let it go," Azazel continued. "You and I both know that anger won't fix what's rotting inside you." He softened his voice, sending tendrils of psychic energy to sift through Baelon's fury in an unobtrusive fog of intent. "If you stay here, nothing will stop the cracks forming in your foundation. Not only with yourself, but with all Krystalii. You must recognize what this dimension is doing to all of you."

"You know nothing of my kind," Baelon snarled, stepping closer. His form shimmered as he grabbed Azazel's wave of psychic energy and made it his own, ripping

into his mind like jagged glass.

"You're nothing but a worthless organic being who does not have the intelligence to comprehend the grandiose Krystalii."

Azazel winced as he blocked Baelon's psychic intrusion with practiced precision and focused his thoughts on a single, unwavering point. Soon the assault rolled off him like water over stone. "I understand more than you think." His tone was cutting and stern. "Your strength... it's borrowed, isn't it? Amplified by this ship, by your constructs. But it's unsustainable. Every moment you remain here, your entire existence will erode around you."

The chamber trembled, and the crystalline glow inside the Krystalii leader intensified. Baelon's jagged features sharpened, but as Azazel watched, he saw tiny cracks along the other's body spread, splinters that ran along the crystal being's translucent skin.

Baelon laughed, a brittle, discordant sound. "You dare to psychoanalyze me? How quaint. Perhaps I should peel away your mind to see where your confidence originates."

Azazel smiled, unfazed. "You could try, but we both know you won't. You're desperate to maintain control—not just over me, but over yourself. Your foundation is cracking, Baelon, and deep down, you know it."

Baelon froze and his mirrored eyes betrayed a flicker of uncertainty. The chamber's hum faltered, the once-perfect resonance breaking into uneven vibrations.

Azazel had planted a seed of doubt—small, but significant. "You can keep me here," he continued with a shrug, "but every second I fight weakens you. Every moment you remain in this dimension, it grinds you down. You've already lost, Baelon. You just refuse to face that inevitability."

The walls trembled, and for the first time, Azazel felt the cage falter. A crack—not physical—but psychic in its structure. He allowed himself the faintest smile.

Baelon's eyes flared as he stepped back. "I assure you, you will never leave this place alive."

"Oh yes, I will. And perhaps I'll take you with me." Azazel allowed a slice of resolve to lace his tone. "And judging by the looks of you, you won't have the strength to stop me."

Before the last word left his lips, a blazing white light engulfed the room. Turning his head, Azazel did his best to shield his closed eyes and waited until he sensed the unexpected intense light had dimmed enough for him to open them. He peeked through slitted lids, and his head jerked as he took in the sigh before him.

It was Toni. Standing in the middle of the room as if she didn't have a care in the world.

And perched on her left shoulder was JR14, as if he'd always been there.

Fists on her hips, she cocked her head. "What are you doing tied up like that?" She looked behind him. "And why is the gemstone jerk lying on the floor?"

The psychic lattice tendrils wrapped around him disintegrated, leaving him free to move. He jumped off the small dais he'd been standing on and spun around to see what she was talking about.

Baelon lay flat on his back, eyes and mouth wide open, as if frozen.

Sending out an exploratory psychic ribbon to the prone Krystalii, Azazel grabbed Toni's hand. "We've got to get out of here before he wakes up. Ready?" Not waiting for her to answer, he teleported them out of the room.

Azazel took them to the only place he could think of—the rebel hideout. If that bright light was what he suspected, things were moving faster than he'd hoped.

"Toni," he turned her so she could look at him. "Did you disrupt the Nexus Core?" He held his breath as he waited for her to answer.

Her eyes widened as her mouth opened.

"You bet she did!" Tharion's clear whoop from behind them answered before she could.

Azazel released Toni but wrapped an arm around her shoulders. He wasn't ready to part from her yet. The pain of leaving her behind tore at him when he hadn't known if she'd be safe or not.

"All the ship's communications are down or sporadic," Laytrii announced. She sat at a command console on one side of the room, her emerald crystal body turned away from them as her fingers flew across the device. "The abrupt silence from the *Nyrlith* to the fleet is causing panic." She turned to look over her shoulder at them. "And no one has to be psychic to know that." With a wink from one of her verdant eyes, she curled her mint-green lips into a smirk. "As the other Krystalii relearn how to use antiquated communications, it's giving Vaeloryx and the others a chance to disrupt the Dimensional Rift Epicenter." Turning back to the console, she resumed her frantic pace on the 3D keyboard floating in front of her. "Unfortunately, I doubt they made it since it's still online. And I can't contact them. I'm afraid we're running out of time."

"Is it because Baelon is dead?" Toni's hand covered Azazel's stomach as she leaned close to ask the question.

Even through the battle suit, Azazel warmed with her touch. He shook his head. "No, he was just stunned by whatever you did. That's why I had to get us out of there before he woke up." He turned to Tharion. "Did you try the Resonant Node to contact either of them?"

"Of course we have." The golden crystals on Tharion's body dimmed. "When we took the Nexus Core out, it somehow interfered with that as well."

"JR14—" Azazel turned to the spider-bot still sitting on Toni's shoulder. "—can you interface with the ship's computer and locate

Vaeloryx and his companions without getting caught?" *If that worked, he'd teleport to their location and help them.*

"Affirmative." The small android jumped off his perch, his wings fluttering out as he buzzed over to Laytrii and landed on the transparent counter. "Attempting interface." One set of his front claws clicked together before a thin wire protruded from one to land on the console.

After a few tense moments, the bot retracted his line and swiveled his head to Azazel. "Analysis: I am now synced with the *Nyrlith* and have complete access to their communications. Elite forces have captured the subjects who are now en route to the detention center." JR14 tilted his head. His multifaceted eyes shimmered in a rainbow of colors. *He must be accessing another part of the network.* "Announcement: Lord Baelon is waiting there for them."

Ezeru!

"Then we've got to disable the Dimensional Rift ourselves." Azazel stood behind the jagged console panel next to Laytrii. "When we do that, it might draw Baelon and his Elites away from them and give Vaeloryx and the others a chance to escape." He looked over his shoulder at Tharion. "Is there anyone else who can help them do that?"

Tharion shook his head with a thoughtful frown, glancing at the ragged group behind them. "I'm afraid not." He gestured to the motley crew. "Vaeloryx took the best we had. I'm afraid the rest of us relied on them in more ways than one."

"Speak for yourself," Laytrii grumbled, then sighed. "But I'm afraid he's right. We'd put them in more danger if we tried and failed." She nodded to the moonstone-colored Krystalii healer, Lyrentha. "While she and I could be of use in the field, our best use is here overseeing operations." Pounding her fist on the platform, she grunted. "Such as they are."

"Interjection," JR14 announced. "I will coordinate with the *Nyr-lith* and keep the lines of communication open, so when Azazel completes his task, you will be informed."

Laytrii's emerald eyes softened as she watched the spider-bot fly back to his perch on Azazel's shoulder. "We would appreciate that."

"While we can't help you in the field, I've got something much better for you to use." Tharion announced with a wide grin. "Can't let you go empty-handed!" He gestured for them to follow him. "Come on. You're gonna love this!"

The golden Krystalii led Azazel and Toni to the same chamber where they'd gotten their form-fitting suits.

"I'm so sorry I didn't think about this earlier." Tharion gushed, looking over his shoulder. "But after you left, I came back in here to look around and noticed this!" He gestured to a pile of strange poles and sticks. "Here are some weapons we, ah, confiscated from an organic race from our dimension. Maybe you can use one of these. Hopefully they'll help."

He handed a weapon to Toni, his crystalline features glinting under the ship's dim lights. "Trust me, this is no ordinary weapon!" His voice echoed in the large room. "The same lattice resonance that fuels the Dimensional Rift powers this baby. It bypasses standard shielding and destabilizes crystalline structures at the molecular level." He tapped the sleek, angular barrel. "Perfect for disrupting Baelon's guards—and the rift itself." He gave a theatrical sigh. "We're lucky Baelon missed this before. I bet he thought he had them all destroyed."

Azazel raised an eyebrow. "Missed?"

The golden-crystal male shrugged. "Well, you know."

Toni chuckled. "Ah, what a good little thief you are. Here, let me try." She held out her hand.

Tharion handed it to her, the bulbous end first.

"All you gotta do is press this here and ka-boom! There she blows." He backed up with his palms raised. "But be careful—damn trigger is touchy as all get out."

Toni raised the weapon away from them and clicked where Tharion pointed. A lightning burst of fire fractured part of the wall into shimmering shards.

"Yeah, now that's what I'm talking about." She grinned, patting the barrel. "You and me, baby, we're gonna save the universe." She glanced at Azazel with a mischievous grin. "Who knew my mom was right when she made me take all those target lessons when I moved out on my own in LA? Damn, what a great movie this would make!"

CHAPTER SEVEN

A zazel didn't like this. He should never have let Toni come with him to the most-guarded place on a hostile ship filled with psychic bullies. He glanced at her beside him. As she clutched the space weapon Tharion had given her, her luscious lips pressed into a thoughtful frown.

But, by the gods, there was no denying she looked like she belonged there, apparently relaxed about the whole thing. While his admiration for her grew, something nagged in the back of his mind. His intuition screamed that nothing about this felt right. Getting to the Dimensional Rift was easier than it should have been.

His inner beast rolled in rising agitation, as if in agreement.

JR14's sharp legs scratched the base of his neck as his wings came out and fluttered before disappearing back under his exoskeleton. Even the bot acted nervous.

Taking shallow breaths, he concentrated on the faint hum of the *Nyrlith's* systems throbbing under his booted feet.

A dim, violet glow from overhead strips cast eerie reflections off the crystalline walls.

Toni pressed close to him, her gloved fingers steady against the edge of the weapon she carried.

"Maybe we shouldn't have split up like we did," Azazel muttered, his voice a bare whisper. Guilt burned like acid in his throat.

Toni's response was soft but firm. "Not that he gave us much of a choice. I'm sure once we cut off this stupid rift thing, we'll go and get Vaeloryx and the others out. Don't worry, Az, we've got this."

Azazel preened at the nickname she'd given him. Sneaking another peek at her, he caught the resolve hardening her features. *Now, that was all kinds of sexy.* His inner beast purred. *Damn thing was acting like a domesticated house kitten with her around.* With concentration, he released the tension pinching his neck. Toni's confidence steadied him. He nodded and turned toward the passage ahead.

The Dimensional Rift Epicenter was three levels below the rebel hideout. Once they severed the Krystalii's psychic network, it should throw Baelon's forces into chaos. Even with the Elites distracted by the Nexus Core being down, it'd be ridiculous to think none of them would be encountered.

JR14 shifted, scanning ahead with his infrared sensors.

"Attention: two Elites headed this way," the droid announced in a low voice next to his ear. "My analysis confirms they carry electro-lances and plasma shields."

And that's what he got for thinking of them. Azazel gestured to back up against the smooth wall with fractured crystal panels. He swallowed hard. The guards' silhouettes loomed through the mist seeping from a ruptured coolant line above them.

"What do you think we should do?" Toni clutched the smooth end of her weapon and aimed it at the ceiling.

"I'm afraid since there's no place to hide, we've got no choice but to engage. Get ready." He whispered, pitching his voice just loud enough for Toni to hear, and stepped forward, palm raised. Since they'd brought the psychic hotspot down, it was time to use his natural powers. The air around his fingers crackled.

The nearest guard faltered as invisible pressure seized him. The second lunged, his lance streaking blue lightning through the mist.

Toni fired, her shot hitting the lance and knocking it aside. She pivoted, sidestepping a slash aimed at her midsection, and brought her pole up in one smooth motion. Another shot.

The guard splintered into clear crystal dust.

Azazel crushed the first under his telekinetic grip, shards of crystal cracking apart.

The corridor fell silent.

"You okay back there, *kalu*?"

"Affirmative. Proceed," replied JR14.

"Good! Let's go before there's more." He glanced at Toni, then sprinted forward with her close behind.

He couldn't put his finger on it, but the fight felt wrong. Defeating those guards was way easier than it should have been. His mouth dried. His inner savage rumbled in agitation, tightening his grip around Azazel's chest. Ignoring the sensation, he pushed forward.

He didn't know how it happened, but they didn't encounter any-one else before reaching the chamber housing the Dimensional Rift. Holding his breath, he peeked around the corner to see if there were any Krystalii there. He held Toni back against the corridor wall. All clear. With a nod in her direction to follow him, he snuck inside, Toni close behind.

A spherical construct sat in the middle of the room and pulsed with an unnatural light. Inside, jagged fissures swirled in a kaleidoscope of pale colors.

His gut twisted. There was an undeniable pull from it. A raw, uncontained energy that strained the very air around them.

"Damn." Toni snorted. "Freakin' thing looks like a crystal ball on steroids." She stepped closer to it. "You know, it kinda looks like a movie prop in one of the fantasy movies I produced last year."

Movie prop? Azazel narrowed his focus on the nucleus. He'd love nothing better than to examine it closer, but time was running out. Kneeling by it, he pulled out a small pulse generator from a pocket in the suit Tharion gave him. "JR14, monitor it while I set these energy dampeners on it and make it overload."

Toni stood guard. Her focus shifted to the open doorway where the pounding of heavy footsteps echoed down the hall.

Had to be more guards.

"How long?" she asked over her shoulder.

"Less than two minutes." He didn't look up. Not that he thought they had two minutes. He stretched his senses outward, seeking the energy signatures closing in. "Here, trade places." His jaw tightened as he sprang to his feet. "You keep watch on this and make sure the energy dampener keeps working. I'll hold them off."

Toni's gaze shot up to meet his. "No! You don't have to—"

"Yes, I do. Let's finish this." He glanced at the bot on his shoulder. "JR14, you stay and help her make sure nothing goes wrong." He turned, not waiting to watch the bot leave his shoulder before he stepped into the corridor. His inner beast now growled in approval, eager for glorious battle.

The first wave of Elites came in fast, their crystalline weapons glinting in the murky light.

Azazel didn't wait. He swept his arm forward, slamming one into the wall with a telekinetic burst. The others charged, and he twisted, dodging a strike before sending another Elite crashing to the floor.

Pain flared through his arm as a lance grazed him. Gritting his teeth, he pushed harder, throwing a wave of force that knocked the guards back.

"Almost there!" Toni shouted from the other room.

Azazel grunted as he blocked another strike. Light flared behind him.

A hum coming from the Dimensional Rift shifted, its rhythm faltering.

"Yay! It's done!" Toni whooped.

Azazel slammed the last guard against the wall and spun, running back into the chamber.

"Okay, we'd better get out of here!" He held out his hand for Toni.

She grabbed it, laughing.

"Yeah, no kidding!"

As they sprinted, Azazel took one last glance behind them and watched as the device collapsed inward. The swirling rift distorted the walls as it imploded.

JR14 leaped onto Azazel's shoulder as they dove through the doorway just before it slammed shut behind them.

A deafening boom followed, shaking the deck.

Azazel leaned against the bulkhead, his breath ragged.

Toni grinned at him. A bead of sweat rolled from her temple.

"Told you we'd do it."

He managed to make a weak smile and clasped her hand in his.

"Next time, let's leave saving the galaxy to someone else."

A resounding boom of laughter, along with the clinking sound of clapping crystals, made Azazel jump.

"That was so entertaining!" Lord Baelon stepped out of the mist and smoke that seeped through the cracked doorway of the Dimensional Rift chamber into the hallway. "My entire crew and I thoroughly enjoyed your show. Didn't we?" The clear blue crystals in his head reflected in the low light as he nodded behind him.

Azazel straightened. His eyes widened when he didn't see any fractures or dull parts of their nemesis's body. Then his attention swung to the fog when a small group of Krystalii waltzed through.

The rebels. Every one of them. Including Vaeloryx.

"Most assuredly, my Lord." Vaeloryx put a hand over his heart, bowing with a smirk.

"Ah, yes." Baelon gestured to the aquamarine-and-silver Krystalii. "I believe you have met my second-in-command, Sentinel Commander Vaeloryx, head of my Elite troops."

Toni gasped.

Azazel straightened, keeping her hand in his as they faced the Krystalii. He ignored the pain his nails created in the palms of his other hand as he clenched his fingers into a tight fist.

The growl from his inner beast was loud enough to hear with his ears and not just his mind.

"You may have played your part well." Azazel nodded to Vaeloryx and the other rebels. "But betrayal has a price I hope you're prepared to pay."

"Oh, I wouldn't worry about that if I were you." Baelon's grin widened. "I'm sure you have more important things to concern yourself with." He tilted his head toward Toni. "Starting with her."

Azazel jerked. His eyes widened as he watched Toni dissolve into nothingness. "Toni!" He reached out to where she'd been, but his fingers only met air. He turned to Baelon, both hands clamped into tight fists. "What did you do to her? If you harmed her..." Taking a step toward the Krystalii, he raised one of his fists as a blinding heat engulfed him.

His inner beast reacted with blinding speed, clawing, desperate to get free.

It took everything Azazel had to contain it. If he gave in to it, letting his primitive urge free, he'd never find Toni.

"Harm her?" Baelon guffawed. "You shard-less vermin."

With a blink of Baelon's neon blue eyes, Azazel found himself frozen.

The sizable crystal alien stopped in front of Azazel and leaned in.

Even with the force of his vast psychic abilities blazing through every nerve, Azazel couldn't move—trapped in place by an invisible weight so crushing it stole his breath. His focus was shredded with icy precision.

"She's where she's always been on the *Nyrlith*. Safe and sound in the regenerating room where I put her when she was first brought aboard. It's you, my friend—"

Baelon sneered mere inches from Azazel's face, close enough for him to smell the Krystalii's putrid breath of metal and dirt.

"—who is not aware of where he is." The Krystalii stood back and crossed his bulky arms with a taunting smirk. "Or how he hasn't accomplished a damn thing since boarding my ship. Pity." His shrug was stilted and unnatural. "You were quite adept at creating an entertaining example for my troops on how organics in this dimension react. But now that we've learned all we need to know, it's time to put you back where you belong."

Baelon turned and walked away. Each step made the blue colors from his body wink across the mirrored and glass walls around the room.

The last thing Azazel felt was JR14 lifting off the back of his neck from where he'd been hiding under his hair.

Not looking back, Baelon waved his crystal hand as if he was dismissing an errant child.

Azazel found himself engulfed by... nothing.

Toni woke with a start, blinking at the feeble gleam of the crystal cage and its towering, faceted, blue-green walls. Swallowing a moan, she draped her arm over her eyes. She'd rather go back to sleep and continue that exciting... wonderful... heart-pounding dream that had been so real than wake up to this nightmare.

That fantasy man... Oh my god, her mind had to have worked overtime to make that hunk-a-luscious up. His male beauty surpassed that of anyone she'd ever met or dreamed of. His soothing masculine voice sent chills down her spine, as did his calm, sharp, intellectual mind. But most of all, she admired how he showed patience when dealing with others. Just look at how he handled that little spider-robot thingy of his. Even after that dream adventure ended, her heart pounded when she thought of him. Her imagination had concocted a classic working-with-a-hero-along-with-some-rebels-to-escape scenario that was everything she could've hoped for. A dull ache settled in her chest as she realized it'd all been a dream. Like a beautiful illusion that slipped through her fingers. Damn, what she wouldn't give to be like that heroic protagonist she imagined she was.

Someone bold. Fearless. Everything she wished she could be.

But in real life, it didn't take much to make her fold. She nodded along with whoever was around her. Biting her tongue, doing her best not to rock the boat or bring attention to herself. That was her shameful secret. She was a coward, and that made her life miserable.

The only thing she was good at was running errands, not chasing dreams. Yep, good ol' reliable Toni. Steady enough to get the job done, but not strong enough to stand up for herself and demand the credit for all the hard work she busted her ass for. And that, ladies and gentlemen, was why she'd never advanced in the movie business.

At least she could admit she'd let people walk all over her for far too long. That weakness was exposed here, raw and ugly. Like a scar that festered under her skin. Joining the alien exchange had been her desperate, last-ditch effort to become someone stronger, someone new. She grunted. Yeah, as if leaving Earth could scrub out who she really was. She hadn't left her flaws behind—she'd just packed them up and brought them along for the ride.

Toni's lips twisted. Sitting here sinking into self-reproach wasn't getting her anywhere. Maybe that blue-crystal-creep Baelon spiked her drink with something that triggered an allergic reaction that created that realistic, lucid dream. Look at her, grasping at anything to keep from thinking about the stupid mess she found herself in.

Expelling her held breath, she watched it roll out in a plume. The room was still chilly. She sat up and rubbed her arms. Damn, what she wouldn't give to have that suit she had on in her dreams. Maybe if she got up and walked around, she'd make herself warmer.

The now familiar, sharp, echoing sound of the wall sliding open caught her attention. Instead of the hulking figure of Baelon, in stepped a Krystalii with different coloring than Baelon's. It was more of a moonstone laced with a notable iridescent shimmer. This one was in female form, complete with feminine features and perky breasts topped with darker nipples. She even had a smooth, human looking vulva.

"Ah, you are awake."

The musical sound of the Krystalii's voice made Toni frown. How could something so beautiful belong to something so monstrous? And why did this creature seem familiar? Like she'd met her before.

"I am Lyrentha. I am assigned as your healer to assure your optimum health."

Lyrentha? Wasn't that the name of the rebel in her dream? How odd was that? She cocked her head and studied the alien. Healer? For her? Toni snorted. She wasn't an idiot. It didn't take a genius to figure out that once she was at 'optimum health', they'd start the genetic experiments on her.

"Here, drink this." Lyrentha held another container like the one Baelon had given her. "It carries all the nutrients and liquid your physiology needs."

Toni stared at the translucent chalice with the pale-lavender substance inside. Even though the first one had been tasteless, her mouth watered as if she'd been offered a succulent treat. With a resigned sigh, she took the cup and looked up at the Krystalii.

"Thank you." Putting the glass to her lips, she muttered, "I guess." She took a quick sip. The same tasteless concoction made her grimace. But at least the rest of it went down easily enough.

"I have also observed the temperature here is uncomfortable for you, therefore I brought this for you to cover your fragile frame."

Toni's jaw dropped when she saw what Lyrentha held up. It was the suit... the formfitting one she wore in her dream. She shivered. It even had the same shimmering gold veins threaded through the deep-midnight-blue fabric. Their intricate patterns ran along the sleeves, legs, and torso. She jerked her head to study the Krystalii. How was this possible?

Her mind in a jumbled fog of questions, Toni stepped off the platform she'd slept on, reaching out with her fingers to rub the fabric with one hand while holding the chalice in the other. A comforting warmth radiated from the material. "Here, hold this." She shoved the empty cup into the Krystalii's hand to grab the suit. Tempting warmth overrode everything else. The cream-colored Hanbok short-sleeved blouse she'd donned with slacks for the alien exchange seemed like a lifetime ago. And the wear-and-tear she'd endured since then showed. Dirt, smut, and God-knows-what-else had torn most of what she had on. To be offered something new and clean was a temptation she'd be an idiot to refuse.

"Where did you get something like this?" She eyed the naked-looking crystal alien. "You don't look like you wear clothes."

Lyrentha jerked her head to the side, the movement stiff and strange. "The Krystalii have no need for such primitive accouterments. We have complete control of our bodies to self-regulate when necessary. This—" She gestured to the suit in Toni's hand. "—is part of the relics we've kept in The Vault of Forgotten Worlds."

Toni startled. Vault of Forgotten Worlds? Wasn't that the name of the place she visited in the dream? Her lips thinned. Hard to believe that was a coincidence. Something funny was going on here. And she didn't need a laugh track to tell her that. "Why would you keep relics from species you've taken over?"

"We are an inquisitive species by nature." Lyrentha's shrug was stilted and unnatural. "We investigate everything about our adversaries for the benefit of the Krystalii race." She stood with her shoulders back, in a posture so perfect Toni would never dare copy. "It is how we uncovered this dimension and the riches that rightly belong to us."

Toni swallowed a snort. Arrogant bullshit aside, she had better things to do. Like getting warm. Who gave a crap about modesty? She couldn't wait to put the suit on. Whipping off the grody shirt, she didn't hesitate to slide everything else off as quickly as she could. Even her shoes. Her shivers increased, making it hard to hold on to the soft material. She checked the suit out front and back—it was obvious it was a onesie. Hopping from one foot to the other, she pulled her legs into it one at a time, nestling her feet into the footies. Once she put her arms through the sleeves, the seam melded over her torso and sealed itself closed. Right up to her neckline.

Opening her arms wide, she examined the formfitting material and let out a whoosh of relief. She threw her head back with her eyes closed, pressing her gloved hands against her skin, savoring the heat like a lifeline. Damn, she'd almost forgotten what it felt like not to be shaking like a leaf. Once her shivering settled, she opened her eyes and looked down at herself. There didn't seem to be any way to open it.

"Hey." She glanced at the crystal woman. "How do I take this thing off to go to the bathroom?"

Lyrentha's face went blank. "I do not understand the question. What is a bathroom?"

All at once, her full bladder felt normal. She no longer felt the urge to go.

Human woman from Earth, do not alarm yourself. A soft, nonbinary voice said in her head. *I am called Sensos, and I am the garment you wear. Now that we've bonded, I will take care of all your physical needs. But please do not alert the Krystalii to my presence.*

Swallowing hard, Toni gave Lyrentha a sheepish grin. "Ah, never mind." She tilted her head and crossed her arms. "So, what now?"

"We will continue to monitor your vitals to determine optimum health. Once we accomplish that, Lord Baelon himself will inform us of the next procedure concerning you." She turned and headed back to the open doorway. "Until then, I suggest you take this opportunity to regain your strength," she said over her shoulder before the wall sizzled closed behind her.

"Opportunity?" Toni's eyebrows rose. "I'll show you opportunity." As the warmth seeped into her limbs, her breath became steady. Her mind cleared. Ah, yes. Now that she felt more like herself, it was time to plan a real escape.

May I assist you in this endeavor? the telepathic voice said in her head.

Oh, you betcha. Toni used her mind to reply for the first time. Hey, talking to it like this was easier than she thought it'd be. *Tell me what you can do and leave nothing out.*

"Are you the human woman known as Antonia Soo-min Choi?"

Toni jumped back with a squeal, holding her hand over her pounding heart.

"What the hell?" She leaned in for a closer look. Was that... the spider-droid-thingy from her dream flying and buzzing in front of her? The one her dream illusion created along with that mouthwatering-hunky-specimen of a man named Azazel?

"Clarification: my designation is JR14." The red-and-gold body of the spider-bot hovered close to her face. "I am here to coordinate with you to liberate the hybrid known as Azazel from the Krystalii."

What? Toni's stomach fluttered. *There really was a guy named Azazel?* With a frantic gaze, she looked around the empty room, as if he were there somewhere.

When JR14 flew in front of her, she jerked her head back and glared at the bot buzzing before her.

"Dang, I'm going cross-eyed with you flying in front of me like that." She shooed him with her hand. "Can't you find a better place to settle so we can talk?"

"Affirmative." The bot replied. With a quick zip, he settled onto her left shoulder. "Proposition: we determine our assets to build rapport. I shall proceed first."

Toni grinned. Trust the little AI to start with himself. He was acting just like he had in her dream state.

"Due to my mechanical makeup that does not give off a psychic signature, the Krystalii cannot determine my existence. Therefore, my physical presence is invisible to them." JR14 fluttered his wings out before folding them under his back panels.

As she watched him, Toni noticed those panels were red, just like a ladybug's. She bit her bottom lip to keep from making a teasing comment about offering to put black dots on them. She doubted the bot would appreciate her suggestion.

He continued. "I have downloaded a significant portion of the schematics of the *Nyrlith* to aid us as we traverse throughout the ship. That is how I located you. In addition, I was able to access what the Krystalii put you and Azazel through in a shared psionic episode in their attempt to study how you interacted with each other when presented with arduous tasks." The bot continued in his mechanical, matter-of-fact tone, "I have also maintained open communication with my father, JR10, who is working with the Federation Consortium to obstruct the Krystalii invasion."

That statement startled Toni. "Wait just a minute. I thought the Krystalii had already taken over the chancellor's palace and most of the systems under their leadership."

She looked down at the bot, who looked up at her, the color of his bulbous, fractal eyes reflecting a pale blue.

The spider-bot shook his head, his front claws clicking. "Negative. That was a misrepresentation in the dream sequence they put you and Azazel through. Approximately 80.32 percent of what you experienced there had no basis in reality. As of now, the *Nyrlith* is fast approaching the heart of the galactic government, the chancellor's palatial space station. Lord Baelon has terminated the research between the two of you to prioritize overseeing the systematic annihilation of everyone aboard that structure to launch his invasion."

Toni pursed her lips and glanced away with an unfocused stare. *Cripe, this was confusing. If what she believed happened didn't... how would she know? Great. Thanks to that crystal-asshole, figuring out what was real and what wasn't just got a lot more complicated.* She closed her eyes and rubbed her forehead. Her cheeks heated. *Not to mention her falling for the most gorgeous man she'd never met. Yeah, trust her to indulge in some kind of pseudo-relationship with a phantom man.* She took a second to wonder what he was like in real life. Well, at least she had the little bot to help her out. Putting her hand down, she sighed. "Let's consider the overall situation. Is it possible the galactic forces can stop the Krystalii?"

"Analysis: 35.09 percent probability of success because they have enlisted a vast alliance with some of the most powerful species in the galaxy. Some are members; some are considered illicit." JR14 answered.

Well, at least it wasn't say... zero.

"Warning: if we are still aboard the *Nyrlith* when hostilities begin, our chance of survival lowers to 13.86 percent. Suggestion: obtain Azazel. He can teleport us off the ship to safety before the conflict begins. That would increase our survival rate to 95.67 percent."

Annnd... that was the kicker, wasn't it? If the good guys won, she and her two companions might get caught in the crossfire. Not to mention what would happen if the bad guys ended up victorious. So, the only way to keep that from happening was to sneak around an alien spaceship loaded with a bunch of psychic-psychotic dickwads, find a well-guarded prisoner, then somehow get him free so he could teleport them off the *Nyrlith,* traveling at an immense speed through millions of miles of space to somewhere safe.

Easy-peasy lemon-squeezy. What could go wrong?

"Yeah, that'd be great." Toni sighed. "But I'm not invisible to the Krystalii like you are. Even if I found a way out of this room, we wouldn't get too far. First, they'd know the minute I left. It wouldn't surprise me if they've somehow tapped into my mind and would know where I was." Talk about a rescue getting cut off at the knees...

The genderless voice of Sensos interjected.

I believe I can aid you in solving that problem.

"Is that so?" Toni asked out loud. Her eyebrows rose as her lips thinned. "How's that?"

Once I cover your head and body, I will make you invisible to the Krystalii. I can then modify your mental as well as physical ethos in such a way they cannot detect you. Thus, you will have free rein aboard the Nyrlith. *And to give you further elucidation,* Sensos elaborated. *I have synced with the construct known as JR14 to enable him to be a part of our conversations.*

"Affirmative of the correlation between Sensos and myself," JR14 chimed in without missing a beat. "Clarification concerning the alien species holding you prisoner. With the approaching galactic government forces headed this way, the Krystalii are not wasting any resources on monitoring you. They assume you are secure and cannot leave this room."

Toni chuckled. Heh, stupid aliens didn't know what *ass-u-me* meant. But wait. "If I'm all covered, how would I see or hear anything?" *And breathe. Let's not forget that important detail.*

I will demonstrate.

Before Toni asked what the suit meant, its material surged forward from her wrists and neck—thick and slow like creeping liquid. She sucked in a breath as it spread and encased her hands, while it climbed up her neck until her head was completely covered. The blackness only lasted long enough for her to expel her held breath, when everything around her became clear.

Holy cow... She was covered by a clear helmet. The darn thing reminded her of an upside-down fishbowl. Good thing it was light and gave her unlimited depth perception.

"Wow," she exclaimed, turning her head back and forth to see how easy it was. Yeah, good to go. "This is so cool."

And, Sensos continued, *this covering will make you impervious to most Krystalii weapons, especially their mental powers.*

"I'm surprised you weren't able to stop the Krystalii from capturing you." Toni mused. "I would've thought they'd never have a chance to catch you."

It was a moment before Sensos answered. When it did, there was a lace of sorrow in its tone. *Unfortunately, they killed my creator before she put me on.*

"Oh, that's so sad. I'm sorry to hear that." Toni threw her shoulders back. "I'll do my best to make her proud."

I know you will. Her suit answered, its tone lighter. *That is why I've chosen to work with you. I believe between the three of us, we will end up victorious in defeating the Krystalii.*

"Assuredly." JR14 agreed.

"Great!" Toni yawned so wide, her jaw cracked. "So, how do we get out of here?" She narrowed her eyes at the wall that opened to freedom where that crystal-bitch had come through. It took her a moment to realize the helmet was gone.

If you don't mind, I believe you are still at a suboptimal health level and in need of additional rest and rejuvenation, Sensos observed. *I advise you to take this time to indulge in a continued sleep cycle to allow me to complete the repairs your system requires.*

Toni yawned again, making her eyes water. Rubbing the tears away, she gave JR14 a sheepish grin. "I'm afraid Sensos is right. I'm beat." She tilted her head toward the spider-bot who now rested on the top of her left shoulder. "So, do you think you can get us out of here when we're ready and lead us to Azazel?"

"Affirmative to the first scenario." JR14's back wings buzzed out before folding inside his back panels. "When I followed the Krystalii inside this room, I analyzed the correct way to manipulate the controls and open it. Negative to the second part of your question. The tentative connection I had with Azazel has since ceased for unknown reasons. I no longer have access to his whereabouts."

I can assist with that. Sensos's voice was faint. *Do not concern yourself with locating this male. While you rest, I will create a private connection between you and the male we need to liberate, to help us track him on this ship. For me to do that, all you need to do is relax. Is this acceptable to you?*

Toni's smile was wistful. *Oh sure, relax on an alien spaceship where the bad guys planned to conduct the dreaded alien autopsy on her.* "I can't think of anything else I'd rather do."

Good. I am happy to hear that.

Sensos's genderless voice had an underlying aura of tranquility.

The tension between Toni's shoulders loosened.

Understand that the dreams you shared with this man weren't all illusion, the alien clothing continued. *While the physical action was not real, the mental and emotional connection was.*

"Really?" Toni sighed. *That'd be nice. Azazel was everything she'd ever wanted in a man. Although, she'd sensed more than once he was holding something back. Hiding something he was ashamed of.*

Concentrate on my voice and think of one of those situations where you and he were in a pleasurable circumstance. Can you visualize that?

Could she? Hoo-boy… the hard part was trying to stop thinking about that. The memory of being on the beach with Azazel was hard to ignore. She breathed. "I have just the place in mind." *Soft, golden sands, and a turquoise sea glistening under a setting yellow sun. The cozy breeze perfumed with the briny scent of the ocean along with blooming beach pea flowers.*

Now you must focus on the male you wish to connect with. Think of not only how he looks, but how his skin feels against yours. The heady fragrance he emits when he holds you in his arms. Sensos's hypnotic voice became slower and softer. *And how he tasted when your lips met his…*

Toni lay on her side as her weighty eyelids slid closed, falling into Sensos's hypnotic narrative.

Trying to breathe took all Azazel's concentration as the suffocating darkness held him hostage. He moaned, his breathing coming in ragged gasps. With a herculean effort, he tried to rub the back of his aching head, but nothing moved. He groaned. Something was preventing him from connection to anything solid. He must be in the in-between place: awake, but not, conscious, but not in reality.

A howling roar jerked his attention behind him. Even though he was in a psychic *Dreamwalk*, the real threat was easy enough to recognize. It was his inner beast, demanding to be set free from the confines Azazel kept him in. Not knowing where his physical body was, he didn't dare risk losing control.

He scrambled to his metaphysical feet and turned around to confront the creature. Instead of seeing the thing in his mind's eye, there was a massive titanium wall that stood between him and the beast. When he first became aware of the monster inside him at a very young age, he was terrified the creature's power was absolute and would take him over. In defense, he'd created an impenetrable barrier. The memory of how he did it was faint, but he'd somehow tricked the beast into the mental cage he'd created. Once the clang of the door rang shut behind it, he'd never let his control slip. No matter how badly they treated him as a slave, he always held tight on the cage. A cold weight pressed in his gut. If that beast ever broke free, the man he was might never come back.

Intense fear sent Azazel rushing to the cold titanium blockade, and he placed his palms over the surface. The indestructible material bowed as something pounded on it. He shuddered in disbelief at the dent it made. That had never happened before.

Sweat gathered at his brows.

"NO!" Azazel shouted. "Stay put!" He pressed his forehead against the cold metal. "Please stay put." Pushing his will from his palms into the wall, he did what he could to strengthen the barricade.

A deafening, angry howl rang in the air, causing the substantial barricade to vibrate under his hands.

Azazel's heart thundered so hard it created a squeezing pain inside his chest.

"Azazel, what in the world are you doing?"

Time stopped. The sweet feminine voice behind him made everything inside him pause. Even the beast became silent. Azazel jerked back with his hands still raised. With wide eyes, he examined the silver-colored wall in disbelief when an unusual sound came from the other side. By *Auu's* stars! Was the damn thing... cooing? He took a step back when the sound changed to a loud purr that filled the air.

"Hey, are you okay?"

Azazel swung around to face the owner of that sweet voice. It was Antonia—Toni. *Here in this* Dreamwalk? *How could that be?* He didn't make this psychic world. So how could she be here? His eyes narrowed. Was she here, or just another construct of Baelon's nasty game? *What was that bastard playing at now?*

He stiffened and clasped his hands in front of him. With a respectful nod, he concentrated on smoothing his breathing and making his face blank.

"What's behind that wall?" Toni looked behind him. She went to it and put her hand on the surface. "Oh, you pretty baby." She rubbed her palm up and down it. Her head tilted, her eyes unfocused. "You widdle snooky-wookims." She hummed as if talking to a favorite pet. "You be a good boy now, and we'll let you out later. Mommy and Daddy have work to do first. 'kay, punkin?" She patted the wall. "Now, behave." Her bright gaze locked on Azazel.

He took a step back, locking his eyes with hers.

"Okay, I'm sure he'll behave himself for now." Toni clapped her hands and grinned. "Hey, how would you like to get out of here and go back to that spectacular beach you took me to before?"

Azazel's eyes widened. *What just happened?* He glanced at the wall as if that would give him some answers. The only reply was the distinct sound of a rumbling purr. His face tightened as he glared at Toni. "I believe you are mistaken if you thought I'd take part in your heinous experiment again, Baelon." He took another step back. Now that his inner beast was once again under control, he'd morph out of this psychic plane to regroup.

As he prepared to leave, the beast bellowed again. It was louder this time, so intense it caused the ground to shake.

"For God's sake, Azazel!" Toni stomped her foot, one hand on her hip as she wagged her forefinger at him with the other. "I just got him quiet. And for your information, I'm real as can be in this crazy place. Baelon didn't create this *Dreamwalk*. I did!"

As she spoke, the beast's roar turned into a low-pitched, wo-woo-ooo melodious song. If Azazel didn't know better, he'd swear Toni's voice soothed the damn thing.

Azazel studied Toni's bright-blue eyes, now dilated as she looked back at him. He grimaced. Not knowing what was real and what wasn't had him second-guessing everything. Which was something he'd never experienced before.

"Hey, listen—" She stepped close to him. "—I've got a great idea! Why don't you do a Vulcan mind-meld so you can be sure it's me?"

Azazel pursed his lips. "A what?"

"You know..." Toni gestured between the two of them. "Join our minds so you can see it's me." She grasped the tops of his arms. "That way you can meet my new friend, Sensos. And you'll find out how I created this dream-thingy-a-booper with no help from that shiny-supremacist-bastard Baelon." Her eyes widened, looking back-and-forth across his face as she pleaded with him.

Azazel's eyebrows rose. *Shiny-supremacist? Dream-thingy-a-boop-er?* His lips quirked into a smirk. "If you're agreeable to that..." It would be nice to let his guard down a little if it was her.

His inner beast purred emitted a low, purring growl behind the wall.

Looked like the animal agreed.

She shook his arms. "Of course I am." She let him go. "It was my idea, after all."

Staring into the ocean blue of her fathomless eyes, he touched his mind to hers. In the blink of an eternity, he had his answer. It was her, the essence that made up Antonia Choi, right here in this *Dreamwalk.* One she'd created with the help of her, ah, clothes. *And how captivating was the concept of sentient clothes?*

"So, you're all good?" She took a quick glance over his shoulder. "Ready to go to the beach?" She grinned, then looked back at him. "We've got lots to talk about. Like finding your body so we can rescue the rest of you." She licked her lips, eyeing him with a slow, seductive once-over.

The promise in her glance made his heart race for an entirely different reason.

CHAPTER EIGHT

A zazel had been in *Dreamwalks* with his brothers too many times to count, but nothing compared to the one Toni, with her friend, Sensos, created, mirroring the one he'd made up before. There was a depth to this place he'd never experienced in any of them before.

The setting sun on the horizon as it kissed the tranquil ocean brought with it a kaleidoscope of jewel-like colors that took his breath away. The feel of the silky sand under his bare feet caressed and warmed his skin. All around, the air carried a perfume laced with the hint of oceanic brine and the overlying fragrance of sea flowers that dotted the shoreline behind them. Seagulls cried above him, flying in loops as they scanned for food under the calm waves. One plunged into the water before surfacing with a wiggling fish in its beak.

Azazel closed his eyes and took in a deep, cleansing breath.

"I can't believe how detailed it is here." He opened his eyes. "You've created a miracle."

Toni grinned and shrugged.

"Well, I *am* a film producer." She waved a hand around them. "Getting the background in any scene as realistic as I could was part of my job." She smirked. "And I was darned good at it."

Glancing around, Azazel appreciated how the imaginary realm complemented all five of his senses. Even the brush of the balmy breeze across his skin was as gratifying as a lover's caress. As the weight of escaping a dangerous situation faded, he let go of the hard tension at the back of his neck, feeling lighter than he'd ever imagined. Even his inner beast rumbled a light purr of contentment.

But the sense of calm wouldn't be possible without Toni next to him. Being with her brought an added gift he never dreamed possible. Taking in a fortifying breath, Azazel savored the taste of foreign freedom.

"Come on," Toni looped her arm through his elbow. "Let's sit over here." She led him to a soft blanket made of short fur that was impossibly free of sand. Plush throw pillows lay scattered across the surface, as if offering comfort. She sat cross-legged with a smile. "Sit. I promise not to bite." She patted the place next to her.

Azazel didn't hesitate. He lowered himself beside her, mirroring her posture.

"Tell me what happened after Baelon zapped me away in that dream," Toni implored, placing her hand on one of his thighs. "He didn't hurt you, did he?"

Azazel covered her hand with his, shaking his head. His long braid slipped over his shoulder, the end pooling between his thighs. "No, he only told me the reason they did that to us was to observe how 'organics in this dimension' reacted to several situations. Then he dismissed me into the *Dreamwalk* you found me in. I'm pretty sure my body is still in that crystal cage somewhere." He pressed his lips together to keep from complaining about how terrified he'd been the longer he was contained—which, in turn, had made his inner beast fight harder to get loose. Thank the goddess Toni showed up when she did. *It was true that beauty could tame the savage beast.*

He grinned as the damn thing continued to coo in the background.

The thought prompted him to find out how. He tilted his head, observing her open expression. "How did you quiet that beast behind the wall?"

"Oh, him?" Toni pshawed with a wave of her elegant fingers. "That big ole softy just wanted some attention." She wagged her admonishing finger at him. "You've been ignoring him for far too long. He only wants to come out and play." She gripped her ankles with a grin. "I told him now wasn't the time for us to meet face-to-face. But I promised him we would as soon as the time was right."

Azazel stilled. *Time was right? For what?*

"And... you talked to him?" How was that possible? He'd never told her about the creature he'd dubbed his "inner beast". Never in his wildest dreams did he consider it was something separate from himself. More like a twisted part of his inner makeup that was prone to uncontrollable violence and animalistic drives.

Toni scratched the side of her cheek. "I'm not sure. Our minds connected as easily as you and I do." She shrugged. "His pain reached out to me, so what could I do? I had to respond." Her head tilted, her bright-blue eyes searched his face. "Where did he come from? I didn't get that he was part of Baelon's group. Do you know why they kept him behind that wall?"

His mouth dried. She didn't know the beast was a part of him. He wasn't sure if he was relieved or hurt about that. He smoothed his expression before answering. "I'm not sure." The lie soured his mouth. "But I think we'd better get off this ship before Baelon finds out we've connected like this."

She nodded. "I agree. Listen—" She scooted closer to him. "—JR14 found me, and we're going to come and get you so you can teleport us off this ship. Think that's doable?"

"It's possible." Azazel rubbed his scratchy chin. "But it'd be easier if we somehow could avoid the Krystalii's psychic sensors. I..." He stopped in mid-sentence when Toni held up a hand.

"What?" she said, her eyes unfocused. "Oh, that's good. Okay."

He waited to see if she said anything else. She must be communicating with her suit, even though it didn't look like she was wearing it right now. The only thing she had on was a skimpy bikini that made his mouth water as he took in all the luscious, bare, golden skin. *Damn, he must be losing his mind if that wasn't the first thing he noticed. Shit, his brother Arakiba would never let him live that down.*

"Oh." Toni's eyes focused on him. She gave him a sheepish smile. "Sensos tells me some of what Baelon showed us in the Dreamwalk was true. Like the Nexus Core, the psychic amplifier, is real. And so is the Dimensional Rift Epicenter." She sighed. "It'd be nice if we could put a wrench in those before you teleport us out. But—" She leaned in, resting both of her palms on his mid-thighs. "—I think JR14 and I should find you and set you free first? Don't you?"

Azazel couldn't help but watch her lips move as she spoke. Being caught in this impossible situation didn't matter. Answering her didn't matter. The only thing that mattered was stealing a taste of those tempting lips before thinking about anything else. Giddy with the freedom to act as he wanted, he cupped her face with his hands, and claimed her mouth with his own.

The sight of Azazel moving closer mesmerized Toni. When he was just a hairsbreadth away, she closed her eyes, aching to feel his touch. The nearer he came, the more the sensual tension pulled low in her womb. It sharpened and turned into something exquisite—decadent, unstoppable. When his lips caressed hers, the impact eclipsed everything else. Even their previous kiss in that last *Dreamwalk* was a pale echo of how this felt. Her body became languid and weak. She gripped the back of his head, holding him fast while she gave herself over to him as raw, unflinching intent took over. She gripped the back of his head, holding him fast. Raw, unflinching intent took over as she gave herself to him. Burgeoning urges for this man consumed her with each swipe of his hot, seeking tongue.

His provocative voice whispering her name in her mind barely registered. Toni was too far gone, lost in a rush of pleasure so intense she wondered if he experienced the same thing. The mere idea of him joining with her on a mental level intensified her own reaction. No longer ruled by reason, she became a living inferno of craving and hunger that devoured every shred of restraint.

Azazel's hand covered her breast, his thumb caressing her puckered nipple through the minuscule fabric of her swimsuit. His mouth left hers and nibbled against her chin before traveling down the side of her neck. She grasped his firm shoulders in a tight grip, moaning, arching closer to him.

"Let me," he implored in a wicked whisper against her pebbling skin.

Toni hissed, too far gone to make a coherent response. "Ah... don't... yes..."

Her heart labored, and she couldn't breathe. His masculine taste—she couldn't get enough of it. More. She had to have more. Shifting her position, she thrust her knee between his firm thighs and ground herself against the hard column of his leg.

Azazel's ravenous growl rolled from deep in this throat, a hungry, edge tone that invaded her mind. She wrapped her arms around his neck and cradled him to take over his mouth once again. When he pulled back to nibble the corner of her mouth, she moaned at the loss. Then, the center of her chin became his focus. His dangerous lips drifted over her skin, leaving a wake of fiery flames everywhere he suckled.

With deft fingers, Azazel brushed her bikini top upward and exposed the puckered skin of her nipples. He gave a sharp hitch and inhaled, taking an agonizing eternity to bend his head to claim what he'd uncovered.

Before she knew how it happened, his long hair became unbound and slid over her like a silken curtain.

With a gentle touch, he captured one of her breasts and lifted the slight weight to his mouth.

His tongue swirled over the oversensitive skin, causing excitement to rock through her. She shook, boneless. Streaks of lightning shot through her, creating a sizzling pathway that drove hard into her very core.

Her core clenched, and a slick heat bloomed between her thighs. Shuddering a labored breath, she explored the contours of the solid muscles of his shoulders and back. With a keening cry, she hummed with pleasure as he lowered her onto her back and covered her welcoming body with his. She sighed, shifting against the rough fur of the blanket beneath her.

When the burning heat of Azazel's mouth left her puckered nipple, her wet skin became chilled. She whimpered at the loss.

"You are breathtaking," he murmured, his deep, guttural voice laced with undeniable desire. "And I crave you more than my next breath." His whispered declaration ended when he captured her other neglected peak in the scorching heat of his mouth.

With an instinct as old as time, Toni shifted to free her legs to wrap them around his solid waist. She squealed when the softness of her sex aligned with the steel of his. A wave of pure wantonness consumed her.

With the skin of her breast engulfed by Azazel's ravaging mouth, his growling laughter came out muffled. "*Hebat.*"

A part of her longed to hear him say it again, with the same reverence. Reaching between them, she wrapped her fingers around him to test his masculine weight in her hand. It was like holding velvet steel, hard with need that thrummed along her palm. She skimmed and danced her fingers over him, capturing his pre-cum to lubricate each tug and pull, creating dominant demands of her own.

"Are you ready for me?" she whispered in his ear. "Are you ready for us?" That was the real question, wasn't it? But how could they have a future when they hadn't even met in person? No... no, stop it. She ignored the sobering question and shoved that doubt aside. Instead, she'd rather revel in the hedonistic pleasure as she writhed, rubbing her sex against his. Why worry about something that might never happen? Maybe this dream was all they had. And she'd be damned if she let anyone accuse her of not grabbing this chance for them both.

With firm conviction, Toni opened herself to vulnerability. Closing her eyes, she savored the freedom of that decision and wallowed in the passionate heat Azazel brought. The next thing she knew, their clothes were gone. All that remained between them was bare, slick skin. A testament born of their shared passion as well as the ocean mist wrapping around them. Keeping hold of his member, she guided him to her opening. With a purr of pleasure, she welcomed him, inch by burrowing inch, into her body. The rightness of him being there, filling her, made her warble a small wail of pleasure. Her hips moved in time with his steady thrusts, and she pushed back with the heels of her feet against the flexing globes of his backside, yearning to take him in as deep as possible.

Her breasts rubbed against the light fur that dusted Azazel's sternum, ramping up the tightening of her nipples that heightened her sexual tension. Yes... this was right. This was perfect. She'd found the one thing... the one *person*, she longed for. Her body demanded every luxurious feeling with him and couldn't wait for that wild ride of completion heading straight for her. She squeezed his fiery velvet sheath, vowing to never let go.

Gasping for air, Toni had the urge to see their joining for herself. With an inborn strength, she forced her eyes open. Enthralled, she drank in every flicker of hedonistic desire that played across Azazel's striking face. His stamp of masculine tension fueled the fire deep within her. Not daring to blink, she watched him watching her. His mahogany eyes glittered with such intent, it triggered a devastating, uncontrollable primal hunger deep inside her.

"I've ached for you since the first time I saw you."

His voice rasped with a rough, dark hunger that made her tremble as his powerful body thrust inside her.

"All I can think about is touching you, tasting you. Do you feel the same? Do you want me?" His demand came out guttural.

As he surged forward harder, faster, Toni groaned and rounded her hips in response. She gazed up at him, enchanted by the sexy, slumberous look he gave back to her.

"I want this," she confirmed with a husky whisper. "I want you with every part of me, with every breath I take." She embraced that truth, letting it guide her to stake her claim on him. Without hesitation, she shoved the last of any doubts or confusion she had and released them into a forgotten abyss.

Azazel gripped her hips and surged in powerful, blinding strokes.

The musky scent of their passion perfumed the air around them.

With a savage growl, he rose to his knees, still gripping her hips, and he continued to forge into her. His driving rhythm increased, each stroke more demanding than the one before.

The steely length of his cock owned her—possessed her. All at once, it was too much.

"That's it, *hebat*. Come for me now!"

A barreling explosion claimed Toni, making her cry his name as an incredible, blinding pleasure tore through her. She held her breath as the blazing sensation took over. Her body rippled and burned as the blinding rush of ecstasy stole her mind.

His release followed hers, his seed spilling deep inside, pulsing in heated waves of breathtaking ecstasy.

She collapsed on the plush blanket, floating in a haze of utter fulfillment.

Her last coherent thought was that she couldn't care less if she was in a dream or reality. The only thing that mattered was the man in her arms and the total completion of him joining his soul with hers.

Toni woke on her side in the refrigerated cold of the crystal cage.

Well, crap.

Waking up in this sideshow nightmare was a real letdown. Thank God Sensos kept her warm. It was hard enough to face reality after that life-changing lovefest with Azazel.

"Antonia, query." JR14 fluttered just beyond the tip of her nose.

Great. She was going to go cross-eyed watching him hover like that.

"Ya…?" She cleared her throat. "I mean, yes?" At the last second, she remembered to speak lower, just in case talking out loud alerted the Krystalii who had to be monitoring her. No need to let them know there was anyone else in the room.

"Are you replenished enough to begin our escape?"

"Sensos?" She took her focus off the bot mere inches from her face. "How about you? Are you ready to hide me as well as create a decoy so they won't know I'm gone?"

Toni sat up, looping her hair behind her ears. It was kinda nice to wake up and not have to do the usual morning body stuff since wearing the alien suit covered that. Still, what she wouldn't give for a hot cup of coffee right about now. Or, better yet, a Korean latte. Yeah, her mouth watered at the thought of the *misugaru* multigrain powder with a dash of honey in her coffee. That would do the trick. *Oh well, first things first. Escape, then hunt down a magical cup of brewski.*

Yes, Sensos replied. *While you were in the dream state with the male, JR14 and I obstructed the sensors in this room to run on a continuous loop. Because I've completed that, the Krystalii will have no reason to suspect your absence. Be prepared, I will encase your head now.*

Toni shivered as Sensos covered her. When she looked around, there was the slightest waver, letting her know her head was shielded.

As she moved, the spider-bot buzzed away and hovered a couple of feet in front of her.

"JR14, can you lead us to Azazel?"

"Affirmative."

Nice. She had no trouble hearing the bot reply.

JR14 tilted his bulbous head. "Advice: stay within eyesight of me."

"Yeah, no kidding, metallic macho," she muttered.

Without another word, JR14 buzzed to the door.

It opened without hesitation, allowing the bot to whiz through.

She followed close behind, sliding her back against the crystalline walls in the corridor, afraid someone might see her sneaking around. The creepy tremor vibrating beneath her feet made her imagine she walked in the belly of an enormous slumbering whale. But... good golly, Miss Molly... Moby Dick had nothing on this place. All around her, prismatic lights refracted off the walls and created fragmented rainbows that danced and shimmered, bending and twisting like an old seventies roller rink with a huge disco ball spinning overhead.

She avoided looking at her mirrored image on the walls and floor since just one glance made her dizzy. Telling herself not to do something was easier said than done. Her eyes kept sliding to the distorted version of her reflection that followed her like a ghost.

"Left at the next intersection, Antonia." JR14's voice remained calm, clinical, and precise as he landed on her left shoulder. "Then proceed twenty-four meters to the access junction."

Toni exhaled, nodding even though she wasn't sure the spider-like AI perched on her shoulder could see her gesture.

Sensos's non-gendered smooth voice whispered through her thoughts.

Steady your breathing. Your heart rate is elevated. The Krystalii may not see us, but I advise maintaining composure. Their resonance fields respond to fluctuations in the ship's vibrational patterns.

"Right," Toni muttered under her breath. She had no illusions about her ability to fight these creatures if something went wrong. Her advantage was stealth—the illusion maintained by Sensos, so she didn't have the option to mess it up.

Edging down the hallway, she followed JR14's whispered directions. She winced at the sound of her walking. Even with Sensos help, she imagined the Krystalii heard every step she took. How could they not hear her shuffling along like a tromping, clumsy elephant?

Tension coiled inside her chest, making it hard to breathe. Unbidden, her mother's chastising voice rang in her head. '*Uri ttal*! Daughter, what are you doing right now? Get a grip and focus.'

Toni bit her bottom lip. Okay, *eomma*. She scolded herself. Trust the memory of her mother's persistent voice to steady her. Her jaw clenched. When she was done with this shit-show, the first thing she'd do was to apologize to her mother for giving her a hard time. Teenage years notwithstanding.

There, ahead, was another narrow corridor.

"Is this the right way?"

"Yes," JR14 said.

"Down this hallway."

Pressing her lips together, she followed his instructions. The farther she went, the more the light faded. Shadows stretched around her, making her squint to see through the growing gloom.

Then the walkway widened, opening into a balcony with a transparent railing.

Toni sucked in a breath and froze.

Expanding before her was an enormous dome of clear crystal that arched high overhead. Underneath it lay a city carved from light and glass. Towers rose in elegant spirals, their peaks radiating soft hues of every color imaginable. Bridges of transparent rainbows arched between them, glittering like threads of silk.

Floating platforms hovered through the space, carrying Krystalii passengers that glided on streams of light. Suspended walkways looped in intricate patterns, creating a lattice of pathways that pulsed in sporadic rhythms. Smaller orbs of light flitted like fireflies as they wove through the city, illuminating hidden alcoves and courtyards lined with crystalline flora.

"Da-ang!" Toni whispered, gripping the railing. "It's a kingdom made of crystal!" She peered at JR14 on her shoulder.

"Observation: a true triumph of geometric precision," JR14 replied. "Analysis would specify that the Krystalii use photonic energy to manipulate matter. Their structures are likely grown rather than constructed."

This is no mere city. Sensos added. *It is a living organism, resonating in harmony with its inhabitants. It's better we remain vigilant. Such beauty often conceals danger.*

Toni tore her gaze away, heart hammering. "Yeah, you're right. It's not like we're tourists here. Let's keep going."

JR14 jumped off her shoulder and buzzed ahead, turning into another hallway that opened onto a vast chamber. Columns of translucent crystal spiraled toward the vaulted dome ceiling, pulsing, as though transmitting energy.

Toni ducked behind one column, her breath catching at the sight of two Krystalii figures parading across the room.

Their chunky crystalline forms refracted light, their bodies in deep hues made up of murky green moldavite.

They were the first she'd seen that appeared androgynous, having neither the form nor figures of male or female. They somehow seemed unfinished.

She shivered as their voices drifted through the air, a strange blend of chimes and whispers. She might not understand a damn word they said, but the tension between them was easy enough to sense.

"Do you understand what they're so worked up about?" She glanced at JR14, who had resumed his place on her shoulder.

"Scanning: they are having a dispute," JR14 stated. "They differ about what is causing the resonance shift detected in Sector 7 that interferes with their connection to Lord Baelon. Opinion: the shift may relate to Azazel's presence. Advice: proceed with caution."

Caution. Right. Toni gritted her teeth as the Krystalii headed right for her, then walked past without so much as a nod. Releasing her held breath with a whoosh, she pursed her lips and swallowed, watching the guards walk away. "Okay, let's 'proceed'."

Edging around the chamber's perimeter, she followed JR14's whispered directions. The coiled tension in her chest eased a bit once she slipped into another narrow corridor. Here, the light from the crystalline walls was even dimmer.

"Warning: we are approaching the containment vault," JR14 announced. "Eighteen meters ahead."

Sensos emitted a low hum against Toni's skin, the suit tightening as if bracing for impact. *I should warn you. Azazel's psychic signature is becoming more difficult to register. I deem the possibility that his restraints are increasing.*

The corridor ended in a set of crystalline doors, glowing with embedded symbols that shifted and pulsed with veins of light.

Toni reached out.

Before she touched them, Sensos spoke sharply. *Wait. JR14, do these patterns show a psychic lock?*

"Analyzing," JR14 responded and flew closer to the doors and extended his antennae. "Live neural waves trigger the lock. Sensos' field should counteract this. Analysis complete. Advise to continue."

Okay, this was it. Now or never. Sucking in a deep breath, Toni stepped closer.

The doors quivered before sliding apart. The chamber beyond was dark, save for a single column of light pouring down from above.

She did a double take. There, in its center, suspended, was a floating figure of a man. Azazel.

He hung in tendrils of light, as if supported by them. Still as a statue, his body was encased in faint energy ripples over the tunic and loose pants he wore. His dark hair floated around his face, and his muscular frame looked oddly vulnerable in the cold light. Chains of glowing crystalline shards looped around his wrists, ankles, and torso. Pulsing.

Maybe the crazy stuff fed off his energy.

"Azazel!" Toni's whisper cracked as she stepped forward.

Please be careful. Sensos's voice cut in. *I suspect the restraints might react to sudden movement.*

Toni swallowed hard, her fingers twitching. "So, JR14. Any advice there, bub?"

"Analyzing. I must determine whether disrupting the containment field's structure will injure Azazel." After a brief silence, the bot continued. "Estimated analysis complete. You do not have sufficient capabilities or the necessary tools to release Azazel. We will have to disrupt the Nexus Core to utilize the release gate hidden on the port side of the cage."

Toni frowned. *How in the hell was she going to do that?*

A moan from Azazel escaped his chapped lips. His eyelids fluttered before they slid open. His dark-brown eyes locked onto hers. Although he didn't speak, his face turned ashen as beads of sweat glistened on his forehead.

"Hang on," Toni whispered, taking another step closer. Sensos tightened its protection around her. "We're trying to come up with a way to get you out."

Azazel's lips moved, but no sound came out. Instead, his voice resonated inside her mind, faint and strained.

Toni... run!

"Observation and opinion," JR14 announced from her shoulder. "Azazel is uninformed of the invisible status Sensos has given you and thus is unaware the Krystalii cannot detect you."

It was hard for Toni to pay attention to the bot. She was too busy panicking as Azazel squirmed, struggling to get loose.

He pursed his lips in a hard line while the tendons in his neck stood out.

Rushing to him with her hands outstretched, she reached the edge of his crystalline cage and put both gloved palms close to the surface without touching it. She shook her head and mouthed, "It's okay," over and over.

"Caution." The bot continued. "If the male becomes overly emotional, it will trigger the encasement he is in and will render him unconscious. Advice: urge him to become still while we continue with our plan to release him."

As Azazel continued to struggle, Toni became desperate. She turned to the spider-android that flew off her shoulder and buzzed over the surface of the clear cage. "How are we going to tell him that without alerting the Krystalii?"

"Feasible solution is about to present itself." JR14 announced as he faced Azazel and hovered in one place. "Suggestion: be on guard. An Elite sentry is about to enter. Back away from the cage to ensure negative detection. Once Azazel is aware the Krystalii cannot detect you, he should become calm."

Right. Just because the Krystalii couldn't sense her, it didn't mean she should stand in the way and allow herself to get tromped by one. She jumped back just as a crystal giant entered the room.

JR14 fluttered and landed on her shoulder. "Observation: interesting development. Instead of clear common crystal, it appears this one is made of danburite material, which will allow the Krystalii to have a higher component of psychic abilities. Advice: stay still and keep your mind as blank as possible. Sensos, if capable, tighten Toni's protection."

Already accomplished. Sensos replied. *However, I would do as JR14 suggests and remain still and calm.*

Toni's breath hitched as she watched the Elite guard.

The thing stomped into the room like a cartoon villain. Its crystalline form caught and fractured in the dim light, creating dazzling shards of brilliance. Composed of pale pink and white danburite crystals, its towering frame glinted with an almost ethereal beauty—one that belied the menace in every deliberate step it took. Each movement was precise, sharp, and silent, as though it glided on air rather than walked.

Its crystal joints ground together with faint, melodic chimes that set her teeth on edge.

The angular planes of its face were alien in their lack of soft curves. All it bore were sharp edges and jutting facets, with two piercing eyes embedded deep within the crystalline structure. Though featureless in the human sense, its face exuded an air of haughty disdain, as if the very sight of Azazel's caged form was beneath it.

Toni couldn't tell if its expression was one of curiosity or contempt. Probably both.

The subtle tilt of its head as it observed Azazel seemed almost thoughtful, but the stillness of its gaze unnerved her. It was like watching a predator assess its prey.

The hands were long and claw-like, hanging at its sides as the tips glowed with an inner light, pulsating like a heartbeat. It stopped just short of the cage, its crystalline limbs bending in a motion that was mechanical and oddly graceful.

Toni shivered as she noticed the faint ripple of energy emanating from the creature's core, like heat waves off asphalt, distorting the surrounding air.

The creature opened its mouth and spoke—if the sound could be called speech. The sound was a mix of grinding stone and chiming bells, a language that seemed as ancient and unyielding as the being itself. The menace in its voice cut sharp and clear—a bully's taunt aimed at Azazel, the way cowards torment a captive who can't strike back.

She clenched her fists, her heart pounding against her ribs as she fought to keep her breaths shallow but steady. The sight of Azazel's face, sweaty and flushed, made her ache to reassure him.

The guard tilted its head again, as if hearing her. Its faceted eyes shifted in her direction for the briefest moment. Their depths caught and held her gaze with an unnatural intensity.

Holding her breath, Toni didn't dare move. She remained still. Every muscle locked in place as the Elite guard straightened to its full, towering height.

The multi-compound lenses turned its focus to Azazel, as if memorizing every detail of the man encased in the serrated crystal cage. Then, with a faint hum of energy rippling through its form, the guard turned with mechanized precision, the motion smooth for something so angular and rigid.

Not daring to blink, she focused on the Krystalii as it headed to the exit. She sucked in her breath and watched as its feet didn't appear to touch the ground. *Darn thing gave an effortless illusion of gliding.*

Chime-like sounds of shifting crystals resonated with each step and sent faint echoes through the cavernous room. The low-watt light from its core dimmed the more it moved and cast longer shadows against the crystalline walls.

Damn, the special effects from the creature gave the surroundings a scary-as-hell edge.

It paused at the doorway, its head tilted as if something caught its attention.

Toni's heart leaped into her throat. Her breath caught against the stifling pressure of her panic. *Did it know she was there? Could it sense her?*

But then, with a low, resonant hum, the guard resumed its movement, and its massive form disappeared through the doorway without so much as a backward glance.

The moment it was gone, she swore the room exhaled. Her eyes remained glued to the empty doorway. The only sound was her deafening heartbeat pounding in her ears.

It took several seconds before she dared to move. Clenching her trembling gloved hands into fists, she let out a grateful breath. "Whew! That was close. Thank you, Sensos."

Daring a glance at Azazel, she almost burst into laughter.

His eyes were as wide as all get-out, his open jaw practically resting on his chest.

Well, didn't that say it all? Maybe now he'd calm down so they could get him the hell out of there and escape.

One could only hope.

Azazel snapped his mouth shut when a line of drool threatened to roll free from his lips. How in the world did Toni escape the Krystalii guard's notice? It was then he noticed the strange outfit she was wearing. If he didn't know any better, he'd swear she wore that unusual suit the so-called rebels had given her to wear from the Vault of Forgotten Worlds in their simulation.

Except, covering her head was a clear—fishbowl? And hovering next to her was his spider-bot, JR14. He'd give anything to hear what they talked about as the droid bobbed up-and-down while Toni spoke with her expressive hands, emphasizing whatever she said. She pursed her lips and glared at the bot with narrow eyes. Apparently, she didn't like whatever the droid was telling her. She put one of her hands on her trim hip while wagging her finger at him before waving it around.

One more bob from the bot before he buzzed to hover in front of Azazel's crystal cage. The droid's eyes changed from his normal pale sky-blue to a vibrant kaleidoscope of colors, a clear sign the bot was examining or processing something.

Toni moved closer behind the droid, now putting both hands on her hips, her lovely lips creased into a frown. Looks like she wasn't happy with whatever the AI droid was doing.

All at once, the bot's eyes switched color to a solid red. Then he zoomed backward until Azazel only saw him as a dot in the distance, then he rushed into view, his bulbous head tilted as if in determination. If Azazel could put his hands up, he would have. *The damn thing looked like he was going to ram into the crystal cage!*

The only thing Azazel could do was twist his head sideways when the bot reached the barrier... then zoomed in without a problem. He landed on Azazel's shoulder as if it were the most normal thing in the world.

Azazel swallowed a hiss when a sharp pain pierced his neck right next to where the bot stood on his shoulder. Did that damn bot just jab him with one of his razor-thin legs?

Query.

Was that JR14's inanimate voice in his head?

Please ascertain and confirm your ability to converse with me in this manner.

The voice spoke to him, not on a psychic level, but more of a mechanical one. Like using earbuds when listening through Bluetooth.

I can. He replied on the same path. Talking to the bot like this was not uncomfortable, just disorienting.

Excellent. JR14 announced.

"However," the bot stated out loud. "It is best to conserve energy by speaking out loud whenever prudent."

Azazel gazed at the spider-bot in amazement.

"How did you get in here? Can I get out the same way?"

"Response: once I determined the vibrational aspects of this enclosure, I adjusted my own frequencies to match it with 99.9 percent probability of success. It only became a matter of intent to do so."

Okay. Not something he could pull off. Gathering his thoughts, Azazel watched JR14 out of the corner of his eye.

The bot fluttered his wings before sliding them under his back panels and folding his legs to settle.

"Now communications can commence," he continued in his matter-of-fact tone. "And we can illuminate you on our escape plans. Bonus: I am communicating with my family now gathered with yours at the chancellor's palatial space station orbiting Zerin."

Azazel's eyebrows furrowed. "How can you talk to them without the Krystalii knowing?"

"I have determined it is possible by bypassing the Krystalii psychic network without any organic or sentient methods."

The bot's blunt response didn't surprise him, but his answer did.

"Since I am of a mechanical design, they are unable to penetrate my unique frequency to intercept. As of now, if you wish to convey any correspondence with the outside forces, you can do so with limited capability.

"That sounds a little awkward." Azazel mused out loud, trying to keep his doubts to himself.

JR14 must have picked up his uncertainty.

"Possibly. Suggestion," the droid responded. "Limit queries and statements to minimal as possible. That would save time and probable confusion. To whom do you wish to communicate first?"

He watched the stunning woman outside his crystal cage, holding her hands together as she watched him.

"Antonia." His voice was lower than intended. "How is she? Does she know who I am? Does she realize we first met in a psychic dream Baelon created?" The questions twisted his gut. Her not knowing who he was gnawed at the pit of his stomach.

"She is as aware of you as you are of her."

The bot's quick reply told Azazel JR14 didn't need to ask Toni that. It had to be something he'd witnessed firsthand.

"Observation," JR14 continued. "I find it fascinating how two sentient entities can connect on such a profound level without a physical meeting firsthand. I believe I will study this phenomenon further to discover if it is an anomaly or if this is natural to organics."

Having a sentient spider-bot study his love life wasn't something Azazel looked forward to. "Let's not get sidetracked, JR14. I think we should get out of this predicament first." Azazel studied the cage casing closer. With his movements restricted, he couldn't run his hands over the surface to get a proper feel for it. The tomb-like pen pressed around him, clamping down hard on his psychic abilities.

Except for his inner demon that stirred when Toni came into the room. Now the damn thing prowled like an animal, looking for a chance to get loose.

"You said you can communicate with your family." Azazel scrambled to get the important questions out first. "Do you mean JR10?"

"Affirmative."

"And who's with him at the chancellor's palace? Are they aware of where I am and the predicament I am in?" He ignored the heat curling up his neck. It wasn't easy to admit being duped by Baelon. But nursing a bruised ego was the least of his worries.

"My brothers, JR15 and JR13, are there with their respective sentient companions. JR12 is approaching the space station with his partner and will dock within the next twelve hours."

Azazel did a quick calculation in his head. Abalim and Asmodel were on the station and Arakiba was on his way there. When the bot didn't expound on their health or lack thereof, it was easy to conclude there wasn't anything wrong with them.

"Where is my brother, Adapa?" His eldest brother didn't have a JR unit.

"The prince consort is on the planet Akurn with his wife, Queen Inanna. They are in continuous contact with Federation Consortium Chancellor D'zia E'etu."

Which made sense. Good to know Adapa was well away from the thick of things. Especially since Azazel suspected the queen now carried twins. Before agreeing to take the assignment on finding Toni, he was tempted to tell Adapa about the children on the way. But at the last minute he decided it wasn't his place to do that. It was something only the man's wife should share.

"JR12 as well as JR13 have gathered specific intelligence from Krystalii allies that will enable us to overtake the hard control Baelon has over his subjects."

Krystalii allies? Now there was an oxymoron if he'd ever heard one.

"The one reality Baelon exposed to you in that Dreamwalk is that there is a Nexus Core on this ship. Not only is it a psychic amplifier for communication, but its primary function is also control. Lord Baelon uses it to maintain an iron-clad dominion over all Krystalii. If disrupted, the restrictions he wields over them will dissipate, giving us an opportunity to free you and allow the ship to be taken over by the Consortium forces."

"So, what you're saying is I have to take out the Nexus Core first to get free from this prison?" Talk about a circular idiom.

"Negative." Replied JR14. "It would be illogical for you to take out the Nexus Core in order to liberate you from your current imprisonment."

"Well then, who..." He didn't have to finish his sentence. His eyes fixated on the stunning figure of Toni standing in front of his cage with her arms crossed, glaring at him and frowning.

"Update," JR14 announced. "JR12 is close enough to send a reinforcement that has the capability of achieving a 73.69 percent chance of success in disrupting the Nexus Core. I must leave to coordinate this endeavor between them and Antonia."

Before Azazel said anything, JR14 sprang off his shoulder and zoomed through the crystal cage's force-field.

A distinctive figure digitized into view behind Toni.

Azazel sucked in a breath when he recognized who—or rather what—it was. "Oh... no," he muttered out loud.

CHAPTER NINE

Stupid, stupid, spider-friggin'-bot. Toni clenched her fists, crossing her arms over her chest. The damn idiot could have smashed into smithereens when he bashed into what looked like hard crystal holding Azazel.

I assure you, Sensos whispered in her mind. *The android analyzed the vibrational makeup of the barrier before attempting such a feat.*

Her suit's reassurance made her feel better. But... still.

"So, why can't I hear what they're saying?" She cocked her head and watched JR14 land on Azazel's shoulder. The pained expression on the man's handsome face lasted only a second before it smoothed out.

The cage mutes outside communications. Sensos explained. *Thus, we are unable to hear them. We must rely on JR14 to inform us of what they discussed.*

Great. She had to rely on the small droid to be an interpreter. She sighed and dropped her arms to her side. What she wouldn't give to talk to Azazel face-to-face. Watching his calm expression drew her closer.

His eyes stared straight ahead, his brows furrowed, and the muscles in his neck tensed. After a hard blink, his face once again relaxed. All at once, he zeroed in on her, and the mahogany color of his eyes deepened to a rich dark chocolate.

The profound depth of desire etched in the dilation of his eyes caught and held her. Heat flared from deep within her core as she responded in kind to his silent entreaty. What she wouldn't give to be with him, touch him, flesh to flesh.

Well... squishy-hot dammit! It took every inch of control she had to keep from stomping her foot like a toddler. Why were there always barriers between them? God, what she wouldn't give to explore this extraordinary man in the flesh. She shivered just thinking about how that would feel. She licked her lips.

And, who's to say what they did in those dream worlds weren't as real as real could get? If so, then watch out, bitches!

Azazel jerked his head toward her with an unfocused gaze. He frowned.

She gasped when she saw his neck bloom into a rosy shade of red. What in the world was he embarrassed about? She crossed her arms and glared at the bot, pressing her lips into a hard line. If that darn JR14 said anything to upset Azazel, she'd... well... she'd do something.

As if the small droid heard her threat, he lifted off Azazel's shoulder, his wings buzzing before he raced to the cage barrier and floated through the clear, hard-looking wall. Then, he flew back to her, slick as you please.

Toni's mouth dropped open. "What in the world are you doing?" She snipped at the bot. Not waiting for an answer, she glanced at Azazel, who had the weirdest expression on his face as he looked over her shoulder.

He'd recoiled with his mouth wide open, and his upper lip curled back.

What in the heck made him look like that?

"I suppose you're the helpless human female I have to work with."

An unfamiliar voice behind her made her jump. This one was distinctively female, with a diva tone worthy of any Kardashian.

Spinning around, Toni faced someone she'd never, ever in her wildest dreams think she'd face on the Krystalii ship. Well, not someone. More like a *something*.

A sexbot.

A bright, neon-pink-like-Barbie sexbot android. Complete with dark-fuchsia nipples that reminded her of erotic cherries topping size 40DD breasts. An impossibly thin waist over hips wide enough to tempt any male to grab onto.

The darn thing even had her feet encased in four-inch stiletto platform heels. Toni'd get a nosebleed if she wore anything that ridiculous.

The mere sight of one of her previous prison guards from that gangster planet FiPan made her see red. Her fingers clasped into tight fists, and her knuckles cracked as she cocked her head, glaring at the thing under heavy lids. Heat flushed through her. Breathing became a second thought as memories of the physical and emotional neglect she suffered while a prisoner there overrode any sense she had.

She only took one step toward the sexbot before she couldn't take another.

What the hell? She looked down at her feet as if they'd give her some kind of clue why they refused to move.

I apologize, Toni. Sensos intoned in its non-gender mental voice. *I am keeping you in place so you may discover that the entity before you is an ally.*

"Yes, darling." The sultry feminine voice of the sexbot matched the seductive smirk on her damn face. "What Sensos is telling you is true. I am a valuable ally sent here by my latest ardent admirer, Arakiba." Her breathy sigh was as phony as believing she took in a breath at all. "I'm afraid that darling hasn't realized yet my heart belongs to another.

But—" She shrugged and waved a nauseating-pink hand in the air. "—that sensitive male's feelings are the least of my concerns. I just cannot allow this dimension to be taken over by those ugly crystal-like brutes." She shuddered. "None of them have enough intelligence to be in complete wonderment about my awesomeness."

Toni had no idea who this Arakiba might be, but he had to be an imbecile if he thought this bubble-headed sex-toy could somehow combat the Krystalii.

"Interjection," JR14's mechanical voice interrupted. "Elemi, please explain to Antonia your purpose here and your role in achieving that goal. As you accomplish that, I will keep Azazel apprised."

"Oh, very well." The sexbot pivoted her head to focus on Toni. "I am Elemi. While my true nature is not this outer casing—" She gestured up and down her form. "—my original form is that of a sentient organic, sleek 11-15 spaceship engineered by the Warriors of Light, once funded by the disgraced Chancellor U'unk to take over the galaxy." Throwing her slender shoulders back, she put one of her hands on her hip and tilted her neon head. The bubble-gum color of her eyes narrowed. "I have since survived being gutted by the Krystalii and re-created in two forms. One as my glorious ship, and one as you see here. I am literally in two places at one time."

The android tapped a gleaming pale-pink fingernail against her lips while she walked around Toni as if judging her.

Toni crossed her arms and returned the favor, keeping eye contact with the absurd automaton.

Elemi stopped walking in circles and continued. "While my 11-15 body is in a nearby orbit not too far from this ship—" Her full lavender-rose lips lifted into a slow smirk. "—I am here in my second glorious form as a loyal citizen of the Federation Consortium to save the day... as only I can."

Azazel couldn't believe there was an actual sexbot standing there on the Krystalii mothership—one JR14 declared was a collaborating ally working with them against the invaders. He narrowed his eyes, studying the nauseating-pink android's interaction with Toni. Where had he seen that one before?

Bro, you there?

A faint masculine voice in his head startled him. It was odd, since the path the voice came on wasn't a psychic one. Cocking his head, he unfocused to concentrate on the sound better.

Bro? Answer me, dammit!

Bro? The only person who called him that was his brother, Arakiba. But... that couldn't be him. It had to be Baelon playing some kind of trick on him.

I know you. All cool and aloof... You act like some great igigi *who believes he shouldn't bother with us mere* namlugallu *trying in vain to keep up with your superior divinity.*

Look, Arakiba. I've asked you more than once not to call me that.

He tightened his gut to hold back the rumbling as his inner beast struggled. He'd spent a lot of time trying to keep the damn thing in check so he didn't end up hurting his blond, smart-ass brother. Good thing Arakiba was nowhere in sight to make things worse.

Yeah, well. Someone should knock you off your self-imposed pedestal so you can join the rest of us mortals. A chuckling snort. *And of course, we all know I'm the best one to do that.*

It took several heartbeats before Azazel believed he might be talking to Arakiba. No one went out of their way to be a bigger pain in the ass than his younger brother. And no one, but no one, could mimic that annoying personality. No matter how powerful a psychic they were. But it didn't hurt to ask. Azazel narrowed his eyes.

How can that be you? This isn't our normal psychic path.

This isn't a psychic path at all, you dork. A bark of laughter. *Boy, for such a brainiac, you sure can be clueless sometimes.*

Dork? What's a dork? Azazel shook his head. *Never mind. If we aren't talking on a psychic pathway, how are you talking to me?*

It's adorable how impatient you've become. Can't wait to tell the bros about it.

Azazel's chest tightened with helplessness. Trying to get Arakiba focused was a constantly hopeless cause.

You know that thing JR14 injected into you? Well, it opened a slight path to my JR12, who snapped one in me. Hurt like a mofo, didn't it?

It took everything Azazel had not to roll his eyes. One tiny scratch made Arakiba whine like a little baby. The injection JR14 gave him on the neck only pinched for a second. He resisted the urge to tell the petulant ass to grow a pair.

And I endured all that pain just so I can talk to you. Now the mental voice had the same tone and inflection his brother had. As if using this means of communication made it easier for him.

Okay, instead of talking so much, why aren't you here to get me out? Let's at least start there.

Working on it, bro. Came the annoying reply. *You just gotta sit tight. I promise things are cookin' for sure.*

Sit tight. *Yeah, I'll get right on that... bro.* He swallowed his annoyance with a sigh. Not surprisingly, Arakiba's remark about Azazel's fraying patience hit the mark. Glancing out of his cage, he clenched his hands into fists as he watched Toni and JR14 leave the room with the neon-pink sexbot. Where were they going? It dawned on him where he'd seen that android before.

*Son-of-a-*lilit*! Was that the sexbot from FiPan you liked so much?* Pervert. *And why is Toni going with her?*

Isn't she the most glorious thing you've ever seen? Arakiba hummed. *Just so you know, the reason I took her from FiPan was to see if I could make her work again. And not for the reason I know you think I did. You're such a perv.*

Oh sure. His brother knew him well enough to throw his words back at him, even without reading his mind.

I wanted to tinker with her to see what made her work. Turns out it was a good thing I did 'cause I used her to save the life of that sentient ship Chancellor D'zia let us use.

Azazel looked out of his clear crystal cage to the empty room where the android had been. *That sexbot houses the consciousness of* Elemi *the ship?* How outstanding would that be?

Yup. Even better, the Krystalii can't see her since she doesn't give off any psychic vibes. Much like the JR units, Arakiba confirmed. *I'm on the ship,* Elemi, *not too far from the Krystalii one you're on. With* Elemi's *ability to absorb the signatures of any ship, organic or not, we remain cloaked from them.*

If Azazel understood him correctly, the ship *Elemi* came across the *Nyrlith's* sensors as part of itself. Finally, some good news. A way for him to escape somewhere safe with Toni. Of course, he'd have to break free from this cage, find her, then either teleport that short distance or steal one of their ships and leave. All without the Krystalii knowing. It'd be great if he had a suit like Toni's that camouflaged his psychic presence. Well, all he could do was deal with one thing at a time.

Can you get us out of here without the Krystalii knowing?

Uh, no can do, bro.

Arakiba's unhelpful answer made Azazel frown.

At least not yet. That's why Elemi is there.

Go on.

See, between the three of us—me, Asmodel, and Abalim—we've come across former Krystalii loyalists who've informed us the Nyrlith *has something called the Nexus Core. It's some kind of device deep in the bowels of that ship, that Baelon psychically uses to control his subjects. Once Elemi disrupts that, me and the bros will come on board and get ya. Easy-peasy, right?*

But why did she take Toni with her? The thought of her traveling throughout the hostile Krystalii ship made the acid in his throat burn.

Toni? Oh, is that the babe you were supposed to find? Ouch! That hurt.

What happened? Why did you say ouch?

Morgan pinched my arm 'cause I called Toni a babe. No need to be so cruel, irnini.

Morgan? That must have been the woman Arakiba was looking for. But him calling her a "sweet smelling lady" in their ancient language was something different. Azazel had never heard his fun-loving brother have such affection in his tone whenever he spoke to someone. Especially a woman.

Can Morgan hear us?

No. She made me speak out loud as we talked so she could hear my part of the conversation. Hey, dude. You are not going to believe where she's from!

Azazel smiled at the excitement in his brother's tone. He sounded like a kid who couldn't wait to share a great secret. Before he commented, Arakiba continued.

You're right, my love. I'll tell him later. Anyhoo, Az. Just sit tight, and as soon as Elemi knocks out that psychic doohickey, we'll be right there to get ya. Later!

Azazel jerked at the notable click announcing the end of their conversation. *Ezeru*! Curse his brother for cutting things off like that! He had too many questions that demanded answers. Trust Arakiba to leave him high and dry, sitting here with no way to find out anything. Much less protect Toni. That *son-of-a*-lilit brother of his had no idea what was going to happen to him when Azazel got his hands around his clueless, smart-ass neck.

His inner beast growled in agreement.

Toni followed the neon-pink Elemi through the gleaming crystalline corridors of the Krystalii ship. The smooth, reflective walls refracted light in an eerie dance of color that gave her a headache.

The faint hum of the ship's systems thrummed around them, punctuated only by JR14's soft, mechanical buzzing as he hovered next to her.

"Darling," Elemi purred, each syllable dripping with diva-level confidence. "Confession time. I know it's strange for me to admit, but playing the heroine is unusual for me. Which I certainly hope you can appreciate. Instead of traipsing around this drafty ship, I should be finding glory, exploring the stars! But alas, I am a prisoner of my own making. I could not allow such an exquisite challenge to unfold without my input, now, could I?" She turned her synthetic head and tossed a theatrical wink at Toni. "I think not. You should feel honored."

"Honored, right," Toni muttered under her breath, rolling her eyes. At first, she worried about them speaking out loud around the ship, in case the Krystalii heard them. But Elemi insisted the crystal creatures wouldn't be able to pick up anything she said since she wasn't organic. The pink bot insisted Toni keep her tone low if she had anything relevant to say at all.

Toni glanced at JR14, who hovered close to her shoulder. "Any idea how long this will take?" She kept her voice just above a whisper. If she spent too much time with her so-called savior, she just might puke. Not the best idea with her head in a fishbowl helmet.

The spider-like android tilted his head, his metallic claws twitching. "Estimated time: 2.6 minutes from the Nexus Core. Barring unforeseen complications."

"And what are the odds of those complications happening?" Toni was almost afraid to ask. Not like the answer would help.

"Probability of interference: 73.8 percent," JR14 replied in his normal matter-of-fact tone.

"Fantastic," Toni mumbled. She relaxed her tightened fists so blood could rush back into her numb fingers.

Ahead, Elemi's heels clicked rhythmically on the floor, the sound both absurd and unnerving in the alien environment. "You're both so gloomy." She huffed with a dismissive wave of her hand. "Oh, for gosh sakes, where's your sense of adventure? It's not every day you get to stroll through the inner workings of a Krystalii vessel with someone as magnificent as me to protect you."

Toni suppressed a groan. *Damn, she'd worked with some serious divas in her day, but Elemi put them all to shame.* "Yeah, I'll make note of that in my diary."

"Childish sarcasm doesn't suit you, dear," Elemi replied, not breaking her stride. "Leave the wit to those who can pull it off with flair. Now, do try to keep up."

I believe her intentions are in the right place, Toni's suit, Sensos, offered.

Maybe. Probably. Whatever. She didn't have anything useful to say to that.

As they rounded a corner, the corridor widened into a large, open space—a junction where several passageways converged.

Toni slowed her steps, a strange unease creeping over her. Through her suit, she tasted that the air was heavier here. Charged with an unfamiliar energy that made her skin prickle.

She stopped. "Wait," she whispered. "Something doesn't feel right."

Elemi paused mid-stride and turned to her, hands on her hips. "Oh, darling, what could go wrong? It's just..."

A sudden, low rumble interrupted her, the vibration rippling through the floor beneath them.

Toni's pulse quickened as she scanned the area, her gaze darting to the reflective walls that shimmered with a life of their own.

"Analysis: anomalous energy signatures detected," JR14 announced. His small head tilted, and the color of his eyes changed from soft blue to a vibrant red. "Recommendation: proceed with heightened caution."

"Yeah, thanks for the brilliant advice, Captain Obvious." Toni snorted. Crap. For once, couldn't she at least act cool and collected like a normal heroine? *But no... not her. As soon as the stress piled on, her sardonic nature ran amok.*

Before JR14 responded, the shimmering walls shifted. What had once been smooth crystal now rippled like liquid, and from the undulating surfaces emerged crystalline figures. Although they might be humanoid, they lacked faces. But the scariest part was how their bodies gleamed with sharp, angular edges that sliced through the low light like razor blades.

"Oh, isn't this just fabulous?" Elemi drawled while clapping with a dramatic flair. "The Krystalii have sent a welcoming party just for us. How nauseatingly predictable."

"Are you saying they know we're here?" Toni bit out.

"Status: unclear," JR14 answered. "However, proximity suggests your query is what you organics call a moot point."

Toni backed up. "You think?" The crystalline figures moved with agonizing slowness at first, their movements jerky and unnatural. Once they stepped into the corridor, their pace quickened.

"JR14?" Toni choked. Were those damn things heading straight for her?

"Suggestion: obtain an energy-based weapon to disrupt their physical cohesion," the android offered.

"Oh, allow me," Elemi interjected, stepping forward. She raised one manicured, gleaming-metal hand, and a burst of blinding-white light erupted from her palm.

The crystalline figures recoiled, then their angular bodies vibrated violently before they shattered into countless shards that rained down where they had once stood.

"You're welcome." Elemi blew on her fingertips as if extinguishing the remnants of her attack. "Honestly, I don't know how you organics manage anything without me."

Toni ignored her and stepped over the shards, her heart still racing. Not wanting to risk the Krystalii hearing them, she kept her voice low. "Thanks, but let's keep moving. JR14, lead the way."

The small android buzzed past Elemi, his sharp claws clicking softly as he moved. "Affirmative. Proceeding to Nexus Core."

They pressed on. The corridors grew narrower and more maze-like as they approached their destination. The hum of the ship's systems became louder, almost deafening.

The air took on a metallic tang that made her throat dry.

"Almost there," JR14 announced in the tense silence. "Nexus Core is beyond the next junction."

"Finally," Toni mumbled, wishing she could wipe the sweat from her brow.

I can take care of that. I will also purify the air for you, Sensos offered.

Toni closed her eyes as a cool breeze floated over her face. Damn, that was welcome. Especially since it brought a soothing scent of lavender with it. She glared at Elemi, who looked as pristine and composed as ever. Even her pink exterior shone untarnished in the low light.

"Oh darling, don't tell me you're tired already." Elemi turned to her with a mock pout. "We haven't done anything to break a sweat yet."

"Sweat?" Toni shot back. "How would you know what that is, you bubblegum Barbie? Or what it means to earn it."

Elemi snorted with a toss of her shiny, pink bald head.

By this time, they'd reached the final junction.

JR14 stopped, his wings buzzing. "Alert: multiple energy signatures detected ahead. Hostile probability: 92.4 percent."

Toni's stomach churned. *Wasn't that just great?*

"Oh, don't worry," Elemi announced with a confident smirk. "I'll go in and handle it so you don't have to worry about perspiring so unbecomingly again." She huffed. "Now stay close, darling. You might accidentally learn something."

Toni opened her mouth to protest, but Elemi turned her back on her and strode forward with her heels clicking with a defiant rhythm.

The corridor ahead opened into a vast chamber where the Nexus Core pulsed with a brilliant, rhythmic light. Just as in the dream Baelon had shown her.

Except for the crystalline figures hemming them in. Their faceless forms moved in unison, guarding it.

Elemi raised both hands this time, creating a flash that made the air shimmer. "Watch in awe, mortal." Her voice dripped with theatrical flair. With a dramatic sweep of her arms, she unleashed another wave of energy, this one a vibrant pink that surged through the chamber.

The crystalline figures faltered, their movements erratic, before they disintegrated.

"And that—" Elemi turned to face Toni and JR14 with a triumphant smile. "—is how it's done."

Toni shook her head, a reluctant smile tugging at her lips. "I gotta admit, you're something else, Elemi."

"Oh, don't I know it." Elemi flipped her glowing bald head like she had a curtain of hair to swish back. "Now, shall we?"

As they stepped into the chamber, Toni couldn't help the flicker of hope spreading through her. If Elemi's over-the-top antics could take down those crystalline guards, maybe they could take out the Nexus Core and free Azazel.

And maybe, just maybe...they'd get out of this alive.

A strange sense of déjà vu made Toni queasy. Taking a deep breath, she followed Elemi inside the Nexus chamber. *How strange that this place is the same as that fake psychic dream the Krystalii forced on me?* As she stepped inside, the cavernous walls were formed from a polished crystal that refracted the pulsing light of multiple towering spires.

Webs of conduits stretched like veins across the room, connecting the spires to the Nexus Core in the center—a crystalline sphere suspended in midair. Its surface rippled with waves of blue-and-violet energy.

All around, the air throbbed with a palpable hum.

The vibration buzzed through Toni, making her teeth ache. She pressed her hand to her chest, overwhelmed by the oppressive psychic pressure in the air, as if the energy emanating from the Nexus was trying to peel back her thoughts layer by layer.

"Magnificent, isn't it?" Elemi's voice carried an edge of awe. Her android form mirrored the surrounding crystals and glass as she moved into the chamber. "Good thing neither one of us is psychic. Being this close to this thing would more than likely destroy us." She headed toward the largest sphere, moving with a grace at odds with her mechanical frame. Her platform stiletto heels clicked softly on the glassy floor.

"Oh sure. Magnificent, like a leopard who can't decide which part of my face to eat off first." Toni mumbled, her gaze darting to the intricate lattice of conduits overhead. *So this is how Baelon amplifies his psychic reach, bending reality to his will.* The thought of disrupting it sent a spike of adrenaline through her. "Are you sure you can turn this darn thing off?"

Elemi didn't answer immediately. She raised her hand, and her left forefinger elongated and thinned into a blade-like probe. With a flick of her wrist, the probe slid out farther. The metallic sheen caught the chamber's light. "Of course I can." The android's tone was matter-of-fact. "Once I disrupt the core's frequency, it'll collapse under its own instability."

As Toni stepped closer to the Nexus Core, the thrumming grew louder, resonating through her very bones. She bit her lip and clenched her fists, watching as Elemi's probe-like forefinger penetrated the crystalline surface.

For a moment, the internal light flickered before a rippling effect pulsated through the inside of the sphere, creating jagged colors of cracking shards within.

Then the Nexus screamed.

Not with sound, but the mental pressure struck Toni like a hammer. She stumbled back, clutching the sides of the orb over her head as waves of psychic energy tore outward, crashing against her mind like a violent storm. She gasped as her vision swam.

As the conduits dimmed, their vibrant blue-and-violet glow faded to a lifeless gray.

The hum stopped, leaving behind a suffocating silence.

The oppressive psychic presence evaporated, replaced by an eerie stillness that made the hair on Toni's arms stand on end, even in the suit.

Cracks spider-webbed across the Nexus Core while a low, ominous groan filled the chamber. The crystalline spires all around them trembled, and some toppled over and shattered into fragments of glittering debris.

The temperature plummeted, and a biting cold seeped through Toni's suit as the room's energy dissipated. "Elemi, is it—" She began, but the android turned, cutting her off.

"No, not yet. Stay back." Elemi's voice was sharper now, her posture tense as she withdrew her probe-like finger from the cracked core.

Sparks erupted from the conduits, minor explosions cascading through the web of connections.

The floor beneath their feet shuddered violently, sending Toni stumbling again. She grabbed onto a nearby crystal spire for balance, and her breath misted inside the clear helmet.

A deep rumble echoed through the chamber as if the entire ship were groaning in protest.

"What's happening?" Toni shouted over the chaos.

"The collapse is destabilizing the ship's psychic network." Elemi's gaze fixated on the spherical Nexus Core. The urgency in her gestures contradicted her steady tone. "I am quite sure Baelon is aware of this disruption. We need to move. Now." With her head down, the android sprinted back the way they'd come in.

Nobody had to tell Toni twice. Staying put was a bad idea on a good day. Sprinting after Elemi, she jabbed a finger toward the exit. "Come on, JR14! We'd better get out of here."

"Affirmative," the bot replied. His iridescent wings fluttered so fast they were practically invisible. "I suggest you accelerate your endeavor to preserve your biological functionality."

"Wow, aren't you just a fountain of good ideas?" Toni glared at the bot as she ran. "Wished I'd thought of that."

Toni's pulse pounded in her ears as the light in the room behind them flickered violently.

Its once-rhythmic glow was now a chaotic strobe. The entire crystalline structure around them groaned and vibrated as though the ship itself was in pain.

Shards of crystal rained down in the corridor, forcing her to duck. Thank God she had a helmet on. "I think we'd better go a little faster." She jogged and caught up with Elemi as the droid headed back the way they'd come.

"Oh darling, must we sprint? It's terribly undignified." Elemi huffed. Her neon-pink exterior gleamed even in the dim, fractured light. Her exaggerated trot somehow made it look like she strutted down a catwalk rather than a desperate escape.

"Expeditious movement is a necessity," JR14 interjected in a calm but firm tone. The small android hovered close to Toni's shoulder, his red-and-gold body glinting. "The structural integrity of this section is deteriorating at an accelerated rate."

"Translation: keep up or we're toast." Toni glanced at Elemi. "You wouldn't want anything to scratch your glorious finish now, would you? Let's get Azazel out of that cage before they have a chance to fix what we broke."

Elemi tossed her synthetic head, the movement insultingly graceful. "Fine, fine. But if I break a heel, you're carrying me."

Toni snorted. *Like hell. She'd never attempt anything that stupid.*

They rounded a corner that stretched ahead into shadowy chaos.

Crystal humanoid figures, once locked in perfect formation, now stumbled and crashed in confusion. Their faceless heads tilted at odd angles, and their movements were erratic and twitchy.

"What's wrong with them?" Toni frowned as she slowed to watch them.

"Hypothesis: disruption of the Nexus Core has accomplished our objective. The severance of Lord Baelon's psychic control over his subjects has resulted in the Krystaliis' tumultuous state," JR14 explained. His metallic limbs twitched as he scanned the figures. "They are likely experiencing a feedback loop of conflicting commands."

"Well, that sounds like fun." Toni grinned. "Let's hope they're too busy falling apart to notice us."

One of the crystalline beings twisted its head as she spoke.

Its craggy limbs twitched, and it let out a piercing, glass-like screech that sent shivers down Toni's spine.

"Oh brilliant, darling," Elemi quipped, stepping close to Toni. "Now you've gone and gotten its attention. Should I applaud?"

"Not helping." Toni hissed.

The Krystalii's movements were fast but jerky as it came toward them. The jagged shards of its body glinted, exposing its lethal sharpness.

Toni tensed, preparing to flee.

"No, no, dearest." Elemi stepped in front of her. "Allow me." With a dramatic flourish, she extended her hand, and a burst of vibrant white-pink energy surged forward, striking the creature square in the chest. It shattered into a cascade of glimmering fragments, the sound like a hundred wind chimes crashing to the floor.

"Efficient," JR14 remarked. "However, energy reserves in your current form are finite. I advise caution."

"Oh please." Elemi waved him off. "I've got enough flair to handle this."

"Let's not test that theory," Toni interjected, grabbing Elemi by the arm and pulling her. "We've got to get to Azazel before this whole ship collapses or something worse shows up."

They raced through the turbulent corridors, weaving between crystalline figures that either barreled past or struck out with wild swings.

The floor shuddered beneath their feet as fractures split the walls, releasing crackling bursts of energy that lit the passage with eerie flashes.

"Query," JR14 said as they approached another junction. "Why does Lord Baelon not take direct action to reassert control?"

"Maybe he's losing it, too." Toni glanced behind her as she bit her bottom lip. "Or, with our luck, he's planning something worse."

Elemi's metallic lips curled into a smirk. "Oh, I'd love to see him try. I'd give him a taste of my magnificence that he won't soon forget."

"Holy crap, Elemi, let's not invite trouble," Toni snapped. "Look, the room where they're holding Azazel is just ahead."

As they neared the chamber, a sudden, deafening roar shook the corridor.

The crystalline walls buckled and cracked, and a massive figure emerged from the shadows. It was one of Baelon's Elite enforcers, a towering construct of crystal and raw energy. Its barbed arms crackled with power as it lumbered toward them, each step sending shock waves through the floor.

"Oh, lovely." Elemi's tone dripped with sarcasm. "Another welcoming committee."

"JR14, options?" Toni's heart raced so hard she barely had enough breath to croak the question out.

"Analysis: direct confrontation is ill-advised. Recommend strategic retreat or diversion," the little android replied.

"We don't have time to retreat," Toni stumbled backward. "Elemi?" She squealed as the Elite drew closer, its crystalline bony fingers reaching for her.

"Darling, if you insist on being reckless, at least let me make your rescue efforts spectacular." Elemi once again stepped between the enforcer and Toni. She raised both hands, and a surge of magenta-pink energy spiraled outward, striking the enforcer.

The blast staggered the massive figure but didn't bring it down.

"Dammit! That didn't work," Toni leaped out of the Elite's grasp and scrambled around Elemi.

"Plan B?" Elemi glanced over her shoulder at JR14.

"Suggestion: target structural weak points to destabilize its form." The pale blue of JR14's bulbous eyes changed to a red-orange as he scanned the enforcer. "Aim for the joints."

With one hand, Elemi aimed and fired at the creature's knee. The crystalline joint shattered, and the enforcer toppled forward with a thunderous crash. Before it could recover, she unleashed another wave of energy, reducing the creature to a heap of shimmering shards.

"Okay. That really was spectacular," Toni admitted with a sheepish grin.

"Naturally." Elemi brushed imaginary dust off her shiny pink shoulder. "Now, shall we rescue your brooding beau?"

Toni startled. *Brooding beau*. With a grin, she followed Elemi as they rushed into Azazel's chamber.

The room was a stark contrast to the chaos outside—eerily quiet.

Stepping through the doorway, her breath caught.

There Azazel was, still suspended in the glowing crystalline cage. His eyes snapped open and widened, locking onto Toni with a mixture of relief and determination.

"Hang on," Toni rushed to the control panel beside the cage. "We'll get you out."

"You'd better get him out now, darling girl," Elemi urged, glancing back at the corridor. "It would be bad form to stick around expecting an encore."

As she spoke her last word, the walls behind Elemi exploded inward with a deafening crack, blowing shards of crystal and glass into the chamber, spraying shrapnel.

Toni shielded herself, putting her hands in front of her clear helmet. The floor shook, making her stumble and fall on her ass. Wincing at the pain, she sat up as a massive crystalline body blazed through the cracked opening, wreathed in an unsteady bluish light that flickered and pulsed erratically in and around him.

Lord Baelon.

His once-pristine clear-blue form was now clouded and cracked, with searing navy-blue lights leaking out, as if he were bleeding. Each step he took sent tremors through the floor, and his clenched hands were radiating energy so fiercely it warped the air around him. His glowing-red eyes burned into her.

"You dare to presume you have bested me?" he roared with raised fists. His voice reverberated with a raw power that shook the chamber.

Gasping, Toni scuttled backward, unable to take her eyes from the towering menace looming over her.

CHAPTER TEN

A zazel exhaled a heavy sigh. It didn't take a psychic to know Toni and the sexbot broke the Nexus Core.

The very air around his cage vibrated with a violent wave, its pressure heavy enough for him to feel, even where he was. Fortunately, it wasn't hard enough to prevent him from breathing, thank the Goddess.

Then something popped into his head. Like a bubble bursting and clearing the air.

Azazel?

The mental clarity of his youngest brother's voice in his head took him aback.

Arakiba?

How was brother speaking to him on their psychic path? What happened to the mechanical setup from his JR unit?

Woo-hoo! Yes, we can talk to each other again.

Azazel winced at Arakiba's gleeful whoop.

I take it Elemi did what she had to and freed the Krystalii from Baelon's psychic hold?

I think so. Azazel hated to admit he wasn't sure. *If that's what happened, they should be back any minute now.* Hopefully.

Great! Listen, Arakiba continued. *The bros and the rest are all orbiting just out of reach of the Krystalii mother ship as we speak. We'll be there in no time to get you and finish phase two. See ya!*

Azazel stifled a groan. Again, his brother left without giving him a chance to ask what he meant. No use in trying to connect with him again. When Arakiba acted like that, he usually wouldn't respond. Asshole.

And just what in the hell was phase two?

A movement outside the chamber caught his eye. There... what was it? He squinted. Yes, it was Toni. By the seven gates, what was she doing? Running through the door as if the wicked god of death, *Uggae,* was hard on her heels.

In desperation, he searched the doorway entrance, expecting to see one of the Elite guards rushing in to stop her. But no. The only thing following her was that shocking-pink android, Elemi.

"Hang on." Toni rushed to the control panel beside the cage that held him. "We'll get you out."

Azazel startled when he heard her. Did that mean that part of his cage had changed with the Core out of commission?

"You'd better get him out now, darling girl." Elemi glanced behind. "It would be bad form to stick around expecting an encore."

A tremor ran through the crystalline cage just before a force shattered the chamber right behind the android. Exploding energy sent cracks racing up the wall as shards of blue, purple, and clear crystal, along with glass rained in a cascade of light and sound.

With a high squeal and her arms crossing in front of her face, Elemi was buried under a mountain of wreckage.

Azazel tensed, his pulse pounding as Lord Baelon emerged from the swirling debris, that massive frame radiating raw, untamed power.

Helpless, he watched Toni as she tried to shield herself, ducking as she raised her hands in front of her clear helmet.

With a violent shake, the upheaval made her stumble and fall.

Frantic, Azazel struggled to free himself, but his efforts amounted to nothing. His body remained a prisoner, dangling, unable to move, much less escape.

His inner beast rolled within him, the menace growing stronger.

Baelon stalked into the room, his once-pristine clear blue form now murky with yawning fissures cracking along his body. Tendrils of steel-blue light discharged from those fractures, like blood oozing down his form. Every thunderous step he took unleashed crackling energy, hurling lightning bolts in all directions. The monster had eyes only for Toni, their red glow blazing in her direction.

"You dare to presume you have bested me?" he roared with raised fists. His voice reverberated with a raw power that shook the chamber.

Mouth wide under her clear helmet, Toni scrambled backward on her hands and feet, the desperation etched on her face.

But she wasn't fast enough. The crystal giant grabbed her.

She screamed and pounded her ineffectual fists against the beast's glass-like fingers.

Toni.

Baelon shook her, then brought her close and exhaled a pulse of energy at her.

Her helmet disappeared, then she stiffened and went limp. Her flaccid body drooped in Baelon's grasp, her dark hair falling in a tangled veil over her face, obscuring the bruises already forming along her pale skin.

The sight of her, unmoving, unprotected, made something deep inside Azazel coil tight. A primal snarl clawed at the edges of his control. He gulped, breathing so hard he became lightheaded. His inner beast became more forceful, as if there was an actual body attached to that part of him, what he believed was his Id—the primitive part of who he was. But this was different. More alive than just a twisted, darker part of his character.

With a casual flick of his wrist, Baelon tossed Toni to the floor like discarded trash.

She landed hard, the sickening thud of impact ignited a violent shudder through Azazel. His fingers curled into fists, his nails digging into his palms as an ancient fury roared to life inside him.

Baelon chuckled, a low, resonant sound that scraped against Azazel's nerves like a dull blade. "Look at you, *Adamou*," he mocked, the labradorite colors that made up his face twisted into cruel amusement. "Caged. Helpless." He leaned closer with a sneer. "And your precious human is not the only one at my mercy."

A searing, unnatural force wrenched at the psychic tether Azazel had shared with his brothers since birth—Arakiba, Asmodel, and Abalim—forcing those psychic threads to open. Azazel recoiled, agony lancing through his skull as Baelon gripped the invisible thread and twisted it with his iron will. The chamber blurred, reality itself bending in the Krystalii's grasp. Azazel strained against his crystalline prison, his breathing ragged.

With a sickening lurch, the space outside his cage folded.

When it unfurled, they were no longer alone.

Ripped from wherever they'd been, Arakiba, Asmodel, and Abalim stood in the Krystalii chamber, their forms flickering in disorientation. When they solidified, shock registered in their eyes as they stared at him, frozen into place like living statues.

Baelon spread his jagged arms in mock magnanimity. "Isn't this better? It wouldn't be sporting if we let you meet your destiny alone, now would it?" His grin sharpened. "Aren't you thrilled that I brought your pitiful family here so you can witness how easily I tear them apart before I do the same to you?"

Azazel's control frayed, and his vision tunneled. The only thing he focused on was his enemy. Every muscle locked as he strained against the walls of his cage.

The crystal hummed with the power that contained him.

His breath turned into heaving, animalistic bursts, his heartbeat a war drum that pounded heavily against his ribs.

He focused on Toni's still form, lying motionless.

Tearing his gaze away, he concentrated on his brothers—his loyal and unwavering clan—as they stood unmoving before the monster, a threat greater than any they had ever faced.

Baelon loomed over all of them. A sneering, gleeful smile exposed his sharp teeth and his jagged features crackled with power.

The unbearable, hopeless sight caused something inside Azazel to snap.

It was the primal force, long buried, long restrained, that answered.

Pain lanced through his bones, searing, stretching, reshaping. Torturous breath tore from Azazel's lungs in a ragged snarl. His flesh twisted, his very essence unraveled into something foreign… primeval and furious.

The crystal cage trembled under the pressure of his shifting form.

Cracks splintered outward, webbing across its surface like lightning streaking through a storm-darkened sky.

Baelon's head whipped in his direction. His smirk faltered.

Azazel's mouth twisted into something that no longer belonged to a man.

His monstrous inner beast awoke.

With a final, earsplitting crack, the crystalline prison exploded outward. Shards sprayed in every direction, and from the wreckage, something massive and inhuman emerged.

Azazel's inner beast was no longer bound.

He was *free*.

Azazel desperately tried to cling to the last thread of sanity as the beast within him tore free. But any control he had ended in a violent rupture—sinew snapping, bones warping, as his mind split in two. His half, that of the man, was shoved into the back seat, reduced to a passenger inside his own skin. The new reality rattled him deeper than any danger he'd ever faced before. The other? A hulking predator, drunk with rage and instinct. His entire being was bombarded with feral, raw fury—along with the sickening euphoria of anticipating the upcoming battle.

His creature turned to the haunting sight of Toni lying motionless on the cracked crystal floor. The sight of her still, unmoving figure caused his monster to roar so loud, it ripped through the chamber and caused the walls and floor to crack and splinter. The Beast drew himself up, his gigantic form that towering over Baelon. A flash of movement caught his eye.

He turned—then froze. The mirrored wall reflected a monster forged of muscle and shadow, a creature carved from a nightmare of rage and ancient instinct. Gone were his human features, replaced by something so untamed and primal—a terrifying transformation of ultimate power that radiated from him.

Obsidian-like scales covered his hulking frame, each plate dark and gleaming with a preternatural sheen that seemed to drink in the light. Faint crimson veins pulsed beneath the surface, the glow spreading in rhythmic waves that hinted at something vile thrumming in his core. Corded muscles rippled beneath the armor of scales with every predatory shift of his stance. His forelimbs—massive and knotted with sinew—ended in claws of blackened steel, each curved talon longer than a dagger and honed to a killing edge. One flex of those monstrous hands promised the power to rend through anything he wished as if it were parchment, and the way they gouged furrows into the crystal floor left no doubt he would.

Gone was the quiet contemplation. In its place was a being made up of wild, frantic, primitive energy that strengthened every nerve, every muscle. His eyes now burned with an eerie, golden fire—eyes that promised utter destruction.

Baelon raised a crystalline arm in defense, but he was too late.

Without a thought, The Beast unleased Azazel's psychic energy, freezing the Krystalii in place before his claws slashed through Baelon's chest. He cut deep into the apatite structure of the Krystalii's body.

A fractured, resonant scream erupted from the tyrant as he staggered backward. Navy-blue energy spilled from the wounds, oozing from him like smoldering lava.

The Beast did not relent. He barreled into Baelon with crushing force, driving the alien overlord onto the shattered remains of the crystal cage littered on the floor.

Baelon twisted, and his jagged fingers sparkled with psychic energy. He lashed out with a concussive blast meant to throw The Beast off-balance.

The air trembled, the force enough to send debris spiraling outward in all directions.

The Beast absorbed the impact as the Krystalii power saturated every cell of his body. Snarling, he clamped one massive, clawed paw around Baelon's throat, lifting the despot off the ground.

The Krystalii's crystalline form flickered, his pulsating glow erratic as if he fought to restore himself.

But The Beast wouldn't allow that to happen. Holding fast to the struggling alien, he brought the helpless tyrant to the end of his snout and howled with a rumbling roar.

The once-omnipotent alien now faced the one thing Azazel had spent centuries restraining. Caught in his impenetrable grip.

With a satisfied sneer, The Beast squeezed, and his claws pierced the fragile crystalline structure of Baelon's throat.

A sickening crack echoed around the chamber as Baelon clawed at The Beast's grip, his fingers scraping against obsidian flesh. Not that it did any good. He found no purchase.

Baelon's eyes flickered as rage and something dangerously close to fear reflected in their crystalline depths.

The Beast bared his set of double-rowed fangs and brought the Krystalii closer.

"Look who's helpless now, *dalkhu*." The heavy words came from deep within him.

With a single, devastating motion, he hurled Baelon across the chamber.

The Krystalii's body struck the wall with a thunderous impact, shattering it into a kaleidoscope of splintered crystals. Diverse colors of blue energy crackled through Baelon's form, flickering like a dying star.

The Beast advanced, muscles coiling, determined to end this.

Baelon sat up, coughing out pieces of his fractured form. He lifted his head and sneered, his voice coming out in a hoarse rasp. "You think this changes anything?" He staggered to his feet, crystalline shards and dust breaking off with each movement. "You are too late. My kind will decimate yours even if I'm gone."

Azazel shook his metaphysical head as he watched the scene unfold. That was going to be Baelon's biggest mistake... taunting the creature.

The Beast roared, a thunderous screech so loud it shook the ground. Then, with a final, explosive surge, he lunged—pure fury in motion. His claws flashed, sharp as unbreakable razors, his primitive hunger howling for Krystalii blood.

Keeping his psionic hold on Baelon tight, The Beast struck. He moved like a force of nature—unstoppable, inevitable. His claws raked across the Krystalii's body, and each swipe sent deeper cracks that splintered through that crystalline form.

Dark-blue energy leaked faster from Baelon like a geyser as he staggered back. His arrogance crumbled alongside his fractured body.

The Beast couldn't... wouldn't stop. He'd waited too long, endured too much to deny his very instinct. Every moment of restraint, every ounce of control Azazel had ever forced over him, was long gone. His rage burst free, no longer contained, and he seized his prize with unstoppable force.

Driving his massive fist into Baelon's chest, he lifted the crystalline tyrant off his feet and slammed him against the jagged wall of the chamber.

The impact sent another shock wave and created cracks that raced across the structure like shards of lightning.

Baelon's glowing eyes widened, and his jagged, sharp teeth bared in something between terror and disbelief. He raised one trembling hand, energy crackling between his fingers.

The Beast's claws came down and crushed the gathered power before the Krystalii could let it loose. "**Enough**," he growled, his voice a guttural snarl, savage and far from human.

Baelon gasped. His crystalline frame flickered, and the once-imposing icy-blue sheen of his body dimmed, its former clarity now turning colorless.

The pressure shifted, growing heavier and charged with something beyond the physical.

Even housed within The Beast, Azazel sensed the way Baelon's presence unraveled.

The fragile balance of the Krystalii's existence slipped through fractured cracks throughout his body.

He wheezed, his words layered in a fragmented chuckle. "You fool. You... cannot... stop what has begun." His voice was weaker now, distorted, as though he spoke through a static connection.

The Beast tightened his grip around Baelon's throat. "**Doesn't matter. You won't live to see it.**"

Rearing back with a roar, he sang in triumph as he delivered one final, brutal blow. His claws tore through the last fragile hold Baelon had on this realm.

The Krystalii's body shattered into a thousand fragments of fractured blue light. For a brief second, the space where Baelon had stood rippled, collapsing inward as the crystal fragments flickered and disintegrated, vanishing into nothingness.

The only thing left was... silence.

The Beast stood, his breath ragged, his massive chest heaving with each exhale. His clawed paws curled, then unfurled. The restless energy of the battle still thrummed through his veins. The weight of his transformation pulsed and lingered just beneath the surface, reluctant to recede. He turned, locking his eyes on Toni's unconscious form. His rage faded and was replaced by something far sharper. Fear.

For Toni.

The battle was over. But for Azazel, deeply entrenched inside The Beast, the actual fight had just begun.

Holy God. Toni groaned. Hopefully, someone got the license plate of the damn truck that ran her over. With a grimace, she rolled over onto her back. Taking a deep breath, she coughed when some fine dust landed in her nose and made her sneeze. She waved a hand over her face, trying to clear the air.

Rubbing her eyes, she took a chance and opened them... and blinked. Several times. Filling her vision were three of the handsomest men she'd ever seen. The blond on her left had steel-gray eyes that twinkled with mischief.

"Well, hello there, pretty lady," he said, placing his crooked elbow on his bent knee. "You doin' okay?"

"Arakiba," admonished the man on her right. "Do I have to bring in Morgan to make you behave?"

"Bro!" Arakiba snorted, shrugging gleefully. "Just being friendly, is all, Aba."

The man who reprimanded the blond had to be the leader of the trio. While his tone was playful, the underlying solemnity was unmistakable.

She took in his striking appearance and swallowed a moan of appreciation.

His skin was so dark it gleamed with purple highlights. His shoulder-length black hair, a mass of corkscrew curls, rested on his massive, muscular shoulders.

"Ignore them," said the man next to the blond. His Native American features were near perfect, a symmetrical creation that was beyond handsome. He gave the other man an admonishing glare before focusing on her and putting his hand over his heart. "I'm Asmodel." He thumbed the blond man next to him. "That's Arakiba, and over there," he nodded to the dark giant across from him, "Is Abalim." He stretched his hand to her. "Can I help you up?" His eyes, an astounding mixture of chestnut-brown and leaf-green with a starburst of gold flecks, gave her an open and friendly look, w

hich helped calm Toni's frayed nerves.

She scrunched her nose. "Yes, thank you." She took his hand and sat up, then frowned as she glanced around. "What happened? And where's Bae...*lon*?" Her eyes widened when she noticed the huge creature over Asmodel's shoulder.

It was some kind of monster. A humongous beast standing on four legs, heaving and snorting as its breath scissored in and out, creating a plume of smoke with each exhale.

Its fierce gold eyes stared right at her.

"What's that?" she whispered, tightening her hold on Asmodel's hand.

The creature's eyes focused on their clasped hands and lowered its head with a rumbling whine.

"What's it doing?"

Arakiba chuckled and separated her hand from Asmodel's. "He knows who his momma is."

She gave Asmodel an awkward glance before staring back at the beast with a huff. "What in the hell does that mean?"

"It means—" Asmodel frowned at Arakiba. "—underneath all that fierce exterior is our brother, Azazel."

Toni stood and faced him. "Brother?" She kept half an eye on the creature. The thing looked like a cross between a panther and a mythical dragon. And it whined. Its serpentine tail wagged behind it, moving so hard it was easy to believe the darn thing's butt would fly off any second now.

"And you're telling me that's… Azazel?" She gasped, covering her mouth with her hand. "That can't be… how… what?" Too many questions. Not enough words.

"Listen." Abalim took her shoulders in a comforting grip and looked her in the eyes. "I know this is a lot to take in. But I assure you Baelon is gone."

Arakiba snorted and crossed his muscular arms over his firm chest.

"But I'm guessing you've been around a lot of psychic activity lately," Abalim continued, ignoring Arakiba. "So, it shouldn't surprise you that Azazel is a strong one. True?"

Toni peered closer at the beast. "I guess so." She swung her attention to Abalim. "Hey, since you claim he's your brother, are you psychics, too?" Crossing her arms, she took in the other two. "All of you?"

Asmodel nodded. "Yes, we are."

"Okay, so does that mean you can all turn—"

"I'm sorry, but there isn't time to answer all your questions." Abalim interrupted. "We're aboard an out-of-control galactic spaceship from another dimension that we have to get a handle on."

"Organic units."

Toni breathed a sigh of relief when she heard the mechanical tone of JR14 loud enough for all to hear as he buzzed to settle on Toni's shoulder. For the first time, she noticed the clear helmet over her head was gone. The air was breathable, but a sharp ozone scent made her crinkle her nose.

Do not worry about the air, Sensos whispered to her. *It is perfectly fine to breathe it.*

"Multiple Krystalii entities aboard this vessel exhibit erratic and destructive behaviors due to the demise of Lord Baelon and the Nexus Core, which now pose an imminent threat to us," JR14 intoned. "Recommendation: immediate neutralization is the most efficient course of action to prevent catastrophic system failure."

"Yes, we'll have to…"

Before Abalim could finish, a horrible realization occurred to Toni. "Oh my God… Elemi!" She rushed to the pile of shredded glass and crystals where she'd last seen the sexbot get buried. "Elemi? Are you there? Answer me!" She dropped to her knees, intending to pluck pieces of the sharp objects off the android.

"Elemi?" Arakiba's anxious voice followed close behind her. "She's under all this?"

When Toni nodded, he put his hand on her shoulder. "Stand back. I've got this."

Glancing up at him, she noticed the determined expression stamped on his face.

A tight line formed on his full lips, and his gray eyes narrowed.

Without another word, she scrambled out of the way when he lifted his palms facing up.

Bits and pieces of the broken shards rose, before disintegrating into thin air. It exposed the pink android lying on her side with her glassy eyes open.

A blast of heat covered Toni's back as the sound of a rumbling purr above her head made her freeze. Out of the corner of her eye, she saw a sea of obsidian right behind her. Something hard nudged her hand, as if begging for her touch.

She trembled. How could she forget that humongous beast right behind her? He was so big, she only came up to its knees as the rest of it towered over her like a massive building.

"Don't worry," Asmodel stood next to her, facing the creature. "He won't hurt you."

"Oh yeah?" Toni refused to turn around. She'd rather watch Arakiba croon and fawn over the unmoving pink android. "Then why is it whimpering and licking its lips like I'm next on the menu?"

A line of drool hit her shoulder. *Thank God she had Sensos on. Maybe the suit would save her from those humongous fangs and claws. Maybe Sensos would turn her into the Flash so she could run fast enough to escape a crunching death.*

Or maybe fish can climb trees.

Do not concern yourself. Sensos told her. *This male is your mate, and he would die to protect you.*

That startled her. *Mate? How could this monster be some kind of mate to her?*

What those men told you is the truth. What you call a monster is the male you know as Azazel. Sensos' smooth reply belied the strange story it told her. *He changed form when the Krystalii threatened you, giving him the ability to eliminate Baelon. I assure you, you are in no danger from him.*

Yeah, but if you're wrong and I get eaten, I'll blame it all on you when I write my memoir, she mentally retorted.

"I'm trying to convince him to change back," Asmodel continued as he studied the creature with an amused grin.

It took Toni a minute to get caught up in the conversation. Talking in two different conversations was confusing.

"But so far I can't get through to him." Asmodel shrugged and faced her.

Toni peered at the handsome man with a frown. She sidestepped, trying to get away from the gigantic beast behind her. The darn thing only shuffled with her, scooting across the floor and snorting a huffing rumble right above her head.

Abalim stood next to Asmodel and eyed the beast with his arms crossed. "I can't get through to him either." He looked down at Toni, then at JR14 on her shoulder. "Any recommendations, JR?"

"Hang on." Arakiba drew their attention before the bot answered.

Toni sucked on her bottom lip when she watched him hold Elemi in his arms.

He stood in a widened stance as Elemi's prone body lay stiff and lifeless in his muscular embrace. "I'm going to take Elemi back to *Elemi* to reboot her. If you need me, you know how to get me. Later."

He and the android disappeared.

The man's declaration of taking Elemi back to Elemi made zero sense. Not to mention how he vanished like that. Toni opened her mouth, but when the beast nudged the back of her head, she stilled. Nope, not gonna move one bit. *Maybe the slobbering thing would go away if she pretended it wasn't there.*

Glancing at the remaining brothers, she gasped.

Without a sound, another creature stood where Arakiba had been.

Toni jerked and put a fist over her thundering heart. *What the hell is that?* Its slim body was the epitome of elegance, with a gooey luminescent skin that she swore glowed. Its two arms had elongated limbs, each ending in long, triple-jointed, elegant fingers. What she found amazing was it appeared neither male nor female.

Studying it made her swallow with a dry throat.

On the top of its oblong head was a crown of golden spines, and it had almond-shaped eyes that shimmered in an array of mesmerizing colors.

"This is Rerqel," Abalim introduced the creature. "He's a... ah... colleague I met on Qorath, where I found your friend Lisa."

"Lisa?" Toni squeaked.

The beast rubbed its nose against her side, purring.

"Is she okay?" It'd be nice to know if one of her friends from that prison cell on FiPan made it out.

"The human female Lisa is indeed in optimal health."

The alien glided close enough it was easy to see it wore some kind of plated armor under its flowing robes.

"And is awaiting the return of her mate." Its gangly fingers waved in Abalim's direction.

For the first time, Toni noticed the strange way the creature talked. The words didn't come out of its razor-thin mouth. Instead, it spoke in her head. Flat and unemotional but layered as though it spoke in a multitude of voices. *Well, wasn't that just eerie as hell?*

"Rerqel and his people plan to take over this ship and house the Krystalii on their planet." Abalim stated.

The firm conviction in his tone told Toni he didn't doubt a word he said.

Asmodel narrowed his eyes at the alien. "You're going to take this ship to your planet and somehow take the billions of Krystalii on it to live there?" He glanced at Abalim. "How's that possible?"

JR14 buzzed off her shoulder until he was in the middle of the group. "Clarification: in accordance with their advanced interdimensional translocation technology"—the bot intoned— "the Xeltrains of Qorath have devised a method to transport the remaining Krystalii through stabilized rift corridors, overlaying their perceived reality onto an artificial construct indistinguishable from their native world. This ensures the Krystalii containment within a controlled dimensional pocket, eliminating their existential threat to this universe while preserving the species inside their cognitive stability."

"How do you know that, gizmo-bot?" Toni slapped her palms on her hips.

"Fact: my brother, JR15, informed me in extensive detail of his interaction with Abalim and the Xeltrain on Qorath," JR14 replied in his matter-of-fact tone.

Oh, sure. That made perfect sense. She dropped her hands when the beast licked the back of her neck. "Stop that!" Without thinking, she turned and swatted its nose that was as big as her head. *Oh shit. Now she'd done it.*

The animal yanked its head back with a sniffle. Its once-gold eyes were now warm mahogany filled with luminescent tears.

How dare the darn thing turn its big, sorrowful puppy-dog cartoon eyes on me? She wasn't maid of stone, you know. "Oh, I'm sorry," Toni crooned and rubbed its springy dark-purple nose. It was soft as a dog's and just as wet. When it didn't bite her hand off, she wagged her finger at it. "Now, stop licking me and behave."

The beast dropped onto its belly with a bone-jarring thud, the sheer mass of its body sending a shudder through the floor. Loose shards of crystal and glass skipped away in frantic little hops, and powdery dust puffed upward in gritty clouds. Beneath its bulk, the ground groaned and shifted, a faint tremor rippling outward as if the ship itself recoiled. Its eggplant-colored tongue lolled from its maw, glistening in the dim light, as a slow string of saliva stretched toward the floor before snapping free.

"That is a fine specimen of a *Ugrota* from the extinct planet of *Nierilia.*" Rerqel nodded his enormous head at the creature behind Toni. "I believe I will take it to Qorath as well."

"That won't be necessary," Abalim interjected, standing in the Xeltrain's line of sight to the beast. "He's my brother who has adopted this shape. He stays with us."

The shrug the alien gave made Toni uneasy.

"As you wish."

"Asmodel," Abalim turned and addressed his brother. "Let's get Azazel back to normal so we can join Arakiba aboard *Elemi* and head to the Consortium palace. Are you ready?"

Asmodel nodded with a glance at Toni. "We're going to need her to do that." His smile was encouraging. "Think you can help us bring him back?"

Toni narrowed her eyes at the beast, looking down at her from its prone position. Falling into its familiar brown eyes pleading for help, she sighed.

"There's nothing I'd rather do."

Helping Azazel shapeshift back to his human form turned out to be easier than Toni thought it'd be. The hardest thing she wrestled with was approaching the menacing, humongous beast with its double-rowed fangs, spiky head, and thick, sharp claws and believing it wasn't going to attack. Her only solace was the undeniable love and acceptance deep in the beast's golden-brown eyes.

"Place your hands on him," advised Abalim.

The sonorous tone in his voice half-hypnotized her, enough to calm her frayed nerves. Without looking away from the rich welcome of Azazel's eyes, she placed her palms against the side of the creature's jaw, threading her fingers through several small spikes protruding across his prominent cheekbones. The leathery skin was surprisingly soft, like a well-worn jacket she'd had since her teenage years. The one that made her traditional mother moan every time Toni put it on.

"That's it." Abalim stood on her right while Asmodel took his place on her left. "Now, close your eyes and feel him. Indulge in that link between the two of you."

His voice lowered, making it hard to hear him. But the solid sense of trust between the brothers told her she had no reason to fear they'd let anything happen to her. If this didn't work, they wouldn't hesitate to pluck her to safety.

Taking a deep breath, she did as he asked and closed her eyes. Her heart raced in the dark—until Azazel's presence wrapped around her, steadying everything. While she couldn't "see" him, she knew he was right there with her.

I am here to assist you as well. Sensos promised.

With the suit's help, Toni merged with Azazel. Her consciousness blended with the very makeup of the man himself. She sensed not only his confusion and panic, but she also caught his overwhelming kindness and sagacity that tempted others to rely on his calm and practical outlook on things.

But he'd lost his way. He feared he'd somehow failed and couldn't go back to being who he was. He believed it was safer to stay as the beast and not have to face his incompetence.

Yeonin. Lover. *Come back to me.* Even with her mind melded with his, she caressed the side of the beast's head, stroking, pouring all her love and acceptance into her touch. *I need you.* Any fear she had of the creature in her hands melted away. She kissed the side of his snout, bathing it with her soft lips. *Remember, you promised to take me to that beach once the danger was gone. You weren't lying to me, now, were you?* She visualized the two of them together like they were on the dream beach, intertwined in the dance of making love. *I want... no, I need you in my life.*

A flash of his masculine strength stroked through her, causing her womb to tighten.

My hebat, came Azazel's firm voice, filled with virile pride. *I would never lie to you. What kind of man would I be if I did not honor my vow to you?*

That's right, bub. You'd better come back so you can keep your promise. She kept her demand firm and non-negotiable. *Don't you want to experience making love in real life? I know I do.*

As my lady so wishes.

Step back! Sensos's cry made her eyes fly open. With a tug from the suit, she jumped away from the beast.

With a violent shake of his head, the spikes along his skull clanged together, echoing like clashing swords in a duel. Then it rose to its four legs, its whole body shuddering like a wet hound shaking off water.

Toni's mouth dropped open, her eyes widening in stunned disbelief as the creature became engulfed in a thousand stars that burst across its massive form.

A blinding spectral light took over before it faded away, leaving a very human, very naked man sprawled face down on the floor. His mouth was slightly parted, and his eyes were closed.

"Oh my God!" Toni raced to kneel beside him. "Is he okay?" She held her breath and glanced at the two men and the spindly alien behind her. Not waiting for them to confirm, she turned back to Azazel.

His silky black hair covered his face.

With trembling fingers, she swept the strands away.

Asmodel chuckled. "Yeah, he's just fine." He knelt beside her with a confident grin. "It's hard to process going between forms the first time."

Toni's eyebrows rose. "The first time?" She looked back at the unconscious man. "You mean he's never done this before?" She waved up and down his spectacular, muscular, mouthwatering male body. She cleared her throat, trying her best to remain detached and not drool over the irresistible sight. Her eyes wandered over the firm musculature of his back before landing on his plump, firm, nibble-worthy behind. Dragging her gaze away, she again studied Asmodel.

"I'm afraid so," Abalim answered behind her. "Not only has he never shifted before..."

Toni looked over her shoulder at him.

He glanced at his brother next to her. "None of us had a clue he could."

She wrinkled her nose and spoke to Asmodel. "Is that true? But weren't you all raised together? Didn't you all claim you were psychics to boot? Like, read each other's minds and stuff?"

Asmodel's prominent cheekbones turned a shade of dark rose. "Yes, and that's why he and I are so embarrassed." He nodded to Abalim. "Now that Azazel changed into this... what did your friend say it was?"

"An *Ugrota*." Rerqel supplied. The alien stayed in the background, watching and unmoving.

Asmodel nodded. "Yeah, that. When he changed into that beast, it loosened all the fears and concerns he had about housing this animal, bringing him to the forefront of his mind. Apparently, he was afraid if he ever let it out, he'd never find his way back." He hung his head. "I'm ashamed we never knew how hard he struggled to keep that part of himself under control. We should've been there to help him through his fears."

"I think you're being too hard on yourself," Toni admonished. She smoothed her hand over Azazel's soft hair. "Maybe it was better for him to wait until I was here to help him work through it." With a soft sigh, she smiled at the sleeping man. "Is there a place away from this mess to let him recover? I've got to be there when he wakes up." She glanced at the men with narrowed eyes and an unyielding smile.

Azazel's awareness crept back in sluggish waves. He smiled when it occurred to him he could move with ease, without pain or strain. His grin slid away as the memory of being taken over by The Beast made him catch his breath. Was it gone? Would it come back?

I am never gone, the voice of The Beast said in his head. *I am a part of you, just as you are a part of me. And now that you have fully embraced my existence, we will live in harmony together, now and forever.*

Azazel relaxed at the admonishing but accepting tone in The Beast's voice. For the first time, he recognized who and what the creature was. While it *was* a part of him, it was also a separate entity that was a natural part of his genetic makeup. He could not deny the beast any more than he could deny the delicate arch of his ears. It just was.

What shall I call you? Continuing to think of him as "The Beast" didn't seem right.

You may call me **Irgon**, the Beast announced. *It means "disrupter" in the* **Ugrota** *tongue.*

A fitting name. The creature sure disrupted his life.

I have taken care of that which threatened us. I must sleep now. Do not awaken me unless you once again find yourself unable to dispose of an impending death threat.

At that last word, Azazel sensed the beast withdrew into a part of him where he'd always been. How strange it was to find himself in a symbiotic relationship with an alien entity. *I doubt things will ever be normal again.*

And speaking of normal... the feel of a warm, supple, naked female curled in his arms grabbed his attention. Her soft breath against his chest prompted him to slide his hand across her curves to her hip, then shift to cup the tempting globes of her ass. His fingers tightened on the pliable skin and pressed her against his larger frame.

"Azazel." Toni moaned his name, wrapping her arm around his neck and pulling him toward her until mere inches separated their mouths. "I can't believe I almost lost you," she whispered against his lips.

"Ah, *hebat*," he crooned. "Do not worry. I don't plan on going anywhere." Keeping his touch gentle, he moved his hand to caress one of her feminine cheekbones before twining her hair between his fingers. He brought the strands to his nose and inhaled, his eyes on hers. He watched the cerulean blue of her eyes dilate until the black pupil usurped the vibrant color, highlighting the love in her gaze. Her cheeks bloomed as a flush of color spread across her skin.

The primal need for the woman in his arms tore through him—an overwhelming sensation he'd spent his life denying he could feel. It was a wildness inside him that had nothing to do with his inner beast. It was all him. This barbaric urge to claim his woman and damn anything else.

But he fought the urge. Now wasn't the time to become some mindless animal bent on conquering the woman in his arms. This courageous, bold woman deserved so much more than a quick tumble from someone acting like a bumbling youth.

"My love, you have no idea what you do to me," Azazel confessed, putting his forehead to hers. "I have always been the inviolable one, a peaceful man who feared no one and maintained his calm in any situation." He licked his lips. "But one look at you, and I melt inside. I never knew I'd feel as strong as this about someone. I not only crave to join my body with yours, but my heart is also full for the first time in my life." He swallowed and ignored the rush of heat creeping up his neck. "I confess I've always been lonely. But now… now for the first time, I feel like I've found a part of myself that was missing." He huffed. "*Ezeru*! It's so hard to express the right words to let you know what you truly mean to me."

Toni's eyelids lowered. Smiling, she wrapped her arms around his neck. "I don't need words, Azazel. Even though I love hearing you say them." She put one of her palms over his chest, where his heart thundered. "But I can sense how you feel here." She leaned in and kissed him, a languorous and sultry kiss of seduction before she pulled back. "Never doubt that I feel the same way." Her half-lidded eyes studied where she petted him. "I warn you"—her voice lowered with a steady tone—"once we do this, you'll never get rid of me."

Her sultry grin warmed him.

"One thing I can promise you is you'll never know the meaning of 'being alone' ever again."

Azazel's shoulders relaxed. "Thank the Goddess," he declared. "I'm looking forward to being with you, no matter where the future leads us. For us, there's no going back."

He propped himself on his elbow to look into her eyes.

When Toni leaned in, his attention was drawn to her swaying breasts.

"No going back." She caressed the side of his face.

Toni grinned as the man in her arms focused on her chest. "Azazel—" She traced her hand across his scruffy jawline. "—why do I feel like you aren't paying attention to what I'm saying?" She put her forefinger under his chin and lifted his head for his eyes to meet hers. "Look at me... not my boobs."

"But I can't help it," he murmured, his dark eyes roaming back to her chest, making her nipples pucker in response. "You're so distracting."

Toni ran her trembling fingers through Azazel's long hair as he helped himself to those quivering mounds, licking first one nipple, then the other. When he tugged her pebbled tips with his blunt teeth, her breath came out in ragged gasps.

He drew her sensitive skin into the blazing inferno of his mouth.

She let out a rough moan.

Through half-lidded eyes, she feasted on the sight of him as his mouth devoured her bosom.

"I love watching you do that," she confessed. "It's the sexiest thing I've ever seen."

After one savage graze of his teeth against her sensitive skin, she threw her head back and squeezed her eyes shut to surrender to the sensation. With her eyes closed, the raging passion inside her rose. Her emotions joined with his, allowing her to experience his building hunger as well as her own.

His every touch, every lick, drove her passion into something tangible and unique. The pull of his mouth on her feverish skin expanded her carnal hunger. With each swipe, he sent a nuclear charge to her sex, dampening and tightening the core between her legs, creating a torrent of cream between her thighs.

He pulled away, his stare intense and direct.

She became lost in the mahogany depths of his eyes. Her breath caught at the sight of the masculine possession stamped there. A man who was the embodiment of desire itself—intent on unleashing every wicked plan he'd been saving just for her.

The slumbering sensuality on his expression made something snap inside her. She pulled away from him and pushed on his chest to make him lie on his back. Not wasting any time, she threw her leg over his trim hips and straddled him, settling her core against his firm stomach. Leaning down, she trailed kisses along his neck.

Underneath her, his stomach muscles tightened as the rigid steel of his cock nestled along the crease of her buttocks. His hand slid up her inner thigh before he slipped a couple of his fingers inside her.

She gasped, and her inner muscles clamped down on him like a vise. He eased his fingers out, and she whimpered at the emptiness that followed.

His magnetic dark eyes brightened as he brought his glistening fingers to his mouth, which curved into a wicked smile. When he drew them out, his lids lowered. "Nothing tastes as good as you do." He whispered.

She sucked in a breath. His declaration made her head swim.

In one smooth motion, he rolled her under him once again and claimed one of her breasts, lavishing them with his talented tongue.

The spicy fragrance of their combined musk filled the air.

He teased and kissed the slope of her breasts as one of his hands explored her body, leaving an inferno in his wake.

She arched into him, writhing with a long, drawn-out cry.

"You have the most beautiful breasts, *hebat*," Azazel murmured, his focus on that part of her. "I could spend all day worshiping them." His dramatic sigh made her giggle. "But, alas, there are other tempting territories that beg to be explored."

He kissed his way down, from the puckered tips of her breasts to navel. With measured movements, he spent some time there, showering her with playful nips before moving lower. Lifting her hips, he wedged his shoulders between her thighs and held her open for his devious exploration.

In a daze, Toni rested on her elbows to watch Azazel focus on her.

In an unhurried motion, he lowered his lips to her straining bud and gave it a gentle suckle.

A keening wail escaped her throat when he intensified his attack, his mouth and tongue propelling her willing body into a tense inferno that caught her by surprise. She exploded into an unexpected, devastatingly wild orgasm.

Her head dropped back to the soft surface. *Damn, that didn't take long, did it? Jeez, how embarrassing was that?*

With her mind stuck in a satisfied fog, it was hard to notice Azazel when he left her quivering and shifted positions to kneel between her spread thighs.

With a quick jerk, he draped her knees over his crooked elbows.

She peered at him through heavy-lidded lashes, and her lips parted with a ragged breath as he entered her in one powerful thrust.

Sobbing his name, Toni held him deep inside.

He suckled the hard tip of her nipple into his mouth, all while his hips jackknifed with steadfast thrusts into her. Powerful surges, again and again and again.

She felt not only his body hammering inside her but sensed his consciousness wrapping around her mind as well. With each powerful drive, he stayed merged with her, mind to mind, in a connection that took her to a never-imagined higher peak. An experience so scorching and profound, she became desperate to savor as much of him as she could. Pressing her inner muscles hard, she clamped on his erection even as her slick heat spilled around his dominating flesh with each claiming drive he made.

She yelped his name in a strangled cry, a heartfelt plea for mercy for him to release her building sexual tension.

"Not yet, *hebat*," he rasped. "You were made for pleasure." He growled. A sound like the snarl from the beast he'd turned into. "For my pleasure."

Each stroke of his body into hers tightened the strain building in her womb, from her clit to her quivering channel. A band contracted between those two pleasure points, then stretched tighter, the need for more growing as each second passed.

"Azazel," she moaned. "I beg you…"

For what, she wasn't sure. The only thing she knew was her body burned as it strove for the final pinnacle to relieve her of the oncoming tsunami she hoped she would survive.

"That's it, Antonia, take all of me." His expression was tight, his eyes razor-sharp with intent. "Now, give it to me. Give me all of you."

"Yes," she hissed.

With her verbal capitulation, Toni let go. Her body released a ripple that stormed through her, shaking her from head to toe. A downpour of intense pleasure rained out from her womb and overtook all her senses. She fell through space and time as her muscles clamped around him, milking him into becoming a part of her.

Then, with a forceful grunt, Azazel's hips jerked, plunging them over the edge with one last forceful thrust.

Her internal muscles gripped his cock, holding him tight as his heated release jetted inside her. In reaction, she closed her eyes and hissed as spasms bolted through her. It was a while before she could let out a sigh of contentment. With sheer will, she pried her eyes open, needing to drink in the sight of the man above her. His smug, thoroughly male grin tugged a laugh from her.

He grinned, then gathered her into his arms, and nestled his nose into the nape of her neck.

Toni wrapped her legs around his taut waist and locked her arms behind the thick muscles of his neck, desperate to keep him deep inside her. Pulling back to look at him, she watched the play of open emotions dance across his face. She didn't need to read his mind to know what he felt. Their inner connection remained strong, giving her a glimpse of his satisfaction with the experience.

Their minds settled into a comfortable alignment with each other. The intense fire hadn't gone away, it only smoldered, waiting for the merest spark to light it once again. She was convinced that no matter how many times he took possession of her or she of him, their firestorm would remain eternal.

"I'm in love with you, Antonia Soo-Min Choi." Azazel pulled back, a tremor in his breath as he searched her face. His eyes, open and unshielded, held his confession long before he spoke.

Toni's grin was so wide it made her cheeks hurt. "And I, you, Azazel." She threaded her fingers through the silky strands of the sepia-brown hair at the side of his head. "I love feeling how fiercely you love me." She cocked her head with a cheeky grin. "And I'm positive we'll grow to love one another the more we are together." With a playful nudge on his shoulder, she pouted. "But... I believe you have some explaining about how I know that."

His playful leer made her giggle.

"Oh, I'll do more than tell you, I'll show you. But first—" He raised his head and looked around with his brows furrowed. "—just where the hell are we?"

Toni threw her arms around his neck and laughed.

EPILOGUE

"**O**h darling."

The petulant feminine voice echoing in the room made Azazel jump.

"I am so hurt you don't recognize me."

The woman in his arms covered her mouth with her delicate fingers and giggled.

He gave her a mock glare. "Oh, you find this funny, eh, Toni?" With a rumbling growl, he wrapped her in his arms and rolled her over and over on the soft mattress in a playful wrestle.

Toni's giggles turned into jubilant laughter.

"Honestly, children." The effeminate voice admonished in an exasperated tone. "Playtime is over." The sound of hands clapping came across like a scolding grandmother. "Your presence is required in the main conference room."

When Azazel found a particular ticklish spot at Toni's waist, he exclaimed, "Aha!"

Toni squirmed with a protesting howl. "Stop, Az!" She pushed his hands away. "I can't breathe!"

He would not be deterred. Instead of teasing her stomach and waist, he rolled them over until she was pinned beneath him. He leaned into her neck and blew a raspberry against the pebbling skin there.

The next thing he knew, she'd grabbed the sides of his head and pulled his mouth to hers. Any attempt at teasing flew away as he sank into the kiss. Then it hit him. Her lush bare skin lay flush against him, ready for him to dive in. With eager hands and mouth, he explored as much of her tempting landscape as he could reach until he found himself pulled away, free-floating above the bed. It was if gravity had taken a vacation.

"*Elemi!*" Toni squealed.

Azazel grabbed the drifting woman and wrapped her in his arms.

She slid her arms around his neck and wrapped her legs around his waist with a tight squeeze.

Keeping in mind how touchy the sentient spaceship was, Azazel took care with the words he chose. "I am so sorry we didn't listen to you, *ninlil*." It was hard, but he kept a smile from escaping as he spoke. "We promise to heed you."

"Humph," the ship responded. "I do like that 'Lady of Airspace' title. Yes, I suppose I'll forgive you. This time."

Thankfully, *Elemi* didn't turn on the gravity all at once. The gradual return of their normal weight allowed them to touch down onto the floor next to the wide bed with sure footing.

"Well," Toni snickered. "at least you know where you are now."

He nodded. "Yes, when my brothers and I went to FiPan to look for you and the other missing women, we came on this ship." Glancing at the ceiling, he continued. "And a most gracious host she was and is."

Wow, he sure can lay it on thick.

It startled him when he heard Toni's thoughts in his mind. While in his beast form, he must've opened a clear, private track that allowed him to connect with her. It took him a moment to get familiar with that psychic channel to see how she reacted to it.

Don't you think it's better to stay on her good side? He tested the link.

Toni smirked. *Yeah, I'd hate for her to shove us out of an airlock.*

"Do you remember how to get to the conference center?" *Elemi* asked, her tone huffy. "Or do I have to assist you?"

"Thank you, *Elemi*." Azazel once again fell into the vivid blue of Toni's eyes. "But that's unnecessary. Please tell my brothers we will be there in a few moments."

"Oh, all right." *Elemi* said exasperated. "But I warn you. Don't make me come here looking for you again."

He sensed when the sentient part of the ship withdrew.

"Um—" Toni glanced down at her naked body. "—think we can find some clothes to wear first?"

By the Goddess, what a wonderful naked body she had. Azazel sucked in a breath, doing his best to divert any carnal thoughts creeping in.

"Let's see what I can do." He stepped back, still holding her hand as they faced each other. "Imagine what you'd like to have on, and I'll create it for you."

Her eyes widened. "Really?"

Azazel gave her a reassuring nod. "Absolutely. Close your eyes and visualize your favorite outfit."

It was easy for him to pick up the clean lines and vivid colors she preferred. He created a fitted brown leather jacket over a soft, slightly oversized dark-red blouse tucked into tailored blue jeans. On her feet were low-heeled ankle boots in the same leather as the jacket. To add a brief flair, he added a bold pair of golden earrings she called urban chic.

He ran his palm over her head to smooth out any tangles, leaving her hair sleek and smooth. "You can open your eyes now." He urged her in a soft tone.

He held her elbow, and his chest tightened, hoping she liked what he'd done. He'd clothed himself in his customary long-sleeved tunic with a high collar in a midnight blue with minimalistic embossed details on the trim, pairing it with loose trousers in the same color. On his wrists, he included a pair of wide leather cuffs the color of deep sepia that matched the shade of his hair. They were a quiet reminder of where he came from as a slave and the strength he'd gained since then.

With an absent thought, he wove his long hair into its customary single braid.

Toni's squeal of delight after she took in his creation was everything he'd hoped for. She rushed to him with arms wide open, embracing him in a tight hug.

"I'm so glad you approve." He stroked the soft hair at the top of her head, and her earrings clinked delicately. "Now, we'd better see my brothers before we upset *Elemi* again."

Walking beside Azazel as they headed to the conference room, Toni took in as much of the ship *Elemi* as she could. With a joyous sense of freedom, she clasped his hand in hers. Her face warmed at the appreciative glance he gave her as he tightened his hold.

The golden streaks in his brown eyes seemed to widen. "By the way, where's JR14?"

"Oh, he's fine." Toni waved her hand. "He's with his, um, brothers at the command center. I guess they're all reporting to their... father?" She wrinkled her nose. "I'm still trying to figure out how a droid has brothers and a father."

"Yeah." Azazel chuckled. "It takes some getting used to. Hey—" He smiled at her. "—since I don't remember coming on board, did the ship *Elemi* introduce herself to you?"

Tearing her gaze from his, Toni looked around at the shimmering walls that had a translucent sheen.

"Yes and no. Since I met her in her robot form, I feel like I know her already." She grasped his forearm with her other hand. "Besides, I was so worried about you, I couldn't pay attention to anything else."

She frowned at the blurred memory of rushing into the bedchamber. After laying Azazel on his back on the soft mattress, his brother Asmodel grasped his face between his palms and closed his eyes. After a few tense moments, he opened his hazel eyes with a slight grin. He looked at Abalim before focusing on Arakiba.

Struggling not to stomp her foot in frustration, Toni didn't wait for him to look at her.

"Well?" she demanded, her fists on her hips. "Is he okay?"

"He's just fine," came Asmodel's annoyingly calm announcement. "Like we told you before, shapeshifting, especially for the first time, takes a lot out of a person." He stood from his kneeling position by the bed. "He just needs to rest to gain his strength."

With that last tidbit, the three of them left her alone with a sleeping Azazel.

No one had to tell her to take advantage of the downtime. It was hard to say a grateful goodbye to the Sensos suit, but she didn't want to sleep in it. Once she was naked, she climbed into bed next to the sleeping Azazel. She might not have shapeshifted, but exhaustion claimed her as well.

Now, walking next to her lover, she took the time to notice aspects of *Elemi* she hadn't paid attention to before. Each step had the faintest give, like it met and supported her weight. What she liked best was how every footfall made the minute bio-luminescent threads through it flicker as if they danced with each step.

And the air! Toni took in an appreciative breath. A soothing scent of jasmine with an undertone of spicy ylang-ylang graced the cozy atmosphere. Her favorite.

"What do you think they want to talk to us about?" She bit her bottom lip. *God, they'd better not try to separate them. No way would she let that happen.*

"I'm sure they're going to fill us in on what happened after we left the Krystalii ship." Azazel lifted her hand and kissed her knuckles, keeping her hand over his firm chest. "But what I'm hoping is they'll provide us with something to eat." At that announcement, his stomach growled. "I'm starving." He put his hand over his flat stomach and gave her a sheepish grin.

When her stomach echoed his rumble, they both laughed.

"Yeah, I'm with you there." Toni grinned and skipped backward, facing him, holding his hand with both of hers. "Come on, let's hurry before it's all gone."

"As my lady commands." Azazel bowed before he swooped her into his arms.

She squealed with delight, wrapping her arms around his neck as he hurried them down the corridor.

They were still laughing when he skidded to a halt at an open doorway.

"Finally," *Elemi's* testy tone announced. "They're here."

Toni's mouth fell open as conversations stopped. Filling the space was a group of people she'd had no idea were on the ship with them.

"Oh, look." Azazel set her down on her feet and nodded at the opposite wall in the large room. "There's food." He grabbed her hand

and headed to the buffet line against the wall with single-minded intent. "Let's eat."

Toni leaned in and whispered as she trotted next to him. "Who are all these people?"

Azazel glanced over his shoulder, then shrugged. "Right now, I don't care. I have something more important on my mind. Like eating."

"Toni?" A woman rushed to her and engulfed her in a hard hug. "Oh my God!" She pulled away and studied her. "Are you okay?"

Toni stepped back and kept her hold on the woman's upper arms. It took a moment, but she quickly realized who it was. "Lisa? Is that you?" The blond woman matched her in height but moved with a quiet, deliberate grace that hinted at a sharp intellect beneath the surface. As a film producer, Toni loved working with talented writers like the best-selling author in front of her.

"Yeah." Lisa laughed. "We're all here!" She turned to the people at the octagon table that took up most of the room. "Hey, guys. It's Toni!"

"What?" Another squeal. This from Latina Izzy, who didn't waste time rushing over and joining in the hug fest.

"Glad you made it in one piece." This came from Morgan, her golden corkscrew curls brushed her shoulders as she came to the group. Her diverse heritage was clear in her striking caramel complexion and golden green eyes. She patted Toni on her shoulder.

Tears filled Toni's eyes. Her cellmates from the gangster planet of FiPan were here. Except... "Where's Althea?" Dread filled her. She stood on her toes to look over her friends, but didn't see the dark-haired woman.

"Oh, you don't have to worry about her." Morgan slid her hands into the back pockets of her jeans. "She's doing just fine with the man of her dreams and living on an out-of-the-way planetoid called Hiigar."

Toni let out a huge breath with a grin. "Well, that's good to hear." She looked at each one of her friends in the eyes. "How 'bout you guys?" She chuckled. "Anyone else find the man of your dreams?"

Izzy's blush traveled from her neck to her cheeks. Lisa's grin was as wide as a river. And Morgan... well, Morgan was her normal cool self. But the slight grin on her full lips said it all.

"Really? All of us?" Toni laughed. "Look at us! Finding love in space after all." She nodded to Azazel and his more-than-handsome brothers.

It was then she noticed a couple of other folks in the room. Some were humans... some not so much. "I think I'd better sit down," she mumbled.

Spying Azazel sitting at the table and tackling the mountain of food on his plate, Toni nodded to her friends and left them to join him. She grinned when she saw he'd brought her a plate of something to eat as well. A strange combination of foods that could be called breakfast, lunch, or dinner. Not that she cared. Spearing a roll that looked like sushi, she plopped the treat into her mouth and moaned. Tuna, her favorite.

"Thank you," she mumbled through the side of her mouth to Azazel as she stabbed a broccoli stalk.

"You are more than welcome, *hebat*." Azazel's dark eyes twinkled as he looked at her before taking a bite out of the slice of T-bone he'd cut. "I will always take care of you."

"Now that we're all here, let's begin." This announcement came from a man who looked transparent.

"That's my eldest brother, Adapa." Azazel leaned toward her. "And next to him is his wife, Queen Inanna, from the planet Akurn. Right now, they're talking to us in holographic form from there. That's why they're translucent."

Adapa was as handsome as all of Azazel's brothers. His features were more Middle Eastern than the others, with clear dark eyes of stern intelligence. Next to him was one of the most beautiful women Toni had ever seen. Her glorious red-blond hair, styled in sophisticated curls around her head, held a small golden tiara. A face as white as porcelain featured unusual turquoise eyes.

"Azazel, since you are the last to arrive, please introduce us to your companion." Adapa tilted his head with a wave of his hands.

If Toni hadn't known he was a hologram, she'd swear he and the queen were sitting in the room with them. Transparency notwithstanding.

"Yeah, now I see why you dragged your butt before coming to join us." Azazel's huge blond brother, Arakiba, spoke up with his muscular arm around Morgan's shoulder, tugging her close. He snickered like a teenager.

Morgan nudged him with her elbow and shook her head.

Toni's face heated. It didn't take a genius to figure out all these psychics had a general idea of what they'd been doing. She humphed and crossed her arms, giving the ass a glare.

Good thing Azazel was more of an adult. He stood and put his hand over his heart, ignoring Arakiba and focusing on Adapa. "Thank you, brother." He faced Toni and placed a warm palm on her shoulder. "Lord Baelon captured Antonia Soo-Min Choi of Los Angeles and held her on his ship." He locked eyes on the group, his gaze sharp and unflinching. "She means everything to me."

Arakiba nodded in response, rapping his fist over his heart twice before extending his arm with his two fingers pointed ahead in a salute of camaraderie. "I feel ya, bro."

Toni stood and gave a slight bow in the tradition of her mother's people. "Please call me Toni."

"Woo-hoo! You go, girl!" Lisa quipped and clapped. "Glad to see you survived Baelon's horrible nightmare."

"Baelon bad... bad... bad!"

A gravelly masculine voice behind her jolted Toni. She twisted around and almost leapt out of her skin.

A giant purple Krystalii sat on the floor with his back against the wall in the corner behind her, legs spread.

Her heart raced until she looked closer. Was he playing with... a slinky?

The creature bounced the toy on his lap and sang a soft ditty under his breath.

"Oh, that's just As'ni," Morgan reassured her. "He's with us." She waved her finger, gesturing between her and Arakiba.

"I go with Ari... I go with Ari." As'ni singsonged and ignored the room as he continued to play with the slinky and a penlight he picked up from beside one of his thighs.

"Um, okay." Toni took one last look at the Krystalii before sitting down. She grasped Azazel's hand for support.

He resumed his seat as well, giving her a tight squeeze.

Speaking of which. "Did Rerqel have any trouble installing the Krystalii on their planet?" she asked Adapa.

"No," he answered with a slight smile. "As a matter of fact, he told us that the Dimensional Rift Nucleus the Krystalii used was comparable to the one they had to control the parallel rifts for the species they oversee. Because of that, they had no trouble dismantling the portal, so there's little chance the Krystalii will find a way out of the parameters the Qorath set them in. He and his people are working on gaining the trust of the Krystalii to guide them on how to govern themselves after the tight grip Lord Baelon had on them."

"I would hope that the Federation Consortium isn't going to just take the Xeltrians' word for what they're doing." Abalim intoned with a frown.

Adapa chuckled. "No, of course not. Rerqel and his people, along with the galactic government, have worked out the best way to keep the lines of communication open so they'd remain transparent on what they're doing. The chancellor promised us an update once they completed negotiations." He glanced at Asmodel sitting next to Toni's friend Izzy. "I believe we should move on to the next issue. Asmodel?"

"Thanks. I'd like to introduce my friend, Raxx Jorlen." Asmodel put his hand on the shoulder of the man sitting at his right. "Without him and his ship, Izzy and I would never have made it off CeluriaVO in one piece." His gentle smile was for Izzy, who beamed up at him.

"Hey, folks." Raxx Jorlen clipped a wave at the group. "Gotta say, I'm stoked to be here." He took a swig from the mug in his other hand.

Toni suspected whatever he had in that mug had a bit of a kick to it. She tilted her head and inspected him.

He looked like a human but wore a strange blend of Earth and alien clothes. His attire, a mix of practicality and style, included a weathered waist-length jacket of hard-to-distinguish material that had seen better days. It sat over a dark, formfitting shirt tucked into durable cargo pants equipped with pockets filled with god knew what.

She stretched to glance at the boots he wore, scuffed and sturdy, that completed the ensemble. Leaning back, she continued to study him.

He might not be classically handsome, but his rugged looks told of a harsh life lived in every line and scar. The piercing intensity of his dark eyes held hidden secrets and sharp intelligence.

If she had to create a tagline to describe him, it'd be *Guardians of the Galaxy* meets *Indiana Jones*. Yeah, she'd cast him as a lead in a film like that in a heartbeat.

"Raxx Jorlen, I have an offer for you from the chancellor." Adapa leaned in with his fingers clasped in front of him.

"Fantabulous, dude. I'm listening." The man leaned back and crossed his ankle over his opposite knee, resting the mug on his thigh.

"As part of the agreement to expunge your criminal record and compensate you for the technology known as the Quantum Lattice Resonator, we offer you the guardianship of the planet known as FiPan."

There were several gasps in the room, including one from Toni. *FiPan, the gangster planet that held her and her friends captive? The place where they were left to rot and die of starvation when the leader died? Could he be talking about that foul piece of hell in the galaxy?*

"Guardianship?" Raxx sat up and plunked his mug with a thunk onto the table's thick, transparent surface. "That's some heavy shit you're laying down." He tilted his head and narrowed his eyes. "So, tell me, dude, what exactly are you offerin'?"

Dang, the guy talked like he was in an old 80s movie.

"It means"—Queen Inanna answered—"it isn't viable to let that site remain without some kind of control. We cannot allow another outlaw faction to move in and take over. So... dude, what we're offering you is a custodial position to run the planet and help guide it to become a viable citizen of the Federation Consortium."

Raxx's mouth dropped open before he snapped it shut. The crunching of his jaw was easy to hear in the now-quiet room. "For reals?" He swung his wide-eyed glance at Asmodel.

Asmodel grinned and slapped Raxx on the shoulder. "You ready to be respectable, dude?"

"Yo, only if you're comin' with me, my man." Raxx's grin matched Asmodel's.

Asmodel shook his head. "Afraid not." He nodded to the queen's hologram. "They have someone else in mind to help you, way better than I can."

Adapa's holographic form tapped a finger on whatever surface he was sitting behind. "We recognize you will need help to turn things around there." He turned his attention to his dark-skinned brother. "Abalim."

A clear monitor materialized in the middle of the table, displaying an image of an alien female Toni had never seen before.

"Ah, yes," Abalim nodded, causing his corkscrews to bob around his massive shoulders. "I'd like to introduce Saphira, who hails from the planet Crichi. I met her and her crew on FiPan. We'd considered Saphira and her crew smugglers, but we have just learned that they were undercover agents for our galactic government. Initially, their assignment was to infiltrate FiPan and gather evidence against a notorious gangster named Zorvok who was trying to take over the underground network."

"That is, until my mission changed when they ordered me to help you find Lisa," the strange female alien spoke from the translucent monitor floating in the middle of the table.

Toni cocked her head in Raxx's direction when she heard him take in a sharp breath. Glancing at him, she frowned at his narrowed eyes and pursed lips. *Looks like there's some kind of history between those two.*

"Not that I minded." Saphira beamed at Lisa sitting next to Abalim. "Lisa was well worth any interruption."

Lisa giggled. "Flattery will get you everywhere, sista."

Toni studied the Crichi and her skin of a deep coral that glistened whenever she moved.

Adorning across her attractive face were intricate patterns, delicate swirls and lines that reminded Toni of tattoos or skin grafts that swooped from her temples, across her cheekbones, before ending down her jawline. But it was her overly large almond-shaped eyes that made her look like an anime character. To enhance the image, her metallic-gold hair was shaped in a mohawk. It was short on the sides with long, silky panels draped over one side and resting down her shoulders.

"Good to see you again, *Jorlen*." Saphira's attention turned to Raxx. She sat back and narrowed those enormous eyes while tapping her forefinger with its tapered golden-brown nail against the amber of her full lips. "Can't wait to work with you once again."

Raxx swallowed so hard it was easy to see his Adam's apple bob. He tilted his head and gave her a lopsided grin, saluting her with his two forefingers.

Well, that was interesting. Talk about unresolved tension.

With that settled, Adapa took over the conversation. "We have some other news we are sure you'll like." He directed his gaze at Morgan.

"Yes, ah, thank you." Morgan stood and leaned on the table with her palms flat on the surface as she addressed those in the room. "I'm sure most of you think I came from Atlanta, Georgia, in America on Earth. I'm afraid only part of that is true."

Her sheepish smile made Toni grin. She'd always thought Morgan seemed like an actor playing a part. Toni leaned forward, eager to hear Morgan's confession.

"While I am from Earth, I'm not from America. I belong to a secret society of Akurn descendants in a hidden city called Aethralis under the Antarctic."

There were several gasps and wide-eyed looks, especially from Azazel and his brothers. Except Arakiba, of course.

"Ever since Prince Murduk tried to destroy the scientific base on Earth thousands of years ago, my great-something grandfather gathered most of the Akurn scientists and the humans they'd helped design to safety." She glanced at Azazel, then Asmodel, then Abalim, as she continued. "As you know, those illegal Akurn scientists also created a species known as the Titans. Thankfully, my grandfather and those with him have kept those beings in stasis ever since." She straightened and crossed her arms. "Now, that's where you come in. Although the citizens of Aethralis include powerful psychics like you, that ability has weakened over the generations. I, myself, only have a small psychic ability known as xenoglossy—the capability to hear and speak a language after hearing it." She sighed and rubbed her temple. "Because our powers are not as strong as our ancestors', the shield holding the Titans is faltering."

"That doesn't sound good," Asmodel muttered.

"Are you asking us to join you and the people of Aethralis to help reinforce the Titans' confinement?" Azazel's voice held a misleading sense of calm.

His act didn't fool Toni one bit. She felt his inner beast beginning to wake up at the thought of an upcoming battle.

"You are correct," Queen Inanna answered. "If those high-powered psychics escape, the mythical accounting of their tyranny will seem like children's fairytales. We have to contain them by any means necessary." Her clear-turquoise eyes glanced at her husband beside her. "Unfortunately, Adapa cannot join you. We need him here on Akurn as we continue to transition from the mess my so-called brother caused. Without us here, my people will suffer and die amidst the chaos."

If these Titans were as bad as they were saying, why let them live? Why not put them out of their misery?

Because we do not have the means to do that. Azazel answered in her mind. *They have unlimited psionic energy, and if we let them out of stasis, even to terminate them, they will take control. Then they'd unleash their narcissistic need to overpower others they deem inferior.* He paused. *Which, in their opinion, is everyone but them.*

Well... crud.

"And that, my bros, is that." Arakiba sat back and rested his ankle over his opposite knee. "Looks like we've got to save the day all over again! All in favor of preventing genocide of everything and everyone on Earth, say, 'aye'!"

Azazel, along with his other two brothers, nodded with nervous laughs.

"Hey, you're not going anywhere without me." Toni grabbed the sleeve of Azazel's tunic. "I may not be a psychic, but nothing's going to stop me from going with you."

Azazel leaned close to her, his mahogany eyes holding her gaze. "I wouldn't have it any other way. So, hold on tight, my *hebat*." His fingers found hers, easing them free from his sleeve, then threading them together in a firm, intimate hold. "Life is about to get very interesting."

"Good." Toni grinned, breathless. "I wouldn't have it any other way."

A low, deep laugh rumbled from his chest, warm and rich, carrying a thousand unspoken promises. Before she took another breath, he pulled her into his arms, claiming her mouth in a searing kiss—a tender and fierce vow spun from everything they had fought for and found together.

In that moment, the rest of the universe slipped quietly into silence, as if the stars held their breath. There were only the two of them—heart to heart, soul to soul—bound by something deeper than time, more enduring than fate.

It was then Toni realized her journey had never been about finding someone to fall in love with. It was about finding the place where her soul fit, where her heart could stand with someone in an unshakable truth. And as warmth surged through her, a new understanding washed over her. The best things in life don't need a happy ending.

Because life doesn't fade to black—it's the next scene waiting to unfold.

A SMALL ASK...

Now that you've finished reading this creation, it'd mean the world to me if you left an honest review wherever you bought it. This type of feedback is an authors lifeblood and helps others find their work.

The adventures can't continue without you!

ABOUT THE AUTHOR

Keri Kruspe, award-winning *"Author of Otherworldly Romantic Adventures"* loves nothing better than writing about romances that feature "feisty heroines who aren't afraid to take a chance on life... or love". Her writing career started when she became determined to indulge in something different in the SciFi romance genre, turning "the alien kidnapping trope upside down" (Vine Voice) in her ***ALIEN EXCHANGE*** trilogy.

After the ***ALIEN EXCHANGE*** universe was born, she created another SciFi Romance series, ***ANCIENT ALIEN DESCENDANTS***, then carried on the adventures in the *ALIEN LEGACY BROTHERHOOD* that continues to mix sensual, romantic themes to otherworldly adventures.

A native Nevadan, Keri is a lifelong avid reader who lives in northwestern Michigan with her hubby and the ruling member of the family, a Jack Russell Terrier (aka the *Terrorist*) named Hestia. When not immersed in her made-up worlds as she listens to classic rock on vinyl, she enjoys discovering the fascinating landscape of her adopted home and pairing red wine with healthy ways to cook. Most of all, she loves finding her next favorite author.

If you want to know when Keri's next book will come out, please visit her at her **website** where you can sign up for her mailing list. You'll get a ***FREE*** copy of the novella, *The Day Behind Tomorrow* that is a prologue to the **ANCIENT ALIEN DESCENDANT SERIES**. Not to mention being kept updated on the life of a dedicated, obsessed author.

Social Media Links:

Facebook

Pinterest

Instagram

BOOKS IN READING ORDER

Claude & Amata

Lok's Love

Alien Legacy Brotherhood

Abalim

Asmodel

Arakiba

Azazel